HONEY AND ICE TRILOGY BOOK I

A COURT
of
HONEY
and
ASH

SHANNON MAYER
KELLY ST CLARE

A COURT of HONEY and ASH

CHAPTER 1

F eet and hands planted in the scorching sand, under an equally scorching sun, I held my position in an awkward downward dog, while I waited for the bellow from the Horn of the Untried. I swallowed hard, trying not to think about what it would mean if I were to fail the final test after so many years of extensive, brutal training.

Eight years had culminated in this moment of do or die.

Did I have it in me to become one of the fae of the Seelie court, or would I be cast out with the weakest of my kind?

"Fuck," I whispered under my breath as bile crawled up my throat.

"You're in a good position for it," Rowan, another trainee,

muttered from my left. Placed as I was, feet and hands buried in the sand, he flashed me a quick smile, but the tightness around his eyes and mouth said it all.

Those who'd ended up in this place knew the consequences of failure.

Those of us who were part human knew it even better.

And mutts like me—*half* human and half fae—knew it best. Sorry for being born, I guess?

I didn't smile back and instead lowered my head to look at the sand between my fingers. The ache of holding this position was more mental than physical, and that was all part of the test. Sweat rolled down my face. The ache in my shoulders crossed to burning throb territory. The braid holding back my thick, dark hair unraveled more with every passing second. Loose strands plastered to my neck and cheeks as I fought to breathe evenly, the minutes ticking by with excruciating slowness while the pain and need to move increased in cruel triple time.

Someone down the line whimpered and I could guess who it was. Bracken. She was *not* cut out for this, but like the rest of us, had no choice but to train and pray she didn't get cast out. Very few women were sent for training to begin with—the low numbers of fae born each year meant that women were kept as safe as possible.

Except when there was reason to hope that you were cast out so you had no part of the fae world—so that your bloodline was ended without the ruling class actually having to raise a finger.

Us bastards and orphans had no family to back us or our training. Here in Underhill, we only had each other, as frightening a thought as that was, and since many of us had come from the same orphanage there were years of history between a number of us.

"Hold, Bracken," I bellowed. "Don't you dare break now. We've only just started!"

She responded with another whimper, and a few of the other twenty-four trainees groaned their agreement.

In the distance, a long low whine built on the air, swelling until the deep keening cut through the sounds of heavy breathing around me and rumbled into the thunderous blast of the Horn of the Untried.

Just like that, I abandoned my downward dog and lunged forward with the others. Sand flew up everywhere as we ran, but my trainer's sharp voice circled in the back of my head. *As soon as you hear the horn, run. That horn doesn't only unleash you, it unleashes Underhill's beasties on your heels.*

Beasties was a polite and totally inaccurate way of putting—

"Monster on the left," Rowan hollered.

As one, our group split through the middle to face the first obstacle of the test.

Our self-appointed troop leader, Yarrow, took the right half, while I took the left. Rowan and Bracken were just behind me.

Our overall mission was to 'collect the coins' hidden on the course, but of course there were monsters involved. The big question was which beasties they'd given us today.

I got my first good look.

Fuck.

"Dragon," Bracken screamed.

Her scream grew fainter as she fled. Damn it. *Bye, Bracken.*

I turned to the left, ignoring the loss of Bracken. I didn't dare take my eyes off the 'small' issue suddenly towering over us.

It wasn't just a dragon, but a *three-headed* dragon. That was two too many heads in my humble opinion. Flames spewed from each mouth in great rolling gouts. With scales of solid black, the beast didn't look real to me—more like someone had cut and pasted it from one of those terrible movies humans liked, and that the orphanage had let us watch on Friday nights as a treat. If we were good.

Its limbs moved strangely, jerking at odd angles as it lumbered toward us.

Slow.

Stupid.

Unbalanced.

"Weapons," Yarrow hollered.

I slipped my bow from my shoulder and drew an arrow clear of the quiver in one fluid movement. Snapping it up and into position, I sighted past the fletching.

The middle dragon head bobbled left and right, almost indecisively. I focused on its furiously rolling eyeball and loosed an arrow. The squelching thud of the sharp tip embedding in my intended target was lost to the surrounding mayhem, but the wet sound echoed in my head regardless.

The dragon's middle head dropped like a wilted flower, but the beast kept coming, the remaining two heads not even glancing at the slumped head between them. I frowned. That didn't bother the beast? There wasn't even a reaction to the pain of a pierced eyeball.

Arrows and spears flew past me, some sinking into the monster's haunches and barbed tail, many missing the mark entirely, and I withheld a sigh. Not-so-secret secret? Fae, even mutts, were shit at fighting with anything other than magic. And guess what rule we'd been given for this final trial to prove ourselves?

You guessed it, no attack magic. And for me, that was just fine seeing as my magic, well, it wasn't what you'd call upper level.

I sighted down another arrow and took the left head.

"Get a move on it, Kallik," Yarrow roared.

Alli. I preferred Alli and he damn well knew it.

"You're welcome to help out," I muttered. But I smirked as the third arrow met its mark. Now we had a bouquet of wilted monster flowers. Kind of.

The dragon heads thudded to the ground. From what I could tell, they were dead. But the body continued to move, staggering in the hot sand, dragging the heads along behind it.

Gross. Not the worst thing I'd seen in the last eight years though. Certainly not the worst thing I'd endured either.

I studied the beast. It was as if the brains weren't connected to the rest of the dragon. The creature was simultaneously alive and *not*. Oddly fascinated, I lowered my bow and arrow to watch the bizarre display.

"Retrieve the coins," Yarrow's booming voice jolted me.

I drew green energy from the nearby trees and used it to fuel my indigo magic, wrapping it around my throat to amplify my voice. "The coins," I yelled at magically enhanced volume to my half of the group. "Get the coins!"

Rowan clapped me on the shoulder. "Did Yarrow just manage to slip in an order before you?"

Yes. And I'd never hear the fucking end of it. Yarrow, the bastard of House Gold—one level below House Royal—had assigned himself as the bane of my existence since nearly the moment I arrived. If I thought too much about it, I could still feel his slimy hands sweeping over me as he pawed at my clothes.

I shuddered. *Nope, not going there.*

The two halves of our troop surrounded the beast.

An excited shout went up, and I spotted our treasure a beat later. Behind the staggering dragon body was a wooden chest strapped in iron.

Rowan reached the chest first, and gingerly holding the wooden edge to keep clear of the iron, flung the lid open. His deep brown hair caught the light, turning it a nice coppery shade as he bent to peer inside. Nope, it wasn't his hair that was reflecting that color. He looked up, the copper shimmer on his face. "Shit. There aren't enough coins." His eyes darted. "Only twenty, tops."

Then this wasn't a 'collect the happy coins as a team' gig. It was a 'get a coin or you're out on your ass.'

He tossed me one and pocketed his own, then backed up as the others scrabbled and fought for the remainder. Yarrow shouldered his way to the front—*dick*.

Rowan tapped my shoulder. We'd been in the orphanage together, and while we weren't tight friends, we'd known each other for years. "We should go. I think from here on out . . ."

I nodded, already slipping my coin into the pouch at my hip. "The next challenge is probably the same way. It'll have even fewer coins, to eliminate more people."

The game had changed.

Breaking into a run beside him, I didn't slow to put my bow away, but instead kept it steady in my left hand, two arrows in my right. Better to have it out and ready before more beasties showed up.

But as we raced from the sand dune, something caught my eye: a crying Bracken huddled to one side of the course, shoulders shaking.

I tucked my arrows into my belt, ran over to her and grabbed her by the arm. "Up and at 'em, Bracken. Maybe we can help you get the next coin."

She bobbed her head, long blond hair unbound and disastrously tangled already. "Okay?"

Rowan rolled his bright green eyes but said nothing, and neither did I. We couldn't leave her behind. Underhill—the ancestral home of the fae—was dangerous even for those prepared to take on its unpredictable challenges. This area of the realm would be extra volatile for the next few hours after the sounding of the Horn of the Untried. Plus—I tightened my hand on Bracken's wrist—it wasn't her fault she got a shitty trainer. Rowan and I had been lucky to snag Bres. Old fart that he was, he was the best at mentoring young fae through this training.

The sand shifted under our feet as we ran, morphing from scalding and gritty to cold, wet, and heavy. A literal ocean appeared before us, extending as far as the eye could see, and I slowed my feet as a wave crashed to our right, stretching up the brand-new shore.

Underhill strikes again.

And this time it had struck me where it hurt. My heart pounded as I studied the choppy surface. I worked to keep my expression clear of the panicked fear trying to claw at my throat, an old memory trying to push its way to the surface.

Cold, the water was so cold and I couldn't breathe.

No, no I couldn't let the past steal my future.

"Bres said we'd have three main challenges. Weapons. Bravery. Mind." Rowan's voice broke through to me. "What do you think this is?"

We'd completed the weapons obstacle, at least that was my thought.

I released a pent-up breath as the waves calmed and the surface stopped moving. "Bravery."

Bracken hugged her arms around herself. "Why? It's just

water. Perhaps it's Mind. It's harder to hold our breath for a long time when danger strikes."

No fucking kidding. That feat was even harder for mutts who had to battle back their human instincts to breathe. Harder *still* for those with a cloying fear of water.

My fists curled as I braced myself inwardly for what had to happen next.

Lifting my chin, I glanced into the water. A glimmer of something silver flicked into the air, end over end, then dropped down to the rolling ocean and disappeared.

"Did you see that?" I croaked.

I felt more than saw Rowan's nod.

"Silver coin," he grunted.

That was enough of a confirmation for me. Better get this over with. Before I could change my mind, I stripped out of my clothes and dropped my weapons to the wet sand.

Rowan didn't question me before following suit, and Bracken stripped down after a brief pause.

"You a good swimmer?" Rowan asked her.

Bracken dipped her head. "Yes."

He didn't ask me—I'd worked hard to keep my weakness from becoming general knowledge. I mean, I could swim, but . . .

I forced my feet through the shallows, hissing as the icy cold hit me.

The three of us were waist deep when the rest of the troop arrived. Rowan and Bracken swam off without further delay. The other Untried would take their cue from us. I couldn't linger, I had to do this. Inhaling through my nose a few times, I clamped down on my panicky thoughts and dove forward.

The water was so cold it clamped iron bands around my chest and the top of my head—or was that panic? Movements frantic at first, I swam as far as I could before breaking the surface for air. Rowan and Bracken were ahead of me. Teeth chattering, I hurried to join them at the spot where we'd seen the flash of silver.

Rowan peered down into the depths, and I looked too, trying to focus on the mission. The water was exceptionally clear, allowing us to see all the way down, and right at the bottom was a chest identical to the one guarded by the dragon. Wooden. Banded in iron.

"Big breath," Rowan said. "This is deep."

Easier said than done, but I took the biggest breath I could manage and dove down.

I pushed hard, but I'd only reached halfway before my tightening lungs screamed at me to take a breath. Logically, I understood that being half-fae I didn't *need* to take a breath for several minutes, but *because* I was half-fae, the human parts of my mind didn't accept this as true, even without my phobia of drowning.

Rowan and Bracken were ahead of me, almost to the chest.

The pressure on my lungs surged. My mind screamed at me to urgently return to shore, but no, I wouldn't give up.

I flat-out refused.

Bubbles slipped from my lips and streamed back toward the surface, but I kept on.

Almost there.

Rowan turned, a silver coin in his hand. He looked past me, eyes widening as he pointed.

I spun in the water as Yarrow caught up to me, swimming fast. Curved knife in hand, he slashed, dragging the blade across my left thigh. A bloom of red swirled up around us, but I barely felt the cut in the numbing cold of the water.

He took another swing, and I pedaled backward, bumping into something soft and squishy.

Yarrow turning tail to bolt was a decent indication of what the soft and squishy thing could be.

Watch for the unexpected.

I slowly turned and forgot about my breathing dilemma.

Tentacles erupted around me. I spotted suction cups the size of my head as the sea creature whipped its limbs outward to hook swimming troop members.

The tentacled monster didn't pay me the slightest attention, instead turning to the other Untried. Was I too close to it for it to see me?

Shit, there was no way it would miss the scent of blood in the water, though. I yanked my belt off and tied it around my leg, then swam below the creature's bulbous, pink body to the chest.

My eyes widened as I snagged the last silver coin. More trainees had swum past me than I'd thought. Grabbing the last coin was cutting things too close for comfort, and from the pattern we'd seen there would be *fewer* coins at the next stop.

I had to get a move on.

Rowan and Bracken swam for the surface, already far ahead of me. The sea beast unfurled a giant tentacle in their direction, and Rowan paused to slash at the limb.

The monster shrieked and recoiled.

It didn't like pain, huh? Good to know.

Coin in mouth, I grabbed the chest and smashed it against the rocky pedestal it had sat upon. The splitting noise rippled outward, and I grabbed a long piece of slat with a jagged edge.

Kicking hard, I swam underneath and behind the tentacled beast. It rose in the water to grab for Rowan and Bracken, and I followed it upward, readying myself to stab the creature if it succeeded in hooking them and dragging them downward like it had done with some of the other Untried. From what I could see at least seven fae were caught in various tentacles. I couldn't save them all, but maybe this would help a few.

Its free tentacles reached out for Rowan and Bracken, and I jabbed its soft underside with the long slatted piece of wood.

The monster shrieked again, the sound reverberating through the water, and diverted its attention to the sea floor, a few of the Untried released from its tentacles. That was the best I could do.

I took my chance and swam out from under it.

Breaking the surface, I didn't dare slow, but swam as hard as I could for the shallows.

Panting for air I technically *still* didn't need, I crawled onto the wet sand, surveying my surroundings.

Bracken was crouched in front of me, but Rowan wasn't there.

He'd gone ahead. Didn't blame him, this was the game.

Bracken watched me closely with those bright blue eyes of hers. She blinked a few times and held out my bow and arrow. "The boys wanted to smash them."

And she'd kept them from being broken? I slipped my silver coin into the pouch at my hip and took my weapon from her. "Thanks."

"Least I could do," she said. "You helped me get a coin. Maybe they'll let me be a tradesperson now instead of casting me out into the Triangle."

I'd gone into this determined to retrieve a coin of each color, but she was right—they'd probably dole out consolation prizes to those who'd succeeded at some challenges but not others.

"Let's go." Limping along, I made myself pick up speed even though my leg throbbed like I'd been kicked by a mule, now that the numbing effect of the water had worn off. A quick glance showed me that the wound was more surface than I'd first thought. That was good.

"What happened?" Bracken asked.

"Yarrow," I spat. Goddess damn him to the depths. "How many got out ahead of me?"

"Fifteen or so including Rowan. A bunch of them banded together though and reached the surface before me and Rowan."

An alliance. Great.

We jogged, and the landscape changed from ocean to a thick jungle that sloped steadily upward. My thigh muscles loosened with the sudden and cloying heat and the wound, while still irksome, wasn't holding me back. As the foliage changed, so did the footing, and it wasn't long before we stood in front of a steep rock face.

"You think we go up?" Bracken asked quietly.

A shimmering gray overlay was on a part of the rock wall. I put a hand to it and a tiny zing of energy slipped up my fingers, all but beckoning me forward. "Yes."

Climbing the steep rock face, hand over hand, carefully finding footholds and finger grips, we made our way up.

No safety nets waited below, and after the hectic anarchy underwater a moment ago, the ascent held an eerie quality.

This had to be the bravery test.

Teeth clenched together, I controlled my breathing. In through my nose and out through the mouth. I wouldn't freak out, heights didn't bother me. This was far more my element than the ocean.

Water pounded somewhere above, but I forced those sounds aside as my hand found the top of the cliff at last. I scrambled over the ledge and turned on my belly to peer down. *Huh*, Bracken was right there.

I held a hand out, helping her up the last few feet. "You did it. Good work."

"Glad you could join us," Yarrow called out.

Whirling in a crouch, I faced him.

Them.

The boys were spread out in a semi-circle around Yarrow, Rowan included in their midst. Fifteen of them.

"As troop leader," he drawled, "I insist that ladies go first. Though I'm not sure that word applies to someone of your . . . dubious heritage."

He was always careful not to call me mutt when higher-ups might be listening in.

Yarrow laughed, and the others laughed with him. Rowan included. Oh, hell no. Rowan hadn't crossed me by joining the winning side—that was just smart—but being an asshole? That landed him on my shit list.

My guess as to why the boys waited for us? Something really dangerous lay ahead, and Yarrow wanted to watch someone else screw it up first. Not an unintelligent idea, though it was a cowardly one.

I gave him a hard smile. "Not what you said the other night, *troop leader.*"

He tightened his grip on the handle of his blade, knuckles tensing, but I made myself walk straight past him as if my leg wasn't throbbing after the climb, and about to buckle.

Because beyond them was the next challenge. And with limited coins on offer, it made sense to go first.

Ignoring their jeers and taunts, I took the only path leading away from the ledge. The pounding of the water swelled to a furious roar that echoed the sudden pulsing of my blood in my ears.

Not *again*.

My eyes rounded.

A vertical waterfall shot straight down what could only be hundreds of feet into a pool of water that looked impossibly small from here. My exhale wheezed out at the thought of diving into it. They couldn't mean for us to do *this*.

Yet the path that shimmered a light gray had stopped at this exact point and there was nowhere else to go.

We were definitely meant to jump.

I slid a foot back. No. No way. I couldn't do it. Just because Underhill often felt like a dream, didn't mean we couldn't die here. If I jumped, I'd either smash against the rocks or drown.

I slid another foot back.

"Alli, watch out," Bracken cried.

I choked on a scream as a large hand shoved between my shoulder blades. I only had a split second to push off with my good leg, catapulting my body away from the cliff face.

And then . . . free fall.

A scream lodged in my throat, filling my mind. Panic hit me, so strong that black crept in on the edges of my vision. I closed my eyes and surrendered to my fate.

Flashes of memories hit me—something that often happened when I was precariously close to death. *Growing up as a mutt outcast. The orphanage. Fighting to get here to this testing.*

Without warning, I slid into a calming warmth that gently slowed my fall, rocking me in its arms. Water. But it was so soothing, my landing so seamless, that for a moment I thought I'd died on impact.

Magic was at play.

I thrashed against the water's peaceful hold as it moved me to the base of the waterfall.

A familiar wooden chest awaited me on a flat rock.

Shaking and moving on autopilot, I pushed back the lid and took one of eight gold coins out, then took another for Bracken too. Those guys could kiss our asses.

Still in shock, I forced myself to enter the water once more to swim to the edge of the warm lagoon and pull myself out.

Land. Glorious, firm, non-drowning land was finally under me. In a crouch, I sank my fingers into the dirt and watched as each of the other Untried hit the water. Not one of them came to harm—which confirmed that there wasn't actually any danger in the landing. We'd just needed the courage to jump.

Or the lucky misfortune to be pushed.

Yarrow was the fifth to take the leap. Still in time for a gold coin. *Bastard.*

Rowan was the eighth to fly the nest.

He trudged out of the water empty-handed with his head hung low.

I didn't give him the extra coin. He'd set the tune, and I'd dance to it.

Bres and the other trainers emerged from the jungle, and I vaguely noted the sopping wet arrival of most of my fellow Untried behind them, those who hadn't made it to the final hurdle.

My attention was fixed on the cliff top. Bracken hadn't come down.

"Dive, Bracken," I whispered.

I doubted she would—*I* wouldn't have if I'd known no good would come of it—but if she didn't complete the challenge, they might give me a hard time about handing over the coin.

A moment later, there was a sickening whoosh and a rapid streak of blond. She hit the water with barely a splash. A few seconds passed before she floated to the surface.

"The coins were all gone, but I thought I'd jump anyway." She shrugged, joining me.

I slid the extra gold coin into her palm and winked at her gaping expression. See how Rowan liked that rotten egg.

Someone clapped, capturing my attention.

Bres stepped forward. "Those with three coins will enter into the Elite of the Seelie. You will receive training in the area of your choosing, along with a stipend, your own home, a crest, and two human servants."

Yarrow puffed up his chest.

I wrinkled my nose, but the deep yearning that had filled me from the second I started training rose hard within me now.

My own home.

My own money.

I had three coins. I'd be an Elite. They could keep the crest and the servants, but the rest . . . that was independence and freedom right there.

Bres continued, "Those with *two* coins will enter into the Middling of the Seelie. You will receive training in the area of your choosing along with a half stipend and shared accommodations with those of your status."

Bracken grabbed my arm, squeezing it hard. "Thank you, Alli."

Better than she could have hoped for.

I couldn't respond, slightly numb from hearing about the future they'd outlined for me.

"Those with one coin—" he called out. Several of the sopping wet group looked up at that. They must've failed to pass the tentacled monster. "—you will be trained as tradespeople and given shared accommodations with those of your status."

There were only twenty-four left in our troop after the eight years of training. Two of the four without coins started to cry, the other two trembling more than Bracken had up on the cliff.

"And those with no coins," Bres announced, "will also become tradespeople."

My gasp joined those from the others.

"I knew they wouldn't do it." Rowan sidled up to me. "They wouldn't cast us out, not with fae numbers so low and human numbers so high."

He was *not* trying to talk to me after pulling that crap. Moron. I ignored him.

Bres spread his hands wide. "Eight years of hard work. If you're still here, you have proven your worth one hundred times over. Each of you is worthy to join the court of the Seelie, no matter in what capacity. All that remains is to take your oath to our revered king. It is my honor to introduce our Oracle to hear your pledges."

A ripple ran through our masses. Most would have seen the legendary Oracle at their sorting—the time when you were put into the Seelie or Unseelie court—but I had not been sorted.

The old, hunched woman shuffled from the jungle to stand between the trainers and our awed troop. A hood masked her face, and I wasn't alone in craning to catch a glimpse of what was concealed in its depths.

The trainers ordered us into a single line, and I tacked myself to the back of the line behind Bracken. Those ahead of me knelt to speak the oath that would bind them to the Seelie king and the Underhill we shared with the Unseelie court. It wasn't an oath a fae could just *un-speak*. Breaking a pledge to the court would see a fae magically bound and exiled.

I released a pent-up breath, having half expected them to rip my three coins away on some bogus technicality. Excitement bubbled in my chest as the line dwindled. What area should I choose to train? And to live? Unimak Island situated in the Bering Sea off the coast of Alaska was filled with beautiful nooks and crannies. Tears pricked at the edges of my eyes.

My whole life I'd dreamed about this moment.

It was finally happening.

Bracken knelt and murmured the pledge we'd all hoped to one day utter when we first entered the Underhill.

When she joined our laughing and grinning comrades, I tilted my chin and knelt in her spot. The last to speak the pledge.

"Your hand," the Oracle demanded.

I tried again to peer inside the old woman's hood, but only glimpsed a strand of long gray hair—a testament to her age, as the fae did not age like humans.

I held out my right hand, and she pricked the palm with the tip of a crystal knife. The blood climbed up the blade.

"Swear your oath now, Kallik," she said in a softer voice. "And may the goddess help us for what comes after."

With a speed that belied her age, the Oracle drove the crystal blade into the ground at my feet.

I frowned. She hadn't done that with anyone else. But the Gaelic words had been drilled into me in preparation for this moment, and they flowed from my lips now, melodic and harsh.

"I, Kallik of No House, do swear to protect and uphold the laws of Underhill." My hand warmed where I'd been pricked, and I rubbed at it. "I bind my soul to her power. I bind my sword to obey the orders of King Aleksandr." The heat grew, spreading liquid fast through my now-trembling body. "Should I ever fail in this, then I shall forfeit my place in this world, the Underhill, and whatever lies beyond."

The final words left my lips, and my magic rolled through me and outward in a blasting wave as the earth heaved. The very air around us cracked with a burst of green lightning. Ice shards of the same color, sharp as razor blades, shot around us as the world exploded.

I hit the ground, hands over my head as the fae screamed.

But there was no hiding from the ground morphing beneath my very body.

Jungle, water, sand, honey, cloud, thorns, ice.

Underhill was unpredictable to the extreme, but in eight years it had *never* done anything like this. What was happening?

As the world continued to shake, I rose onto all fours, staring down at what was now a very normal dirt floor covered in pine needles. Too normal. It was unlike anything I'd seen since ... since I'd traveled here.

I lifted my head and my gaze slammed into the Oracle's. She'd removed her hood, and while one eye was sealed shut, a great slash across it, her other eye was filled with every possible color.

She regarded me in condemning silence.

"What's happening?" I whispered over the screams and thunderous rumble.

Somehow she heard me.

"Underhill is no more, Kallik of No House," the Oracle replied. "You have destroyed it."

CHAPTER 2

I stood, staring around the space that had been Underhill only a moment before. Icy cold wind cut across my face, freezing the leftover water from my high dive in a matter of seconds.

Shouts went up all around as the trainers bellowed orders.

Bres's voice was over them all, but I stood there, unable to move as the Oracle stared up at me. She said nothing, only pulled her hood tighter around her face, turned her back on me and walked away.

"Get over here, Kallik!" Bres roared. "There's a storm coming!"

A howl screeched through the air and snow fell so heavy I could barely see through it. I forced my feet to move, unable to truly process what the hell had just happened there.

The Oracle had to be wrong. I . . . Kallik of No House and one of the worst magic users of my troop, could not have had anything to do with . . . destroying Underhill.

Through a two-foot-deep snow drift I stumbled up to Bres and the others who'd just come through.

Across from us were two other troops with trainers. Another Seelie group, and one Unseelie group. We'd never seen each other before this moment, kept separate from one another within Underhill for our training.

"Follow me!" Bres snapped, his voice magnified with his magic to be heard over the storm.

A thought slammed into me, almost stealing my breath. "Was anyone hurt?"

Bres glanced over at me, his eyes steely. "No."

Sudden, sweet relief flowed through me. The death of another fae was no tiny thing with our small population. While sometimes such a thing was necessary, I didn't think I could face myself in the mirror if something I'd done—maybe done—had hurt another of my people when death wasn't warranted.

As the head trainer of our troop, Bres led us down a pathway to a massive log cabin, the same massive log cabin we'd met in eight years ago before we'd stepped into Underhill. Designed as some sort of retreat setup, there were twenty rooms on the second floor, and the main floor was easily five thousand square feet of open space and massive kitchen.

We burst in, all but falling over ourselves, the other two

troops pushing in behind us to get out of the weather.

A fire was quickly built in the huge stone fireplace and heat slowly began to circulate. Just being out of the storm was enough, though, to improve things.

The Seelie trainees stayed to the left, the Unseelie to the right. Lines of division that would always and forever be so.

I found my way to a window and stared out into the growing storm, only half listening to the whispers circling the room like a murder of crows.

"What happened? Is our training done?"

"Do we get to go home to Unimak?"

"Is Underhill really gone?"

One of the other trainers spoke, not one I recognized. A quick glance over my shoulder and I pegged him as Unseelie, and for just a moment I thought he was someone I knew. Dark hair hung to his shoulders, but his eyes were a deep green. His magic was dark green and matched his eyes, as so often was the case with a fae. So dark of a color it barely counted as green. Swirling it around his throat, he used it to magnify his voice.

"Underhill is not gone. The birthplace of our magic and our source of power does not just disappear. It does on occasion get finicky." A smattering of chuckles followed that. I did not laugh. I stared at him, thinking about another Unseelie, one who'd been my friend before he'd been sorted into the dark court.

I rubbed at the center of my palm where the Oracle had nicked my hand.

My thumb rubbed over another scar, one that took me further back, all the way to my childhood, when I'd met my first fae, before I knew that it was half my heritage too.

A ridged scar that ran along the full length of my index finger was the only indication that I'd almost died long before this moment.

"This way, Kallik," my mother whispered in Tlingit, gripping my chubby hand tight.

We were creeping to the top of a rise behind a line of other tip-toeing adults and children. We didn't live with any of these people—but we saw them from time to time.

Like during the winter solstice when we snuck from our part of the island to spy on the fae festivities.

I giggled as she hoisted me into the fork of a tree, but quickly fell silent at the sight below.

Pretty.

Their clothing flowed and flared in time to their spins as they danced on the banks of the dividing river. A bridge spanned the tumultuous, white-tipped water, and the danger of that only made their grace all the more pronounced.

I leaned forward and nearly toppled from the tree.

"Be as quiet as a mouse. The magical folk would not want us watching," Mother said. Smiling at me, she held a finger against her lips.

Nodding on autopilot, I barely blinked as the magical folk celebrated under the steadily darkening night sky.

Their movements called to me, pulling at something under my tummy.

I cast a glance to where my mother spoke in undertones with a group of elders.

Just a quick look from closer. I'd be a mouse and come right back.

Slipping from my tree, I stole into the cover of the shrubs and enchanted trees, picking up my pace when the others were left behind.

I worked my short legs as fast as they'd go, jogging at points when the rise flattened. My heart thumped in my ribs, and my rapid breaths rose as fog in front of me in the freezing dusk air.

But excitement warmed me and spurred me onward.

I had to reach them—the fae.

Sliding down the last of the rise at last, I snuck closer until I lurked in the last line of trees. My inhale caught.

Beautiful.

Their hair gleamed under the soft moonlight. It was as though stars were trapped inside their bodies, giving their very skin an impossible glow.

The music faded and my heart sank as their dancing slowed in response. I glanced back up the rise and took a step back toward my mother.

Harsh music blared, and I crouched, returning my attention to the river.

The fae had parted.

I couldn't see.

Chewing on my lip, I peered over my shoulder again. Mother would be disappointed in me. She'd make me clean all our catches for a month.

The fae fell silent, and the clop of hooves arose from beyond the wall of their bodies. I could just make out the helmets of a group riding in.

I just had to see.

Leaving the safety of the trees, I scurried to join the row of fae and then eased between them, doing my best to be like a mouse. They didn't pay me any mind, solely focused on the mounted group.

Breaking through the front, I got my look too.

My mouth bobbed in an O. A man rode at the front of the group. If the fae around me shone like they contained stars, then this man contained the very sun. He scanned the masses, a wide smile upon his face.

His smile was only slightly larger than that on the face of the woman by his side.

She was the most beautiful person I'd ever seen, and I could only stand frozen to the spot as they passed by and dismounted before walking onto the bridge.

I couldn't tear my eyes from them as the sun man began to speak, his powerful voice pouring over the space like the river water raging beneath him—except where the water was rough, his voice was smooth. Like cinnamon butter.

A smile rose unbidden to my lips though his words were the adult kind and didn't make too much sense to me.

He outstretched his hand, palm up, and royal blue shot from his skin there, bolting upward before it split into hundreds of tendrils and started weaving around those in the clearing.

Around me.

I gasped as white-hot heat exploded in my chest. Not painful, but so hot that I couldn't fathom how it didn't burn my tunic and thick fur coat away.

A royal-blue tendril stopped before me and bent at the top as though tilting its head in enquiry.

I jerked as it darted forward and wrapped round my fingers, curling and caressing. What was happening? Lifting my head, near panic, I stared at the man on the bridge . . .

To find him staring back at me.

Was he doing this on purpose? I didn't like it. Tears welled in my eyes, and I sniffed, shifting my gaze to the woman beside him.

But unlike him, she wasn't looking at me. The ethereal woman was fully facing the man, her fingers gripping his upper arm tight.

Was she upset?

I looked back to the man in time to see him curl his fingers to a fist. The magic shut off, the blue disappearing from the night sky and my fingers as quickly as Mother blew out a candle.

He started to speak again, but I couldn't tear my gaze from my fingers. They were just the same as they'd been. Did that happen to anyone else?

Trying to stay like a mouse, I peeked at the surrounding fae. None of them seemed uncertain like me. No one stared at their hands. They just watched the beautiful couple on the bridge.

I wanted to see the blue tendrils again.

Children were lining up, flowers in their hands. They were dressed in bright, flowing garments like the adults. Peering down at my brown fur coat and boots, I nevertheless crouched to scoop up a few white flowers that had no business being alive in winter—but Mother said some fae created such things with their magic. Maybe their dancing grew the flowers.

Head down, I skirted forward and tagged onto the end of the line.

It moved swiftly. Swift enough for me to realize that if Mother hadn't been aware of where I'd gone, she'd have an unobstructed view of me now.

Too late.

Maybe if I got close enough to the man, then the blue would come back and I could ask him what it was.

Smiling in anticipation, I reached the bridge, only a few children in front of me. The beautiful woman accepted their flowers with a smile that stole my breath clear away. Raising her head, she blinked at the sight of me.

Oh no, my clothes weren't nice enough. Would she send me away?

I fidgeted on the spot, but she simply spoke to a male fae behind her who had a gold helmet on. He dipped his head, and she returned to accepting flowers.

Three children.

Two.

One.

Forcing my cold legs to move, I approached, unable to meet her eyes as I extended the three white flowers. "You're pretty."

She smiled and took them. "Thank you, child."

Her voice was like bells. How was that possible? The question bounced between my ears as I peered up at the man beside her.

His face was so much harder this close.

I didn't like it.

I wanted my mother.

Tucking my chin, I hurried away to escape his company. But a rock was kicked into my path. Tripping over it, I stumbled sideways, reaching for the railing of the bridge.

But it was as though it melted away, bending and rendering it impossible to clutch.

Head first, I toppled over the edge of the bridge.

A scream left me, because in the mere seconds before water closed over me, fear gripped me. A fear every child like me was taught from a young age.

Water on our island was deadly.

Winter water most of all.

I plunged into the depths and everything was robbed of me. Up and down. Light. Air. Feeling.

My coat dragged me down, simultaneously cushioning me as the water threw me against hidden boulders.

My lungs tightened, and I tried to move my arms and legs like Mother showed me. Swimming. I had to swim!

The water was so strong.

Too strong.

And I was tired.

My legs and arms felt funny—the way they usually did when I first woke or feel asleep. My eyes closed, and even a sudden tugging and jerking on my coat couldn't open them.

Hands hauled me from the river and I hit the riverbank hard.

Coughing and sucking in what air I could, my eyes popped open and met with the darkest gaze I'd ever seen.

The pretty boy's eyes were black, just like his hair, and water dripped from the strands. "Are you okay?"

He wasn't speaking Tlingit, but mother had made me learn the fae language too. My lips wouldn't move, though, and I simply chattered in response, doing my best to nod.

"Son?" A nasally and bored voice rose from behind the boy. "Is the human alive?"

The pretty boy tensed but didn't look at the person speaking. "She's alive."

"Then leave her there."

A frown marred the space between his brows. "I will take her back to her people."

Soft chuckles drifted up around us.

The nasal voice spoke again, this time a hint of laughter in the woman's voice. "Just like his grandfather."

I took the boy's offered hand, mine slippery with blood, stumbling on shaking legs. "My m-mother—"

"Up on the rise," he grunted, wrapping an arm around my waist.

"Y-yes." I sniffled, blinking back tears. "I j-just wanted to s-see."

He hushed me softly, not in an unkind way, but no one else stopped to help me, none of the beautiful people sent me smiles.

I wish I'd never come.

I rubbed at the scar on my finger. An Unseelie boy had saved my life, all those years ago. Perhaps it would have been better if he'd let me die. At least then . . . I looked over my shoulder at the group of fae gathered here in this cabin. Fear lay heavy on them, I could almost see the cloud of it above their heads.

They knew—as did I—that no matter what the Unseelie trainer said, something had happened to Underhill.

And more than all that, I knew it was somehow, impossibly, my fault.

"We'll ride out the storm here," the same Unseelie trainer said. "Then we'll head back to Unimak in the morning."

The door banged open and a pair of men stumbled in, covered in furs which were covered in snow head to foot, and that included their thick beards.

Beards.

Humans.

My hand shifted over my body and I pulled my magic around me, so that my glamor covered anything that made me look less human. Like the weapons I carried, and the leather armor I wore.

Not exactly what you'd call normal for being in the middle of Alaska.

"Goddamn it, Gary, I told you we were going the wrong way!" The first of the men stomped his feet, knocking a layer of snow off.

"You were the one who said that the bigfoot went this way,

you were tracking it!" Gary grumbled and then he lifted his eyes. "Um. Gord. We aren't alone."

Gord—apparently—pulled his hat off. "Long as they ain't fae I don't give two figs who is here."

Ouch.

I took a look around and saw that the trainers had masked a bunch of the trainees' gear as well. Our twenty-four, twelve in the Unseelie camp, and another fifteen newbies from the more recently brought in Seelie troop. Just over fifty people all told.

Gary dusted off his cap showing a bare skull—shaved, not bald. "You all got caught in the storm too?"

"We're here on an executive retreat," Bres said smoothly, adding a little charm magic to his voice.

Gary grinned. "Nice! We were hunting bigfoot. You know that the Triangle is loaded with them critters? I think we were onto at least a pack of ten before the storm hit."

Bres nodded. "Truly, we'd love to hear the tale of two mighty hunters."

Gord and Gary grinned, shucked off their furs and took front and center stage right near the fireplace.

Rowan slid back to stand next to me. "Can you forgive me?"

I glanced over at him. "Yes. But don't except me to trust you."

He grunted. "Fair." And then he nodded at the two humans, oblivious to the fact that they were surrounded by fae. "You think they don't like us for real?"

I shrugged. "I think fae scare a lot of people." I knew that they scared my mother. She'd kept me as far from that boundary between us and them for as long as she could.

"Gray," Gary whispered. "The beast was gray from the top of his head to the bottom of his oversized feet, with fur hanging off him like an old man's beard, tangled and snotty with food. Teeth like broken daggers, and when he looked at me," he shuddered, "I could feel him stare right through me." A few of the younger fae leaned in and I tuned out.

"How come you don't like fae?" Yarrow asked suddenly, breaking his way right into the conversation.

Ass.

Gord leaned back and looked at Yarrow. "'Cause one of these days, they're going to want to go back to the old ways."

I frowned and Yarrow snorted. "What old ways?"

"Where humans were slaves," Gord said. "They want to make it like they aren't dangerous, but they are. They say they can't lie, but I'm not so sure that isn't in itself a lie."

The human wasn't wrong. Since the fae had come out to the human populace roughly a hundred years before, right after the end of WWII, we'd encouraged the old beliefs that the fae couldn't lie, and that we were a gentle folk. We'd split our people up all over the world, to keep our numbers down.

It made it easier for the humans to trust us, which we'd needed at the time.

Of course it wasn't true. Fae could lie just as easily as any human. But what Gord and Gary were correct about was that the fae were far more dangerous than we let on.

Especially when we believed we had no other way out but to fight.

A truth which I was about to learn all the way to my core.

CHAPTER 3

Eight years ago, I'd been full of anticipation and eagerness, and the journey to Underhill had seemed endless. Today, when I had a dire secret to keep from the world I was returning to, the flight home from the Triangle passed in a flash.

The private jet circled us high above Unimak Island, and I peered down at the tiny blip of land, dread filling me at the familiar sight of the twin mountain ranges jutting north like a two-pronged fork. A massive azure-blue crater lake rested at the base of the central peak, where the ranges merged to one.

Whoops went up from the other Tried occupants in the craft at the sight of our island, but their cheers were muted. Those of the newer troop were silent. The Unseelie had taken their own plane back to their side of Unimak.

The truth of it was, we all knew Underhill had shattered yesterday. That dimmed the glory of our return significantly.

The fae of both courts *and* all outcasts would clamor for answers.

I couldn't blame them. Aside from the obvious 'how the hell did I annihilate a realm' aspect of what had happened, I had the same question as everyone else.

What would befall us now?

The fae had existed on Earth in our human-designated pockets of land for more than one hundred years, and for longer than that as free-roaming beings, but we'd *always* had the fae realm to return to when we needed magical replenishment or a rest from human politics. We relied on Underhill.

And, according to the Oracle, I'd somehow destroyed it.

Me.

The half-fae mutt.

A bastard left by her father's guards at an orphanage.

A good number of the fae had some human blood in them—it was what had kept our people going after the last great war. But very, very few had more than a small percentage. Me? I was full on fifty-fifty. Something that hadn't happened in a very long time.

And yeah, maybe I came to grips with that reality long ago.

But seeing Unimak after so long, after working so damn hard to change my reality during training . . . turns out some cracks still remained.

I jerked as the tires screeched and we landed on the short airstrip at the northeast tip of the island.

A heartier cheer went up from the other Seelie from Unimak Island, one of the four territories of fae, represented by our class of trainees, but I didn't join in. As the door opened and Bres led the way out of the craft, I tightened my resolve.

Nothing—*nothing*—would get between me and my independence.

Not a father who'd ordered his minions to chuck me in an orphanage instead of claiming me when my mother died.

Not a stepmother who loathed me.

Not this current nightmare.

Taking a breath, I grabbed my patched duffel and tagged behind Yarrow as he rolled his carry-on luggage between the aisles. Lugh help me, the case was customized with his stupid-ass name. In what looked like rhinestones.

Fae aircraft were made to accommodate our greater than human height, but Yarrow still ducked his head to get out. I walked through unhindered and blinked twice at the waiting crowd.

It was normal for the families of Tried to show up, but some of those below were blatantly Unseelie officials. The laws around Unseelie and Seelie mingling were strict so for them to be here was . . . serious.

"Bet they're here for answers," Fern said from in front of Yarrow.

Of course.

They'd already heard the news about Underhill from their own trainees and trainers, and were rightfully pissed. It had been during a Seelie ceremony that the breaking had happened, and they knew it.

I schooled my features to blandness, scanning the masses of fae.

"Looking for your family, mutt?" Yarrow tossed over his shoulder at me as he waved to a large group of golden-haired fae. "Wait, they're dead, aren't they?"

Pretty sure Daddy wouldn't turn up, not that Yarrow knew who that was. And if my stepmom stepped out of the masses to greet me, I'd die from shock.

"Nope," I replied. "Just looking at the stain on the back of your pants."

I dodged around Yarrow as he stopped to check and joined the other Unimak Tried.

Maybe I hadn't fit in with the other troop members, but after eight years as a band of twenty-four, it felt strange to be parted from the others, who would be dropped off at their various Seelie homelands. I'd like to say I'd miss the constancy of their company, but I wasn't so sure that would be the case. But with Unimak being the official residence of the Seelie king, maybe some of them—like Bracken, and possibly Rowan—would visit from wherever they ended up.

Of course, that depended on me surviving until then. And

there was one massive problem with that.

The Oracle knew what I'd done, and she'd disappeared without a trace amidst the chaos yesterday. Just walked away like it was nothing.

Was she a danger to me? Would she tell the king that I'd destroyed Underhill on purpose? Of course I hadn't, but I knew without a doubt he wouldn't believe me.

There sure as shit wasn't anything I could do against a woman of her power. She might have already told the king and his advisors. Maybe the Unseelie were here because their queen knew too. My guts twisted up and sweat broke out along the back of my neck.

I couldn't help searching the flocks of fae for the king's guards.

"Your attention, newly Tried of Unimak," Bres boomed.

The crowd quieted.

I faced my old trainer, trying not to read too much into the way his eyes rested on me for a beat too long.

He studied the five of us who'd gathered all three coins. "You have earned your place amongst us. And this feat will be recognized. There will be a feast in your honor tomorrow night at King Aleksandr's castle, where all Seelie shall look upon you. You have earned the right to choose your area of training, and this is where you will announce your decision. I urge you to choose wisely. This choice cannot be undone."

Damn it. I hated seeing my father.

Mainly because he hated seeing me too. In truth, it was not

public knowledge who my father was—I'm not sure I believed it myself sometimes.

The bastard daughter of the king, half human no less? What a disgrace. What a terrible mistake. My guts clenched with that old pain, superseding the fear that the guards were looking for me.

When younger, I'd yearned for his approval, for a home where I would be loved—especially after losing my mother. That had bled into a stage of angry denial, where I'd wanted nothing from him. Somewhere along the line, I'd realized that there would always be a yearning for his acceptance. And that his refusal to claim me—his only child, to my knowledge—would always hurt. But now I'd finally earned Elite status, something that would give me control over my future for the very first time.

That's why I'd always imagined this moment would be filled with triumph and vindication and feelings of acceptance and equality. I'd gone into Underhill believing that I would survive, believing that I would come out on top—one of very few women to ever do so. I had, except *now*, I hadn't.

In the end, I felt none of the things I'd expected to feel.

"Please approach one by one for your accommodation assignment," Bres commanded.

We'd been asked for our requests yesterday night as we'd hunkered down in the big cabin, all but stacked on top of one another, and after everything, I couldn't recall what I'd blindly written down.

Third in line, I frowned when Bres purposefully moved

around me to speak with Fern and Yarrow first.

Unease crawled up my spine, and I scanned the dispersing crowd anew. They were converging on the other Tried, welcoming them to their midst.

"Kallik," Bres said once everyone else was gone.

I faced him, straightening my spine so I could look up into his face. "Sir."

He studied the small scroll in his hand. "You're first tier, just outside the castle."

My lips numbed. *What?* "That's not what I chose."

Sure, I couldn't remember exactly *what* I'd chosen, but there was no way I'd have selected anything near the castle. My request would have been more along the lines of 'the enchanted forest farthest from the castle,' or 'at the sea inlet farthest from the castle,' or 'along the river *farthest* from the castle.' Hell, I would have taken a spot on the Unseelie side of the river over a home near Father Dearest's castle.

Bres wasn't the warm and fuzzy type, but he'd loosened up somewhat in the last year as I'd taken my spot in the troop as a leader. There wasn't a trace of that now. "This has been assigned to you from higher up. You have no say in the decision."

My spine stiffened, and blood poured into my cheeks. I swallowed my temper down before it could spill over—practice made perfect. Fighting against a king was a waste of time. "I see."

I took the slip of parchment from him. Gold glitter was embedded in it, a sure sign I was on Unimak again.

KALLIK, ELITE TRIED OF NO HOUSE
666 FIRST TIER,
SEELIE COURT
UNIMAK ISLAND
ALASKA 99638
UNITED STATES

The 666 wasn't a coincidence. The other fae didn't know who I truly was, but the king's wife had set the standard for how to treat "the mutt" from an early age. This was the same old crap I'd grown up with. If it wasn't last-minute exclusions from festivities that all other Seelie were invited to, it was jeering comments from her on my shabby dresses during parades when no one else could hear. It was glares when no one else was looking. It was ordering her guards to use their magic to push and jostle and make me look like a fool after she'd passed through—just like the day on the bridge long ago when I 'fell' into the river.

But I wasn't the same sixteen-year-old girl who'd left.

I refused to be.

"Thanks, Bres—" I lifted my head, "—for getting me through training."

His lips pressed together. The old fae glanced around, but we were largely alone. Everyone else had gone off to celebrate and relax with their families. "What happened to Underhill, Kallik?"

My insides froze, but I'd half-expected him to interrogate me. Which was a problem. Bres had made an oath to the Seelie court and Underhill long ago too—if he had serious concerns or suspicions about what had happened, then he *had* to take information to the king. Which meant I had some serious convincing to do. "Have you heard something more?"

He narrowed his gaze. "The Oracle drove the blade with your blood on it into the ground. Why?"

I sighed in relief. "You saw that too?"

Bres leaned in. "Tell me what *you* saw, what happened?"

I shook my head, goddess, I did not want to do this. I'd sworn an oath to protect my king and Underhill. "I don't know," I answered that part honestly. "The Oracle. After cutting me . . . I think she cut herself too." The lie fell from my lips and I wanted to puke. I shrugged to cover my unease. "Then she shoved the blade into the ground. Everyone was behind her, and I didn't think anyone else saw. I didn't want to say anything—she's the *Oracle*. Who is going to believe me?" I didn't overplay my role too much. Bres knew me better than most and he knew I was shit at lying.

Even though I'd stuck to the truth as closely as I could, doubt flitted over his features.

I drew closer. "Did you see where she went? It looked as though she disappeared after it happened. She turned and just kind of . . . faded away."

Bres pursed his lips. "She has ways of disappearing. And no, no one knows where she's gone."

"I didn't know if that was normal." By his expression, I'd say not.

The trainer established distance between us again. "Dismissed. Don't forget the feast tomorrow night."

How could I? "Yes, sir."

Scroll in hand, duffel slung across my shoulders, I strode for the large building that was literally made of twisting red vines woven thickly around one another, purple leaves spreading as wide as palm fronds. Blue and gold flowers adorned the over-the-top display. A bit tasteless, but if there was one thing fae excelled at, it was making money—and rich human tourists loved this shit.

I eyed a royal-red banner as I passed through the building.

WELCOME TO WORLD FAE-MOUS MAGICAL ISLAND!

Silver glitter coated my brown leather leggings and simple tunic by the time I escaped outside. *Great.*

I dusted it off, not knowing why I bothered. This was just the start of my glitter woes.

"Alli," a puffed shout reached my ears.

My heart leaped as I spotted the enormously busty woman bearing down the hill toward me.

"Cinth!" I picked up my step and dropped my duffel. My one true best friend, Hyacinth, bowled into me and the air rushed from my lungs.

The sweet smell of fresh bread and spices clung to her and wound around me as she held me tight. Her dark blond hair was pulled back in an intricate braid, but the end of it rubbed against my face. She held me at arm's length, grimacing, dark blue eyes crinkling around the edges, pulling on the old burn mark on the left side of her face. It had faded in the last four years. Because for her it had *only* been four years. Because of some intricacy of the magic, eight years in Underhill was half as long here. "I meant to be here when you landed, but the last batch of cherry and beetroot tickles weren't ready. Are you well? I can't believe you're finally home!"

Tickles were a fae biscuit—my absolute favorite treat. Maybe I hadn't tried cherry and beetroot tickles before, but if Hyacinth baked them, I'd no doubt they'd be delicious.

"Oo," she exclaimed before I could answer, clapping her hands together. "I made a sign."

Her face fell as she held up the crumpled banner reading, *Welcome Ho*—.

"It said 'Welcome home, Alli,'" she murmured. "How did that get torn off?"

I smiled. Hyacinth was just the same—the four years for her hadn't change her an ounce. And even though we hadn't talked in all that time, it was like we'd never been apart. We picked up right where we left off.

She held up a finger. "I snuck you a tickle too. It's just here . . ."

Hyacinth groaned as she extracted the crumbed remains of the smooshed biscuit. What was left of it dissolved between her fingers to shower the ground.

My smile widened as I pulled her in for another hug. "It's so great to see you. I *missed* you."

My voice was muffled against her large chest—Hyacinth was normal fae height, aka several inches taller than my measly five foot seven.

"It may not be obvious from the ruined sign and cookie, but I really missed you too. Let me have another look at you."

I was thrust to arm's length again, and she turned me around as if we were doing a little dance.

"Those are some serious muscles, Alli. Hey, did you hear Underhill is gone? Oh! We need to get moving. Head Chef only gave me an hour, and I want to see your new place. Where are you now? Please tell me you're near the third tier. We'd almost be neighbors!"

Like a favorite coat, I'd already slipped back into our friendship, but that didn't mean I could tell her everything. So I didn't respond to her question about Underhill. "First tier," I said and shoved the glittering paper at her.

She scanned it and her mouth bobbed open. "First tier by the castle?"

I grunted and didn't quite make eye contact. "I got to choose. Elite Tried right here."

She gripped my arm tightly and gave a little squeal. "I *knew* you'd earn Elite status. One of the only women ever to do it! Hold on, you hate the castle, why would you choose there? Hey, tell me everything. I want to know it all. *Goddess*, I've missed you so much. No one here compares to you, Alli."

She tugged me along and I followed dutifully as she talked nonstop. I strode beside my friend as we walked to the nearest Seelie trolley station that would take us through the city.

The two fae courts may depend on each other to maintain magical balance, but they didn't like to share toys. They had one side of the island, and we had the other.

The trolley was blissfully free of human tourists today. That was the last thing I needed. They could be so rude, and damn loud. And the cameras . . . always with the pictures and selfies!

Almost as bad as Gary and Gord demanding pictures with us before we left the cabin. Humans were strange, they bonded so quickly with others.

I listened to Hyacinth babble as we began to magically move up the jutting east range that belonged to our court. An enchanted forest—blue and gold today—covered a good chunk of the Seelie territory. Another tourist gimmick. Seelie fae didn't care what color the forest was—we just cared that *life* fueled our magic.

As the gradient steepened, I peered out the back window of the trolley to where the fae abodes were now visible below. While my father's castle sat halfway up the incline of the mountain range, well above our current position, his subjects' homes sprawled down the mountainside and through the enchanted forest to the ice-cold Pacific Ocean. Our court inhabited all the land east of the dividing river in Unimak.

" . . . so now I'm the deputy chef," my friend declared proudly.

I tuned back in and smiled at her. "That's great, Cinth. You deserve every bit of that title. In no time, you'll make head chef and be running the whole kitchen."

She blushed, making the burn mark go deep red, and hugged me again. "I hope so. It's a dream, you know."

As a full-blooded female fae, she hadn't had to jockey for status in our world. She could have chosen any role or home she desired . . . if her parents hadn't lost their minds and tried to slaughter some of my father's guards ten years back. They'd started a fire, and she'd been caught in it, unable to escape. After her injuries healed, she'd ended up in the orphanage with me, and it was there she discovered her passion and innate skills for food.

She kept looking me over as if she thought I would disappear. "You know what's weird? You're the same age as me now."

We'd joked about it before I left. She'd started out four years older, but we were both twenty-four now. "Does that mean you won't try to mother me anymore?" I grinned. "No more trying to tuck me in?"

She whacked me lightly. "I mother fae twenty times my age, so it's highly unlikely you'll escape that."

The trolley lurched to a stop. "*You've arrived at the first tier! Have a fae-tastic day!*"

"I have not missed that," I muttered, grabbing my duffel.

We wound around the perimeter of the castle's inner walls. Right at the back, completely bereft of sunlight, sat 666 First Tier.

My home. Yeah, I wasn't so sure how I felt about that.

"That's an interesting number," my friend murmured, checking the address against the scroll in my hand again.

"Funny, huh?" I said without an ounce of humor. In the human world, the number 666 was the number of the devil, we all knew that. It meant something different, although not necessarily better, in the fae world: chaos and bad luck.

So, no matter which side of my heritage I looked to, the number wasn't an auspicious one.

The door opened at my touch, and I pushed inside, Hyacinth hot on my heels. We walked down a short hallway that opened into a room with a table and a single chair. Really, they couldn't have given me two?

There was a sink there, along with shelves containing a plate, bowl, and cutlery. The single chamber branching directly off the central room contained a bed and copious amounts of bedding.

On the opposite side was a door leading to a bathroom with a threadbare towel, toothbrush, and soap.

We'd been warned not to expect anything other than the essential furniture, and they hadn't exaggerated. Living in the first tier clearly didn't give me special perks.

Fine by me. Maybe I could trade this place with another of the Tried? Others might think it a boon to live so close to the palace. That thought had some merit. I could get a place closer to Cinth once the final ceremonies were all done.

"Some homey touches and this will be yours in no time. I have a few spare things that I'll bring over after my shift tonight. Oh wait, we're on double shifts because of the feast tomorrow. Are you going? Of course you're going. It's *for* you." Cinth's cheerful voice echoed from the bedroom. Walking out, she set the torn welcome sign on the kitchen table. "You get a stipend, right?"

I brushed a finger over the countertops, the granite thrumming under my hand, still vibrating from being pulled from the earth with fae magic. "First payment tomorrow."

"Well then, you'll be up and running soon." She beamed, and I could tell she was exuding extra cheer on my behalf. Hyacinth always had possessed an uncanny ability to detect what I really felt. She didn't know about the particulars of my birth—I'd tried to tell her on multiple occasions, but someone must have put a magical binding on me when I was young. No matter how hard I tried, the words just wouldn't come out. Even so, she always sensed the way it impacted me. The conflict that seethed and twisted in my heart.

I'd expected to return home as one of the Seelie court at last.

Expected freedom.

Expected to *feel* so much more when I stepped into my very own home.

But now I understood the truth. This was just a bittersweet taste of what could be ripped away.

Determination filled me, and I strode to the table to pick up my 'Welcome Ho' sign from Cinth. I set it above the door frame to my room and stood back, folding my arms.

I'd convinced Bres to abandon his suspicions earlier—hopefully. If the Oracle kept her mouth shut, then this would all go away in time.

No one would be any the wiser about what I'd supposedly done to Underhill.

I just had to keep my head down, play my part, and play it as though my life depended on it.

Because it did.

CHAPTER 4

I didn't stay in my assigned home more than three minutes after Hyacinth left for her shift at the bakery. There was somewhere I needed to go, someone I needed to see.

My Tláa.

Grabbing my bow and arrow, I slipped them into my empty pack . . . but it didn't seem like enough after years of fighting in Underhill, so I slid a short, curved blade into a sheath on my thigh.

Bres had warned us that when we came back we'd be big on overkill with the weapons—a latent effect of the constant danger in Underhill for eight years—but he'd said the need to go fully armed would fade in time.

"You were right, old man," I muttered under my breath. The

urge to grab my throwing knives and the grappling hook I'd made in Underhill itched at my fingers.

But would I encounter a three-headed dragon here? No.

I could do without them.

Hurrying out of the shadowed home before I could change my mind about the grappling hook, I debated taking the trolley back down the mountainside. But then I'd have to listen to *"Have a fae-tastic time, we can't wait to Seelie you again!"*

I rolled my eyes and walked through the streets instead. This would give me a chance to see what had changed since I'd left. Here in the first tier, the shops were about as high end as they were on the infamous Fifth Avenue in New York City. To be fair, this was also where most of the human tourists shopped—where we allowed them to be—so the selections were somewhat geared toward them.

The windows boasted fae clothing—thick cloaks of velvet or fae silk (lighter than feathers and warmer than wool), leather arm bracers studded with polished copper, handmade hiking boots, and custom-made pants made from the hide of fae oxen (or foxen as Cinth and I liked to call them). Every article of clothing was something fae *could* wear here, but probably not in that shade of bright purple with glittering onyx buttons, or the lacy black number with brown feathers. These were our castoffs at best, gaudy tourist trap knockoffs at worst. The humans didn't seem to notice. They came here seeking a fantasy. We gave it to them, and they paid dearly for the honor.

The weapons stall past the clothing stores caught my eye, and the smell of ash and smoke filled my nostrils, slowing my feet as I approached it. The sound of the hammer falling rhythmically on the metals we used was only interrupted by the soft nicker of a horse waiting to be shod.

I shook off the call of the sharp steel and picked up my pace to a slow jog down the range and into the enchanted forest.

The cobblestone pathways were interspersed with bursts of wildflowers in every color of the rainbow as if nature were pushing her way into every crevice she could. The multitude of flowers filled the air with layers of perfume. Rose, jasmine, lily, vanilla, chocolate, cinnamon, and other scents not found in the human world had been woven through the petals with deft hands. I found myself pausing to pick a few, choosing the brightest reds and pinks.

Tucking the flowers into my empty pack, I broke into a faster run, drawing in deep breaths.

A thirty-mile run was required to get out of the Seelie court, out of our enchanted lands. For a human, it would take four or five hours; for me, barely two. That was a serious investment of time, but I needed to feel the wind in my hair and let the events of yesterday fade.

I needed to pretend I didn't feel the weight of chaos coming for me.

I needed my mother.

Tiers two and three were a blip on my radar as I descended

the mountain. I passed tier four without pausing at the orphanage where I'd grown up. That shithole could burn for all I cared.

"What's on fire?" someone yelled as I tore past, picking up speed again.

I flipped them off and they laughed. I couldn't have gotten away with that in tier one, but tier four? Yeah, the trade fae didn't care who you were or what you looked like as long as you paid them for their wares.

The gradient plateaued as I reached the bottom of the mountain, and I ran west to find the river.

River Danaan was the divider between the Seelie and the Unseelie, and following it was the best way to find your way around on Unimak, especially if you wanted to land yourself in the world of humans.

The world of my mother.

Around me the bloom of color continued, sans the glitter that covered everything in the tourist areas. This was pure enchanted forest, full of little creatures as well as flora that was beyond anything natural.

The trees spread high above in every color imaginable—leaves of pink, purple, blue and blood orange. Flowers that were brilliantly gold, silver, and bronze with centers that looked like perfectly placed jewels. Everything was real, everything was alive, just . . . it was magical too.

Birds swooped through the branches, flashing their equally bright colors, calling to one another in dulcet tones that beckoned me to rest, to ease my tired mind and body.

"Not today, my friends," I breathed as I continued on.

The river wound to the left, and I slowed. Not really tired, but this far from the mountain I could safely stop to catch my wind.

Voices tugged on my ears as I slowed, and I immediately dodged behind the massive green trunk of a tree close to the water's edge. I wiggled my fingers against the smooth bark, feeling the essence of the tree. I narrowed my eyes to pull up my ability to see magic, and the green threads of energy that tied it to our world bloomed into view. In response to my plea, the tree's branches grew longer, drooping low, like a willow, until they covered my hiding place.

I mentally thanked the tree for its help, absently noting the flowers that had sprung to life beneath me, and lowered my hand.

The voices pulled me forward.

"What do you mean Underhill is gone? That's not possible. A trick from the Seelie. Aleksandr knows that we outnumber them," a woman said. "What do you think, young Faolan? You grew up there; could this be a ruse they have put into play?"

I blinked a few times, my stomach swooping. *Faolan* was here?

He'd been eight years older than me when I left for training. And yes, I'd had a major teenage crush on the much older guy with the brooding good looks. Classic bad boy.

I winced even though they couldn't see me.

"I doubt they'd try a ruse of such a magnitude. They are not aggressive when it comes to making a move, at least he is not. If it was the queen consort running the show, perhaps . . ." His gravelly voice sent more than a few shivers down my spine, straight to my . . . no, *no*, I wasn't going there.

It had been a huge crush, built on childhood hero worship after he saved me from drowning in the river, but it was still *just* a crush. Though his kindness in the years after saving me hadn't helped matters at all.

"Back straight, Kallik! Seelie don't slouch." The orphanage *matron whipped her magic across the back of my legs.*

I yelped and straightened. With Matron Bethalyn, it was best to pick your battles aka commit transgressions when she wasn't around to witness them.

From beside me, Hyacinth scowled at the older woman's back.

"What is this?" I muttered.

Cinth sighed. "They're bringing in kids with parents to buddy with us. Makes rich people feel better about themselves, I think."

I hadn't known the girl many months, but Cinth was usually cheerful as could be. When she got down like this, she was normally thinking about her parents' deaths.

That made me sad for her.

Reaching out, I took her hand in mine. "Should we sneak out?"

A tiny smile danced on her lips. "We could. If this wasn't going to be a monthly thing until further notice."

I groaned, wiping at my dripping nose. Great. The last thing I wanted to do was hang out with a person who either pitied my fate or looked down on me.

The half-rotted double doors of the orphanage swung inward and a crowd of Seelie kids—all a few years older than me by the looks of them—walked in. Their sour expressions told me what kind of day this would be.

I groaned again, but the sound snapped off like a piece of toffee when I saw a boy with dark hair and dark eyes right at the front of the incoming group. "Hey . . ."

Cinth shot me a look, but the matron started to talk.

The boy was so familiar.

Like I'd met him.

My eyes widened and I squinted at him in earnest. It was him. The boy was older now, and much taller, but there could be no doubt.

It was the boy who had saved me from the river.

He frowned and glanced at me, and I quickly tore my focus from him, planting it firmly on the matron.

"Each of you from the first and second tier will walk forward and select an orphan. This will be your buddy for the years to come." She paused. And when no one moved, snapped, "Get to it."

The Seelie standing opposite weren't immune to her sharp tone either. Even then, the dark-haired boy was the first to cross the divide. He looked up and down the row of us, and I'd never felt shabbier than in that moment though I played in these clothes each day without a second thought.

His eyes landed on me once more.

Did he remember me?

"She's a mutt," a boy said from next to me. Rowan. He'd been here for years. Longer than me. And he settled upon generosity or ruthlessness at random.

For the most part, I didn't mind him, so I didn't glare. I'd pour a bucket of water over his blankets later.

Rowan's comments did elicit several muffled giggles from the other orphans—and the well-dressed Seelie opposite. I just sighed. Now I'd be the last one chosen.

The dark-haired boy approached and stopped immediately before me. "I'll be the judge of that. Your name?"

His voice wasn't at all as I recalled. Far closer to how I remembered his mother's voice sounding when she told him to leave me on the riverbank.

"You don't need to be the judge of anything," I replied, sending him my coolest look.

He merely smiled. In a flash, it disappeared again. "Your name?"

I rolled my eyes. "Kallik of No House. Who're you?"

"Faolan. Grandson of Lugh."

My jaw bobbed. "Of Lugh? The Lugh?"

From his tone until this point, I would've expected him to enjoy the awe I'd accidentally let slip, but the frown that had smoothed over returned in full force. "Is there another Lugh I'm unaware of?"

Fair point. "Okay. Well . . ." I stared down the line. "Honestly, there aren't many in here that won't be torture to buddy with, so better get to it. Or Cinth here—" Turning to my new friend, I saw she was already talking with another boy in nice clothing. "See, you gotta be quick."

The boy was shaking his head when I returned my gaze to him.

Blowing out a breath, he extended a hand. "Kallik of No House, perhaps we can get through this together. What do you say?"

Me?

The mutt?

Rowan muttered something, and it didn't take much imagination to guess it wasn't complimentary.

Swallowing hard, I took the hand of Lugh's grandson, hardly believing my luck. "Sounds okay to me."

I gritted my teeth at the memory. Not because of it directly, but what had come after. The older I got, the more distance he put between us, which had only made my crush ten times worse. At least he'd been sorted into the Unseelie court two years before I left for training, and after that I knew nothing could come of it. There was no mixing between the two courts—it was strictly forbidden.

Even knowing that didn't stop sixteen-year-old drunk me from making a fool of herself.

I groaned, recalling the last time we'd seen each other, at the one pub that stretched across the river and allowed Seelie and Unseelie on the premises at the same time.

A few eyebrows had winged up as I crossed over from the Seelie side of the building. Normally, that might have put me off, but Cinth had urged me to try the Fae Honey—apparently the best around. And then there was the whiskey made from the human herb, nepeta.

The drinking horn I carried had some sloshing in it, but my attention was focused on my target.

Depending on how training went, I knew it might be the last time I saw Faolan, and I wanted answers. He'd completely brushed me off the previous week when I'd snuck across the river to see him.

Treated me as if I were just a little girl making a fool of herself.

I clutched the drinking horn in one hand and slapped the table with the other, drawing his eyes to me. "So I'm not good enough because I'm half human, is that right?" At least I tried to say that, but my words came out weird and slurry.

Faolan looked at me, dark eyes narrowing as he looked me up and down, his lips pulling tight. "Orphan, what are you doing here?"

"Going to training tomorrow." I ignored the fact that he hadn't used my name. "Last night before I die, and you're the hottest guy on Unimak, which means we need to talk."

Joking about dying in Underhill was bad luck and considered rude, but the drunk Unseelie around him laughed and clapped him on the back.

"Better kiss her goodbye, Lan," one said.

He frowned and shook his head. "You're too young, Orphan. Too young to go to training by two years. Too weak to survive. You're a little girl. Go to the kitchens with your friend if you can, that's a better place for you."

A few of his buddies laughed and echoed his words. "Get out of here," one Unseelie barked. "You aren't wanted here. You don't belong here, mutt."

But the thing was, I was more than a little drunk myself, and only one of his objections penetrated. That I was too young.

Too young, my ass.

So I grabbed his arm, jerked him around, and then bodily dragged him out of his seat to a chorus of oohs. Closing my eyes, I planted a kiss on him that I'd dreamed of for years . . . except it didn't feel quite like I'd expected. Weird shape. Squishy.

Opening my eyes, I stared at his left eye.

Which I'd apparently just kissed.

I bit back my groan, and strongly considered asking the tree that had covered my hiding spot to just bury me on the spot.

Why did Lan, of all people, have to be here now?

"Guardsman, I want you to find out what happened there. Use whatever connections you have," the woman said. "You will be my eyes and ears and will report directly to me."

"Yes, my queen."

Oh, shit. Queen Elisavana was across the river? I crouched lower so I could peek through the bottom of the tree's dangling branches. A dark brown shimmering skirt flared out at the edge of the far bank. I spotted a flash of black leather pants and boots behind the skirt before they both moved closer to the forest on their side of the river.

How long before I could move? I *really* wanted to visit my mother, but if there was one thing capable of distracting me, it was an encounter with Faolan or the Unseelie queen.

Grabbing the lowest branch of the tree, I silently hauled myself up and worked my way through the branches until I reached a perch that gave me a view of the river and those who walked beside it.

There.

The queen of the Unseelie strode upriver along the thin edge of the trees, toward her west-range castle with Faolan not far behind. He paused and turned, and I ducked on the off chance he'd look up instead of at the banks of the river.

Heart hammering, I stayed low and held still until I was sure they'd both be gone, then I slid down the tree and hit the ground with a light thud.

The hairs rose on the back of my neck. I turned and snapped a fist out.

I caught Faolan in the left side of his face, knocking him back several feet.

"Lugh's left nut, what the hell are you doing on this side of the river?" But I already knew. He must've seen me duck down, dammit. My hand barely throbbed as I shook out my fingers.

Left hand, too, that was my weak side.

He rubbed at his face, looked at me and then looked closer, his eyes widening a fraction. "*Orphan? Is that you?*"

I frowned. *Ouch.* He didn't even recognize me? "What, hoping I wouldn't make it back?"

"Still joking about dying in Underhill, I see." His lips thinned. "To be fair, I'm shocked you made it through the training."

His eyes swept over me as they'd done that night in the bar, and once again, I felt like I'd been judged and found wanting.

Whatever. I pushed my way through the long hanging willow

branches I'd created, the soft pink of the leaves far prettier than anything I'd seen in these last eight years. "You shouldn't be on this side of the river. You could get in trouble. Wouldn't want to mar your record."

Faolan caught up easily and strode alongside me, keeping a good three feet between us, ignoring my verbal jabs. "At least your reflexes have improved."

I snorted and kept my eyes on the path ahead of me. My schoolgirl crush was long gone, but damn if he wasn't still a fine piece of ass. Which was why I refused to be caught ogling him. "What are you doing over here? Where you aren't wanted." Yup, look at me go, using the same words he'd spoken to me against him.

His body tensed, and from the corner of my eye I saw his jaw tighten. Score one for me.

"Still rude as fuck, I see," he said. "Seems to me you'd want to apologize. As is our custom for when someone makes a fool of themselves."

Ah, fuck, he was going to talk about it, wasn't he? The eye kiss.

I fought to keep my face blank. "I have no idea what you're talking about." There. Let him think I'd been drunk enough that the moment hadn't stuck with me.

"Hmm." That rumble from his chest was all male ego. "Here I was thinking you'd want to improve on our last kiss. See if you can aim your mouth a little lower." The asshole laughed.

The double meaning was not lost on me.

I spun on one foot and swung the other leg in a perfect

roundhouse. None of the other trainees—not even Yarrow—had ever been able to block this move.

Faolan caught my leg at the knee and threw it away, one slash of a dark eyebrow arching. "Don't start something you can't finish, *little girl*."

He didn't just call me—

"Lanny," I purred the nickname used by his mother and that I'd used as a child when he'd visited me, enjoying his wince, "you're on the wrong side of the tracks, *little* boy."

Yeah, that was a low blow—we were both short for fae—but he went there first.

Faolan scoffed. "That's the best you got? You think that, of all the things you could say about me, is going to injure my feelings? You're obviously a child. Still."

I whirled away. "*Not* nice seeing you. Go away, Unseelie."

He turned with me, easily keeping pace.

"Did you hear about Underhill?"

That was obviously the only reason he was still talking to me. He knew where I'd come from, and when.

Faolan was under oath to the Unseelie queen, just as Bres was under oath to the Seelie king. There were serious consequences to breaking that, which meant anything I told him would go directly to her. I had to be very careful. "Hear what?"

"Don't play dumb, Orphan. You would have been there when it happened." I noted that he had not used my name, not once. "What happened? You were there. Who was with the Oracle when . . ."

I turned and faced him, once more smoothing my features. I wasn't the best liar, but when push came to shove I could fake it. My eyebrows rose. "When what?"

His eyes searched my face as if he were looking for the answer on my forehead, typed neatly in size 12 Times New Roman. "Something has happened to Underhill, and like the rest of the fae I want to know what." Just like him to not give more information than needed.

It seemed not much had changed in the time I'd been gone, but fishing expeditions were a tricky thing if a person didn't have the right bait, and Faolan was not dangling anything I wanted to bite.

Well, okay, maybe I wouldn't mind biting parts of him, but that was neither here nor there.

I shrugged. "Nobody tells me shit, remember? Kallik of No House, orphan and immature girl, remember? I'm just out here to see my mom, so if you don't mind, I'd like to be left alone."

His eyes locked with mine, and I thought I saw a ripple of color in their dark depths. He snorted at me, as if he didn't like what he saw in my lilac eyes.

"Maybe I'll come with you."

That had *not* just come out of his mouth. I blinked hard and stared at him. "Why?"

"I don't trust you, Orphan," he said.

"Maybe you should get a new hobby. Crocheting. Molding chocolates." I broke into a run again, but he kept up easily. Because while he might be short for a guy, I was extra shrimpy for a fae woman. Petite is a word I'd heard bandied about in reference to my height more than once, though by human standards, I was pretty normal—and actually far above average for my mom's people.

"How was training?" he asked a few minutes later.

Small talk, really? The old me would have been ecstatic to have his attention, but twenty-four-year-old me was just . . . wary. He didn't truly like me, and we both knew it. The time spent with me during the mentorship program had been forced on him. The grandson of Lugh doing his duty for the poor unfortunate ones.

As soon as he'd been able to leave those doors and never come back, he had.

Rowan had turned against me in the final test. Bres had closed himself off during our last conversation. Yarrow . . . well, I wasn't even going to bother thinking about that toad's ass. Aside from Hyacinth, I didn't know who I could trust. Or maybe I just knew she was the only one and wished it were different.

"It was fine." I took a deep breath. "Hard. It was hard."

The Untried were the mutts and part breeds of our world. Like the other, more pure-blooded Fae, Faolan had trained in the Unseelie court after he was sorted. Of course he'd started off in the Seelie court and begun his early training there. Either way, in both places he'd trained with the best of the best so he could be all he could be.

You know, like the human marines.

They didn't have a chance of dying in their training.

An uncomfortable quiet reigned after that, and we reached the distinct edge of the enchanted Seelie forest.

As if a giant had laid his finger in the earth and drawn a thick trench, there was a deep gouge in the ground. On our side the plants were vibrant and alive, thick and verdant like a wild jungle. On the other, a barren plain extended all the way to the southern tip of Unimak. Winter still held its grip on the human side of the island, though the season was nearing its end.

I stepped across the divide and the temperature dropped thirty degrees, easily.

Wind howled across my face, numbing my skin in a matter of seconds. I drew a red thread of magic upward from deep underground to warm me. Heat radiated through me, and in response to my Seelie magic, moss erupted over the stones I stood upon. I smiled, thanking the red energy quietly, and walked out onto the plain, heading directly south toward the cluster of rocks that awaited me.

Faolan didn't follow. Not many fae willingly crossed the divide. The emptiness here was abhorrent to them, and they considered it dead for more than the humans who lay buried under the earth.

There in the middle of the plain stood an inukshuk—rocks stacked in the rough form of a person. This was the place where my mother had been laid to rest, alongside our ancestors.

I crouched at the base of the inukshuk and pulled the flowers from my pack. A little crumpled, they were still a bright contrast to the dull brown palette out here.

"Hi, Mom," I whispered. The wind whipped my words away from me.

It hadn't been long after I'd fallen through the ice that she'd died. I'd woken up one morning and found her asleep in her chair near the dead fire. I closed my eyes, trying not to see that last moment with her. Touching her cold hand. Patting her colder cheek. Curling up in her lap and knocking her mug out of her stiff hand. Cringing when I saw the mess I'd made, still thinking she'd wake up.

Hunger had driven me to move. To pull on all my outside clothes and make my way to the place that was warm—where the pretty people lived. It wasn't until I was older that I recognized it was strange to live in a place where there were no other humans. That it had always been just me and my mom.

And then I didn't even have her.

It had been Faolan who'd found me at the edge of the boundary. He'd taken me to the orphanage, holding my hand, speaking softly to me. As if he cared.

I swallowed hard and tried to fight back tears, feeling Faolan's gaze burning into my back, but it was no good.

I remembered very little of my mom, having lost her before I turned five, but she was the only loving family I'd had in this world. And though my memories of her were fleeting, I recalled her love and her voice and the feel of her callused fingers stroking my cheek. The songs she used to sing to me at night still came to me in my dreams.

There was enough there to feel ample regret at the loss of her in my life, the wish to have her with me still.

Things could have been so different.

"I screwed up," I murmured softly. "Bad this time. I don't know what to do."

The only answer was the howl of the winter wind whipping across my face, freezing my tears to my skin.

CHAPTER 5

I idly twisted the tip of my dagger on the tabletop, digging a small hole into the surface, considering the options laid out before me, options that would define my foreseeable future.

Protector of a fae ambassador. That would place me in regular political meetings with humans. Not my favorite pastime.

Low-ranking guard leadership position. Less than ideal, but it could turn into more in time.

Personal guard of a fae royal—yeah, right.

I scanned through the list of options, nixing most of them.

I could become an outpost scout, but then I'd never see Hyacinth. Or *Faolan*, a ridiculously dumb voice whispered in my head.

I scowled. I'd only spent an hour in his company yesterday, but it had been long enough to leave my mind awhirl. Nothing had changed. He was still Unseelie. I was Seelie. There was no possibility of anything between us, not ever. Except Faolan from a young age always had possessed an annoying mix of brooding sexy charm and bad boy. Well, maybe sixteen-year-old me hadn't found the combination annoying, but twenty-four-year-old me didn't like how she'd come out of the exchange yesterday.

I doubted he'd lost any sleep over the back and forth.

I sighed and flipped my dagger, barely noting the familiar thud as the hilt landed in my palm.

The air around me felt charged, like the brooding of a storm before it unleashed on the world. Outside the sun shone brightly, which meant the feeling had nothing to do with the actual weather and everything to do with what had happened with Underhill.

My body tensed at a booming knock.

Dagger in hand, I answered the door and glanced at the male human. A servant, judging by his gold and silver livery. "Can I help you?"

He peered at my weapon and hastily lifted the large purple-wrapped box in his arms. The servants that were to work with me wouldn't be sent my way until after I chose my vocation. So, I was on my own for opening my own door.

"Delivery for Kallik of No House."

This was the second delivery today. Food had arrived this morning—a courtesy package to tide me over until my first stipend was ready.

I flicked the dagger behind me, ears picking up the *thunk* as it hit the opposite end of the hall. "That'd be me."

I took the box, judging its weight. Who the hell had sent me a gift?

The old man squinted over my shoulder. "Took me a bit to find this place. Didn't know they had homes at the back of the castle. Kind of an unlucky number, isn't it?"

"It's the asshole of the castle," I corrected. "You can say it."

He bared his teeth in a wide grin. "Your words, not mine. Good day, ma'am."

After kicking the door shut, I returned to the table and tossed the box down, staring at the thing. Gold glitter all over the purple wrapping. Embossed card. Blue ribbon.

I tore into the package and my brows shot up at the contents. A dress.

I grabbed the card.

KALLIK OF NO HOUSE.

YOUR ATTIRE FOR THE FEAST TONIGHT.

SINCERELY,
CASTLE ADMINISTRATION

Feasts weren't a leather tights and tunic occasion, clearly. Had all of the newly Tried received 'attire,' or just me? In other words, was this a personal gift from Father Dearest or another of my winnings?

Not that it mattered. No matter how I looked, he wouldn't claim me. Certainly not at an event like this.

Still, I wasn't fool enough to think I had any choice. I had to wear it.

The dress only expanded as I pulled the yards of material from the magicked confines of the box. A soft lilac, an exact match for my eyes. I rested the tulle against my arm. I'd inherited bronzed skin from my mother's side, and I had to admit the color of the gown brought out a hidden glow.

I held the dress up and grimaced. How the hell was I meant to fight and run in this thing? I mean, not that I should have to do either at a feast, but eight years would not leave me overnight. Any place could end up being deadly.

The dresses I'd occasionally worn at the orphanage were more like sack shifts compared to this tent of a garment. Whisper-fine transparent lace made up the top half, its sole purpose to be the backboard for a cascade of lilac sequins that would presumably cover up the girls. The sequins dotted the shoulders too, and the full-length sleeves that ended in lilac feathers—yep, *feathers.* They also trailed down some of the huge tulle skirt that would cascade to the floor.

I mean, it was stunning, and it would look gorgeous on someone else. Not a grubby mutt like me.

"You're not in Underhill anymore," I croaked.

A brief chirping sound filled the house, and then a burlap

pouch appeared out of thin air and fell onto the table with a metallic clatter from the interior.

I rested the dress over the only chair and swiped up the pouch to loosen the tie.

Gold coins glimmered up at me.

"Yes," I hissed.

My first stipend had officially arrived. Literally the first coins I'd had of my own *ever*. I shoved aside the dress box and gently poured them out onto the tabletop.

Ten of them. Just for me. And there would be ten more every two weeks from here on out.

If I really scrounged on food, one of these would last me a week. I'd need to use a couple of them for new clothing, but I wanted to save as much as possible. Coins didn't mean as much to fae as money did to humans, but on Unimak I'd need currency to make a good life for myself, and I was not going to go without again. I'd take care of Cinth too. I knew that she was barely scraping by on her income, even with her new title.

Once upon a time, fae relied entirely on their magic for clothing, furniture, and household objects, but we didn't dress in leaves and vines anymore, and possessing items from the human world, instead of stone cutlery and wooden bowls, was a status thing. Not that I bought into that, but the courts frowned upon the use of magic for unnecessary items or purposes. Balance had to be maintained, after all; the worlds of the fae ran on it.

I collected my coins and returned them to the pouch, glancing around. There really weren't many hiding places here. After searching the house, I settled on a couple of places.

First, I cut a slit in the quilt and tucked seven coins inside the lining. Jingling the other three, which I'd spend tomorrow, I placed them behind the kitchen pipes under the sink. Then I turned my attention to making myself more presentable.

Which took an unflattering amount of time.

"You just need to get through tonight," I told my reflection after showering.

Each day that passed between me and what had happened in the final test was a good sign.

A great sign.

This was just a wave I had to ride. If only the wave didn't feel like it was ready to crest and drown me.

My stomach rolled, and for a moment I struggled to breathe as if I were indeed deep underwater. "Focus, girl, one day at a time," I whispered to the mirror and my too-pale face.

I forced my thoughts to return to my career options as I brushed out my shoulder-length brown-black tresses—also courtesy of Mom's Native heritage. If there was something more I could do to style my always straight hair, then I had no idea how to manage the feat. But I'd leave it down for once.

A knock sounded on the door while I was still fighting my way into the dress tent. I winced at my completely bare back—well, the transparent lace covered it, but it did bugger all to hide anything.

At least the sleeves fit around my muscles.

"Hold on," I hollered down the hall.

Matching slippers had been sent with the dress, but I took one look at them and swiped up my supple hiking boots. The line had to be drawn somewhere, right?

Shoving into them, I laced the fronts and swished my dress back into place.

Weapons, weapons, weapons.

I buckled the sheath for my curved knife at my thigh and slipped the weapon inside.

The knock boomed again.

I swung the door open and glowered at the person on the other side.

The castle guard cocked a brow. "I'm to escort you to the castle. Don't keep me waiting."

His arrogance bounced off me. Other than Hyacinth and Bracken, I'd never encountered a Seelie who didn't have a stick up their butt. All Seelie were afflicted by the tendency, even those on the fourth tier.

To be fair, the Unseelie weren't a lot better, but they'd be more likely to stick a knife in you from the front, rather than the back. There was a certain honesty to that I could get behind.

I followed in his wake, and the nerves I'd managed to force aside all day wove though me until they fully occupied my stomach. My father was in the castle. Was this man taking me to him?

The last time I'd seen my father was from afar at sixteen. He'd watched as his guards interrupted the convoy of sixteen-year-old fae as we were brought to the castle for sorting into Seelie and Unseelie courts. I'd spotted him from a window.

They'd plucked me from the trolley, and an hour later the orphanage matron had informed me I'd be leaving for Underhill training the next day, two years earlier than most— unless I had an objection—which I didn't. No sorting for me.

He'd done me a favor, really. I'd dreaded the sorting for months, certain my half-fae status would disrupt the process somehow. Or that other fae would find out I was his child, and he'd punish me for spilling his secret. Or that I'd be cast out into the Triangle for some reason.

A ridiculous thought, really, now that I was old enough to think it through. Magic wasn't as second nature to me as it was for a full-blooded fae—just like the ability to hold our breath for longer periods of time underwater—but I'd never had massive issues learning to wield the indigo threads of power within me. It took me time, but I always got there in the end.

My years in Underhill had helped me figure that out.

The guard guided me through the back parapet and up the servant stairs.

Unease had just started to stretch up through my chest when he pushed aside a curtain to reveal the four other Elite Tried.

Never thought I'd be glad to see Yarrow.

Fern, Aspen, and Birk waved, chummy now we were to this point, and I joined them.

"Didn't recognize you," Birk joked, nodding to my dress. "Can you fight in that?"

I eyed their attire—fancy, but functional. "Debatable. Swap?"

He cracked a grin.

A woman in a skirt suit and heels clacked through the wide entryway at the opposite end of what appeared to be a sitting room—or at least the royal definition of a sitting room. It was three times the size of my new abode, but who was measuring.

"I'm castle administration," she said in a no-nonsense voice, tapping her pen against the notebook she carried.

She didn't have an actual name? Her eyes swept over us behind a pair of glasses I was pretty sure she didn't even need. But it did complete the look of being administration, I suppose.

"Our guests are being seated. In a moment, you will follow me to the ballroom where you'll announce your chosen vocational area to King Aleksandr and repeat your oath."

Fuck. Last time I spoke that oath, things went belly-up in a big way.

She looked at each of us in turn, and I wondered if she could tell I still had no idea what 'vocational area' to choose.

We fell into a single file line behind her, and I took up the last spot gladly, scanning the huge and empty halls we passed. My fingers itched for my curved blade as the rumble and murmur of a crowd trickled to me from ahead.

The rich aromas of roasted meat and herbed vegetables filled my nostrils, and I inhaled deeply. If Hyacinth had anything to do with what was out there, I knew what I'd be doing for the rest of the night. This dress wouldn't fit come morning.

We were paraded through the round tables of high-class fae and royals, and I highly doubted any of the guests at this feast supposedly held in our honor shared our part-fae status. Their eyes fixed on us as we passed, but their attention didn't linger—as though bored, they returned to their conversations after a beat.

"Await King Aleksandr's entrance," Castle Administration said as she left us at the edge of the raised dais.

Yarrow swaggered onto the stage and claimed the position closest to the two thrones. He waved to some of the nearby tables, calling out to them and winking.

Vomit. For a brief second at the beginning of training, I'd thought our shared bastard status might bond us together. Though he had been claimed by his father in House Gold, Yarrow was still a bastard and had entered training to consolidate his place among the high-born and prove his worth.

That *could* have been something we shared.

If Yarrow wasn't a douche canoe. As it was, I was almost certain he hated me *because* I reminded him of what he was—strike that, I was sure of it. I was everything he hated about himself, which had made me his favorite punching bag in no time.

No sooner had we formed a line to the left of the king's throne than the herald who'd only muttered a weak announcement for our entrance brought down the tip of his golden staff on the ground three times. "King Aleksandr and Queen Consort Adair!"

Poor guy must live for that moment.

My father and his wife both had to know I was here. They hadn't prevented me from coming. If I kept my head down, they'd ignore me, per our unspoken agreement. Other than the small part of me that still wanted to be acknowledged—and loved—by my only surviving parent, I didn't want to be known as the king's bastard kid, and 'Dad' and his bitch of a wife didn't want anyone knowing either. It was win-win to ignore one another.

Her glares under her obviously fake eyelashes wouldn't hurt me any.

I released a pent-up breath. I could get through this. I had to. Surreptitiously, I wiped my clammy palms on the lilac tulle skirt and watched as the royal pair drew closer.

The king didn't acknowledge those he passed. A deep line marred the space between his brown brows, and he seemed lost in thought. I seized the chance to peruse him. A few strands of gray disrupted the glossy chestnut of his short, wavy hair. He'd always been grave and foreboding, but those qualities seemed accentuated tonight.

We did not look alike. The shape of his eyes reflected my own, as did the slight curve of his lips, but that was about it.

Good ol' Stepmommy waved grandly at her inferiors, gracing them with a curve of her red-stained lips and an ever-so-subtle dip of her magnificently coiffed head. She was a classic fae beauty with white-blond hair, brilliantly blue-green eyes, and a fine-boned body with soft, feminine curves. She seemed to have two modes: simper and smirk, but her minions lapped it up. Guess they wanted to kiss the ass of the most powerful woman in the Seelie realm. Personally, I didn't think she held a flame to the Unseelie queen, who had ruled alone since she took control of her court some fifty or so years before.

The pair ascended the stairs from the opposite end of the stage—thank Lugh—and took their thrones.

I exhaled slowly.

"All hail King Aleksandr!" the herald cried.

The booming reply shook the very castle, and I dutifully murmured along with the other fae.

Bres stood from a table in the middle of the gathering and ascended the stage to bow low to the king. He faced us afterward. "Tried. The king will now hear your choices. We will begin with the Middling Seelie. Birk, Fern, and Aspen, step forward."

My mind scrambled as they faced the king and lowered to their knees, speaking their vocations in clear, confident voices.

Crap.

"I now present our two Elite Seelie," Bres told the king.

There was a polite smattering of applause.

Were there really only two of us in the Unimak division? I'd thought there would be more. I hadn't paid attention, what with the demolishing of Underhill.

"Kallik and Yarrow, please step forward."

Yarrow sauntered to face the king, somehow making the act of lowering to his knees seem cocky too.

Steeling myself, I approached my father and stepmom, looking each of them in the eyes before I lowered to my knees also, the tulle cutting into my skin.

King Aleksandr's gaze settled heavily upon me, and I fixed my sights on the ornamental epaulette covering his left shoulder.

"Yarrow, speak your choice," Bres commanded.

"King's guard," Yarrow declared.

The crowd erupted into shocked murmurs. That was not on the list of vocations.

"You do not have the power of that choice," Bres reminded him in sharp tones.

Yarrow smirked. "That's just where I'll eventually end up. I'll start in an army leadership position, of course."

I'd strongly considered doing the same, but eight years and two days with this jackass were eight years and two days too many. I wasn't about to willingly take one more minute with him than I had to.

The audience laughed at his response.

"Simply charming," someone exclaimed.

Oh, brother. These people might kill me one day.

I licked my lips as Bres glanced my way. The coldness blanketing his features was something I'd never experienced from him.

Fear squeezed my chest.

"Kallik. Speak your choice," he ordered.

"Protector of a fae ambassador." The words slipped from

my mouth, but I didn't feel any resounding rightness about the choice. It had been a simple equation in the end: I didn't want to be in the castle or with Yarrow, and I didn't want to be totally away from Hyacinth. That only left one job.

Was it the job for me?

No, but it offered security, and I could live with that.

The king still hadn't glanced away, and I shifted my gaze to his wife. Her loathing slammed into me, and my lips curved slightly at the rare glimpse behind her carefully maintained mask.

I quickly lost my smirk—not smart to piss her off more than my existence already did.

Yarrow murmured from the corner of his mouth, "I give you an hour tops."

"We both know you'd only need a minute," I replied under my breath.

The king's lips twitched.

Unrelated to my response . . . surely.

"Kallik of No House will be assigned to protect a fae ambassador," Bres relayed to the audience. "She will attend negotiations with humans and Unseelie fae."

Birk, Fern, and Aspen returned to kneel with us, and we chanted the oath to the king together.

My shoulders relaxed when the castle didn't fall down around my ears.

Then *he* spoke for the first time. "Thank you all for your future service and the hard work you have put in to attain your positions. The Seelie court honors you for your service."

I'll bet they do.

After another smattering of applause, Castle Administration popped up again, and we were led to a table at the back of the ballroom. Guests of honor—but not *that* honored, obviously.

I didn't care and was glad to be out of the limelight.

Dinner was served. While the other Tried left our table to mingle with their relations and friends, I dug into the succulent lamb and baby potatoes swimming in rosemary and butter, perfectly content to blend into the background.

"Psst."

I lifted my head and beamed. "Cinth."

"I don't usually serve, but I had to see you all dressed up. Alli, you're so beautiful! I didn't know a person's back had that many muscles either. Interesting. Here's a tickle."

She deposited the biscuit on my plate, and I lost no time stuffing it into my mouth.

I groaned. *Goddess.* The base melted on my tongue, quickly followed by a tart note of cherry and encore of earthy richness I assumed was the beetroot.

I wiped my mouth. "Seriously delicious."

Her cheeks pinkened. "Thanks. I came back to your place yesterday, I'd forgotten my cloak. Where did you go?"

"I went to see Mom." I straightened. "And I saw Faolan by accident."

Hyacinth's jaw dropped. "Faolan aka the one you crushed on

from afar for years?"

"Yes."

Her grin was so wide it pulled at her burn. "Faolan who was eye-kissed by you?"

"Yes," I said dryly.

She whacked me lightly. "Is he still hot? Did you talk? Did you kiss his other eye to make up for lost time?"

I snorted. "Not yet. He's . . . still hot. We talked."

"I'm surprised he could string two words together around you. I mean other than 'Orphan, get out of my way.'"

I snorted. She wasn't wrong. "Faolan has never had an issue keeping his wits about him around me." More like the other way around.

I'd wanted to come across as a sexy panther lady, but based on his reaction, I'd projected more of a pouty schoolgirl image. Which I seriously did not like.

She planted her hands on her hips. "Not before, perhaps. But Alli, my friend, you are *all* grown up now. Boobs. Butt. Confidence. Makes for one sexy sandwich. And now you're old enough, if I recall his original hangup, especially with the years of difference between here and Underhill."

She was forgetting the whole half-human mutt thing *and* the Unseelie-Seelie thing, but I let that slide.

My lips curved. "Sexy sandwich?"

"My life is food." Hyacinth yelped at a scowl from a nearby server. "Time's up. I'll come by your place tomorrow? I have stuff for you."

She deposited another tickle on my plate and skedaddled.

I took my time with the second sweet, nibbling at the buttery pastry. I surveyed those nearest to me, working my gaze steadily toward the stage. Yarrow was guffawing up there like a damn donkey.

My stepmom squeezed the king's hand, then stood in an elegant swish of fabric. I watched Adair cross the stage and descend. Bres immediately joined her, bowing low.

Ah. Not good.

But possibly not terrible. I shouldn't assume anything.

His mouth moved fast, and as their conversation progressed, their heads drew closer and closer together. Adair's expression was increasingly grim, and sweat trickled down my spine.

Judging by the simple fact that I was sitting in the ballroom and not the dungeon, I could assume the Oracle had decided not to divulge the truth to my father. At least not yet.

But Bres . . .

If Adair discovered my part in the demise of Underhill, that was checkmate right there. She'd take any chance she could get to have me removed permanently.

The pair straightened, and as one they turned to look at me.

Fuck.

I could assume a whole bunch from that. I lowered my lashes and sipped meekly at my crystal goblet of water. Peeking up to watch them on the sly, I spotted the queen consort delivering an order to the old trainer with a snap of her fingers. This man had guided me through the last eight years, and now he was handing me over at the damn finish line.

His eyes drifted to the nearest guards, but he made no move other than to nod in reply and bow again.

My stomach plummeted through the floor as they separated. She knew.

My stepmom knew or at least suspected, courtesy of Bres, that I was the one who'd shattered Underhill.

My hands curled into fists as my inner storm raged, and I fought to catch my breath.

I'd hoped to fly under the radar until this blew over, but if Bres's quick glance to the guards was any indication, my days of freedom were extremely numbered. If Underhill had taught me one thing before it crumbled, it was the ability to think on my feet. To strike before someone struck *me*. To make pre-emptive moves.

My attention settled on the grave figure sitting on the throne. As if compelled, his green eyes met mine. His gaze was impenetrable, but I gathered one thing from the haste with which he looked away.

Just like always, I was on my own.

I steadfastly *refused* to give up my new freedom, yet I couldn't clear my name from a dungeon cell.

No. Something had destroyed the fae realm, and regardless of whether I was actually at fault, I had to figure out how to get it back.

That was the only way I could have the future I'd dreamed of my whole life.

Which meant it was time to move.

CHAPTER 6

I stood and pushed my chair back as slowly as I could, not wanting to make a scene. Basically, I didn't want Bres or Adair to think I was making a run for it. Which was why I'd waited for the first five courses to wrap up before leaving the table.

"Leaving already?" Birk looked up from his seat to my left. "What about dessert? Didn't you say that your friend is baking and you wouldn't miss it for anything?"

Excuses piled up at the back of my throat, and I stumbled out with the dumbest one possible. "I've got to go see someone about . . . something."

Birk blinked his baby blues up at me. "Yeah, so that's not weird at all."

Shit. I turned and strode away from the table, glad I'd worn my hiking boots. *Extra* glad I'd taken at least the one knife with me.

My skin itched all over, and I wanted to shuck the dress, but I had enough presence of mind to realize running naked through the castle would be a less than subtle way to leave.

I faced the main doors and my heart gave a terrible thump. The king's guards hovered there, two to each door, hands on the hilts of their swords.

And they were watching me.

A string of curses flowed from my lips, and the Seelie matron seated to my right gasped, putting a hand to her throat. "Well, I've never heard such foul language—"

"Not even in bed with your hubby?" I tipped my head at her gray-haired companion, whose eyes bugged a little too wide. Sure, his lips twitched, but I didn't have time to point it out to his wife.

Three servers headed past me with empty trays, and I fell in behind them, weaving my way through the tables, skirts brushing against everything.

Passing by our table again, I touched Birk's shoulder. "I'm going to get more of those tickles, okay?"

I gave him two thumbs up—very human of me—and he smiled. "No complaints from me. Get a whole plate if you can."

A simple opening covered by glittering light-blue material formed the exit into the kitchens. The cloth barrier rose as I drew closer. Stepping through, I listened for the whisper as it lowered, then immediately broke into a run, following my nose, scaring the servers who'd been ahead of me.

"Sorry!" I called over my shoulder as they muttered and cursed in my general direction.

The scent of roasting meat, spices, a thread of sweet baked goods beckoned to me, and as I got closer, I heard the clatter of pans and murmur of voices.

The kitchens were well lit and laid out like the progression of the served meal. Appetizer stations in front, salad and then soup, main meal and dessert at the back. My massive skirts brushed against everything, getting covered in sauces in a matter of seconds.

"Get out of here," someone yelled. "You're going to light yourself on fire."

As if his words were prophetic, my tulle skirt brushed up against an open flame. I swore as the blasted thing caught on fire.

I grabbed the material on either side of the flames and smashed it over the piece on fire, pressing it against my hip. Heat shot through my skin, not enough to burn, but enough to remind me that I could melt.

Flames out, I kept running, feeling the prickling threat of the guards at my back. I ducked under a serving platter, then danced around two more cooks. The thing was, despite all the mess and chaos I was causing, no one really tried to stop me. They mostly just ignored me. Which, let's be honest, was my whole life. Ignore the girl who doesn't fit in—until she's done something we can legit kick her ass out for.

I slid to a stop at the dessert section and scanned the heads for my bestie. "Hyacinth!"

She popped up like a damn gopher, her eyes wide. Flour dusted her nose. "Alli, what are you doing here? I can't give you more tickles. We're running low."

I shook my head and hurried toward her, ignoring the side-eyes I was getting from the other line cooks. "I need you to hide me."

"What?"

"Just ten minutes. Guards are going to come through here looking for someone. I need you to hide me or give me one of your secret exits."

She stared at me like I'd lost my mind, and maybe I had.

I grabbed her by the upper arm and bodily dragged her out of the main section and into a side pantry. "Guards are coming to throw me in jail, Cinth—at the least. I need to avoid them long enough to get back to my place and grab my stuff."

She put pastry-covered fingers to her temples. "This doesn't make any sense."

"I'll explain later. *Please.*" I leaned in closer. "I know there are places back here where you and Jackson . . ."

I didn't want to rub it in because Jackson had been one of the loves of her life. She'd had many. *Many.* And she'd used the cavernous kitchens as a makeout place more than once.

Lips pursed, she dragged me off. "You don't think anyone else noticed you running through here? The others will tell on you faster than a fat kid squeals for candy."

We hurried into the depths of the kitchens, moving deeper and deeper into the immense pantry, the light dimming. When we stopped, she shucked her clothes. "We'll switch. Men won't think to check hair color, all they'll see is the dress. Go on, get naked, girlfriend."

I blinked. We could not be more different in body size and shape. She was curvy to the max, all boobs and ass, and I was . . . not. But I did as she said and stripped out of my dress, handing it over.

She quirked an eyebrow at me. "Really, hiking boots and a knife under there? How in the world do you think you'll ever catch a man like that?"

I grunted. "Not really worried about catching men right now." But if I changed my mind on that front, Hyacinth was absolutely the person I'd consult. Men flocked to her like flies to foxen shit despite her burn, despite the fact that her parents had gone crazy.

Cinth flung her clothes at me. Sure enough, they hung off my frame, but I used the apron strings to tighten them.

I looked up. My dress was, uh, different on her. The back was completely open because her chest was so much bigger, and the tops of her rounder-than-mine ass cheeks peeked out. The front was a whole other issue. Her spillage out of the dress was such that I could see definite nipple color. Top that off with the hem of the dress hitting her at mid-calf and it was quite the look.

"You're lucky I love you," she muttered, bustling back the way we'd come in. She paused at an intersection of spices and fruits. "Follow this path. At the very end is a delivery entrance. It'll take you out on the west side."

I kissed her on the cheek and then swatted her on the ass for good measure as she rushed back out to lead the guardsmen on a merry little chase. With the smell of spices thick in the air, making my nose twitch, I made my way down the slim passageway.

What the hell was I going to do? I had ten gold coins to my name, and that was assuming I'd be able to sneak back into 666 First Tier and get them. Was I really running? Or was this a panicked knee-jerk reaction? There was a chance the guards were pursuing me for a reason completely unrelated to Underhill, but if that were the case, I could easily blame my running act on the fact that I'd lived under a constant threat of death for the last eight years.

Only I didn't think I'd be given the opportunity to speak at all. One of the Untried had stolen a jar of healing balm from a mentor during training. The hunt had gone on for weeks, but they'd persisted and finally caught the thief a month later. Drake had no left hand now and had been cast from the court to live as a lone fae in the human world. North, specifically, to the Triangle.

I reached the exit and pushed a hand against it. Well oiled, there wasn't a single creak as I let myself out of the ginormous pantry.

With one hand on my borrowed pants to keep them up, I bent at the waist and adopted a limp. Head down, I hobbled slowly around the side of the castle, hopefully pulling off a lame and tired worker vibe.

A clatter of weapons and boots on the cobblestone path behind me tugged at my ears, but I didn't pick up my pace, just kept on moving in the same fashion.

Speed, especially sudden bursts of it, draws the eye. Bres might have turned me over to Adair, but his training was still with me.

"Where did you get this dress?" a man shouted.

"A girl—woman, I guess—traded me. It's lovely, isn't it? I think I can make it fit if I let out the seams." Hyacinth's voice rang out clear as day. "No one in my position would ever get a dress so fine as this, you know."

"What did you give her to wear?"

I was almost to the corner of the castle.

"Wait, who's that?"

Well, fuck me, Lugh, I was in trouble.

It took all my self-control not to react.

"Oy, what's your name?"

Nope, not answering.

I reached the corner and clung to it as if I could barely move before stepping around. As soon as I was out of sight, I *bolted*. This side of the castle was covered in produce gardens which fed the rich, and would help hide the desperate.

I went straight for the corn. The brilliant green stalks and leaves were easily twelve feet high, and the foliage was thicker than with human plants, more like palm trees than corn.

Into the field I went and immediately dropped into a crouch, slowing my pace to a crawl to ensure I didn't disturb a single stalk.

The gardens backed onto the asshole of the castle—aka my side of things. I just had to get to the far end, and I'd be free and clear.

Voices rippled through the air, and a burst of light lit up the sky. Search sparks.

"Damn," I ground out. There was no way they'd go to this much effort if they just wanted a friendly chat about my choice of vocation.

They all knew I'd played a role in Underhill's demise, even if I had no notion what I'd done. This was the excuse Adair had been waiting for my whole life—a reason to off me.

The search sparks trickled downward, and I eyed their trajectory. If a search spark landed on a person, it illuminated them entirely. Walking glowstick Kallik would not make it out of here because she'd light up an entire room by herself.

Near the base of the corn stalks, the ground was soft from all the weeding and care. Flipping onto my back, I scooped dirt over my legs, body, and arms. Seconds. I had only *seconds* to act, and I moved as fast as I could without disturbing the corn and alerting them to my position.

Cinth would be pissed. She hated dirt on her clothes.

I bit back a laugh as I lay in the dirt and layered it over my neck and face, finishing by tucking my arms in under my body. This was insane. *Insane.*

I left one eye uncovered to watch.

The search sparks fluttered down around me, one landing on my middle covered in dirt. I didn't dare breathe.

But the brilliant blue light fizzled after a few seconds and didn't penetrate my protective covering.

"She ain't in the corn," a gruff voice said.

"Then check the forest boundary at the southern tip. And speak with that Unseelie guard from yesterday."

I froze anew. They were going to my mom's burial ground, and they knew about Faolan following me. Questioning me. The only way they could know about either of those things was if they'd already been watching me.

Bres must have set them on me just in case.

Except why let me walk around freely at all then? Just to see what I'd do?

I rolled, and the dirt poured off of me as I hurried through the corn, less careful now the guards had turned their attention elsewhere. At the back of the garden stood a massive stone wall. Twenty feet high at least, maybe more. Once I started climbing, I would be totally exposed.

I pulled off my hiking boots and slung them tied over one shoulder. Fingers and toes were needed for this.

I found footholds and finger grips easily enough. Of course, I'd faced much harder climbs while training in Underhill. Again, Bres might have betrayed me, but his training was helping me.

Partway up the wall, I dared to glance back. The castle glowed from within, the windows lit up as I crouched and fought my way to freedom out here in the darkness.

Up and over the wall I went, dropping to a crouch on the other side. I'd never been happier to see house 666. Go figure.

There were no guards out front, but I couldn't take any chances. I slid through the back alley behind the properties closest to my home.

No, not my home. It wasn't mine anymore.

Not now.

Not yet.

Not until I fixed this mess. *If* I could fix it.

Heart pounding, I let myself into 666 but didn't risk turning on a light. I stripped out of Hyacinth's clothes and found my own, grabbed my coins from their hidey-holes, tucking six into the pouch at my hip and twisting four in a strip of cloth to fasten under my shirt, then gathered my weapons.

A new conviction burned within me. If I wanted to avoid being jailed or killed—or at the very least having my hand cut off like Drake—then I had to leave Unimak.

A tremor started low in my body.

Oddly, this decision felt right in a way my chosen vocation had not. Because the winds of change were pushing me, like it or not, and part of me knew I would never be accepted here until I got the bottom of what had happened to Underhill.

Unfortunately, the only place left open to me was one that I'd been taught to fear from childhood. The place the orphanage had used as the nightmare to keep us in check. The area of the world even humans had learned to fear in recent times.

The Triangle.

CHAPTER 7

Those winds of fate that were pushing me out of Unimak also pushed a little good luck my way. I crept toward the hardpacked airstrip where the cargo plane was loading up one of its weekly runs of goods to be sold to the human world. Ready to leave in a matter of minutes if what I was seeing was on point.

The two pilots slammed the cargo hold shut, and climbed into the cockpit. I ran for the cargo hold door as the engines turned over, and the props began to spin.

The door was over my head, the handle well out of reach. "Shit."

I drew magic from the plants along the edge of the airstrip and wove it through the metal of the door, which my magic didn't like. Iron, the plane had iron in it and it was negating my magic.

So much for a little good luck.

The plane began to roll and I bounced along on my toes like a kid reaching for a cookie jar just out of reach. I shoved my magic hard into the locking system of the door, hoping a little brute force would help me out.

Nope. Nothing.

The wheels were picking up speed now, which meant I really had to get my ass in gear if I was going to make something happen. I slid back under the belly of the plane, crouching, running with the stupid thing. Yes, it was my ride out of here, but only if I could get my ass onto it.

The body of the plane passed over me and I was suddenly looking at the back end.

And the door of the cargo hold, handle well within reach—assuming I could keep up with the taxiing plane.

I put on a burst of speed and leapt, grabbing the handle. I twisted it hard and the door popped open, flinging me to the side. "Goddess!" I hissed as I dangled from the door, my feet barely touching the hard pack as I bounced and fought to get myself up and into the belly of the plane.

At this rate I was going to be seen, caught, and tossed in jail.

No, I couldn't let that happen. I pushed off with the tips of my toes and threw my body up and into the hold, like one of those human high jumpers. Grabbing the inside of the door, I pulled it shut and locked it tight.

The little bit of iron that was woven through the metal stung my fingers, but that was a small price to pay for freedom.

I stumbled over a tree branch and landed on my butt. "Trees?"

Finding my way through the semi darkness, my belly rolled as the plane lifted off. I'd only just made it on in time.

My relief was brief as I found a pile of loosely woven blankets also being sent for sale. I pulled one out and wrapped it around me. The cargo hold was going to get cold, and the air thin.

Hunkering down between the branches of the trees, I closed my eyes. I needed to sleep while I could, or at least get some semblance of rest. But my mind was working through all the challenges I faced ahead of me.

First being how the hell to find the entrance to Underhill. It was hidden from the trainees on the way in for the Untried, and on the way out. Even when Bres had brought us away from the cabin after Underhill's demise, we'd been blindfolded.

Eyes closed, I spent the first hour chasing my thoughts like a fox after a rabbit that was just too fast. What would happen when they—my father and Adair—announced that I'd been the one to destroy Underhill? What would Cinth think? What would Faolan think? I shook my head.

"Why in the world would his opinion matter?" I muttered. "It doesn't. Everything you thought he was, was a lie." I closed my eyes as if that would help shut down my racing thoughts.

Sometime in the second hour the heavy rumble of the engines, the smell of the trees and the thin air sent me into a light doze.

"Are we going to the sorting?" I tugged on Hyacinth's shirt, unintentionally tugging it down over one boob. At fourteen she was already drawing the boys' eyes with her bigger than average bust. She took my hand and adjusted her shirt.

"No, we aren't allowed to go to it until we are old enough, you know that."

"But Lanny is going to be there, I want to see him sorted," I whined softly. "He said he'd look for me."

Hyacinth brushed a hand over my head. "He'll come see you after, I'm sure."

I frowned and tried not to be petulant—that was the word the orphanage nanny used on the other kids. Don't be petulant, it's unbecoming.

I followed Hyacinth through the orphanage to the kitchen where she took a few ingredients and began mixing them together.

"You're quiet, Alli," Cinth said as she squashed some seeds with a mortar and pestle.

"I just feel like I should be there. What if something bad happens?" I pushed around a few flower petals.

A soft knock on the door of the kitchen turned both of us around.

Faolan stood in the doorway, dressed from head to toe in more finery than I'd ever seen him in. A white shirt that laced up the middle, dark gray pants tucked into knee-high leather boots and a deep blue cloak that hung from his shoulders. His hair was tied back at the nape of his neck making it look like he'd cut it short.

"I came to say goodbye," he said, his voice different. I didn't like it.

"My time with the mentorship program is over; you'll have someone else come and read to you now."

I took a step toward him and Hyacinth put a hand on my shoulder, stopping me. I looked up at her and she shook her head.

"Lanny—"

"Faolan," he corrected me. He'd never spoken to me like this before.

"I thought you were my friend," I whispered.

One eyebrow lifted and he stared down at me, not a single drop of emotion hidden in the depths of his eyes. "Friend?" He laughed, the sound harsh, and it cut into my tender heart. "I am the grandson of Lugh, and I have done my duty by helping here, in the orphanage. Nothing more."

My lower lip trembled and Cinth stepped in front of me. "You don't have to be an ass about it. We know where we stand."

"Do you?" he asked. "I don't think she does. I think she believes that I came here for her, when I could have been here for any of the orphans."

The tears slid down my cheeks, hot and scalding, and a sob began to build in my chest. "But you said that I was . . ."

"Special?" He rolled his eyes. "That's because we're coached on what to say, Orphan."

I reeled back as if he'd slapped me. That's all I was to him. A charity case that he'd had to read to every week, that he'd had to pretend to like. To be kind to.

Cinth grabbed a rolling pin. "Get out!"

"No," he said. "I promised her I would say goodbye, so here I am.

Goodbye, Orphan. May the goddess watch over you." He bowed from the waist and I stared at the young man that my rescuer had become.

"You saved me from the river," I blurted out. "Why?"

He lifted his head and turned his back on me, speaking over his shoulder. "I would not let a dog drown in that river if I could save it, why not save a mutt? Perhaps one day you'll make something useful of yourself."

Cinth threw the rolling pin at him but it bounced off the door frame and he was gone.

The sobs rolled out of me then, great heaving sobs that were caught on Cinth's shoulder.

"Oh, Alli, don't listen to him."

Only how could I not? He was the one I wanted to be like. I'd heard the orphan nanny whisper words like hero worship around me. Lanny—Faolan—had been my hero. He'd saved my life. He'd been my friend through the mentorship program. He'd always been a little distant, a little quiet, but never cruel.

He thought I wouldn't be useful.

My tears slowed as I clung to Hyacinth. "I'll show him, Cinth. One day, I'll show him."

I pulled back from her arms to see that she was crying and I wiped her tears away. "We'll both show him what we're made of. Then he'll be sorry he's not our friend anymore."

She gave me a smile, and I could see the belief in her—she knew I wasn't useless. "I know you will."

CHAPTER 8

The tree saplings rustled and bumped into my shoulders as the aircraft screeched to a landing. I remained crouched in the cargo hold, teeth chattering, as the pilot navigated down the runway. Even though I'd had that thick blanket, the ride had been frigid.

I knew where I wanted to end up but had no idea what my actual current destination was. My main concern had been getting off of Unimak before the king shut down the airstrip to trap me on the island.

By my reckoning, we'd traveled around four hours.

That suggested I was still in Alaska, and the frigid temperature in the hold backed that supposition up.

The aircraft had halted, and the thunderous rumble of the engines diminished into a whine and then silence. Focusing, I picked up the beeping bustle of luggage carriers and other planes outside.

Sneaking *onto* the plane hadn't been so hard (if I didn't consider that I almost hadn't got the door open) at a tiny regional airport where no one was on the lookout for people doing suspicious and shady things. Wherever we'd landed sounded larger and busier, which meant more stringent security.

A ringing grunt of metal was followed by light streaming into the cargo hold.

I ducked lower, sheltering behind a cluster of silver and red saplings some rich human must have ordered.

"What've we got?" one of the baggage handlers hollered.

The voice of the man clambering into the hold echoed. "More weird fae shit."

"Glitter?"

"Yeah. That shit is fucking everywhere."

Both men cursed.

As they set to work unloading the goods, I skirted against the wall, behind cases of Fae Honey and boxes of spiced fireweed truffles. Once they'd filled the carts, they drove off, and I inched forward to peer outside.

Rolling plains filled the horizon to my left, covered in tall trees, but I couldn't see beyond the terminal building to see what lay off to the right.

Fairbanks International Airport, a sign on the building read.

I spied maybe seven gates—not as big as I feared. I'd worried for half the trip that we'd land in Anchorage. And then, that the plane was bound for the lower forty-eight.

Fairbanks put me toward the east section of the Alaska Triangle, which covered the land area between Juneau to the east, Anchorage to the south and Barrow at the very northern tip of the state.

Until recently, the Triangle had contained Underhill.

And it still contained far more than that—it held every cast-off fae ousted from our world.

I stayed in the hold as another flight rolled out and the aircraft marshal returned to wherever it was they hung out between flights.

The luggage guys would be back soon, which meant I had to make my move. I slapped my thighs, driving a bit more blood to the muscles. The cold of the flight would make me dull if I wasn't careful.

Flicking up my hood, I hoisted myself from the cargo and dropped onto the balls of my feet, silent as a slight breeze.

Those pine trees were my best bet. I couldn't go through security.

I hugged the shadows of the craft. Then, after swiveling around to look for company, I aimed for a lone jet bridge fifty strides away.

Now came the hardest part.

I walked at a fast clip to the terminal building, aiming for an 'I'm meant to be here' vibe. Maybe the hood discouraged that image?

Too late.

Heart thumping, I reached the building. I'd only taken one step to begin working my way around the side of the terminal when the doors slid open and five security guards stepped out.

They stopped at the sight of me.

I tugged down my hood. "Is this the terminal? There was no one to guide me off . . ."

One of them smiled and started to raise an arm, but a narrow-eyed stout woman cut him off.

"There was no other passenger on the plane that just came in," she said with a glance at her clipboard. "The pilot. Co-pilot, and one passenger. That's it."

Well, dang. "Yes, so is this the correct place to go through security?"

The guards spread out.

She rested a hand on her holstered gun. "It would be. If the passenger hadn't already gone through. You'll need to come with us, girl."

I considered breaking into a run right there. Five humans didn't really compare to the monsters I'd fought in Underhill. Don't get me wrong, humans *were* a danger to fae due to their numbers, their guns, and the sheer amount of iron at their disposal. It was why we hadn't resisted when they'd assigned us to live in barren

KELLY ST CLARE *and* SHANNON MAYER

pockets of land spread across the globe after WWII, but in a one-on-one fight—or one-on-five fight as it were—a human didn't stand a chance. Nor could they hope to catch up to us on foot.

But I could either run here, *or* I could let them lead me through the terminal and then run where there were more human civilians for cover.

I nodded. "Of course. I'm as eager to have this cleared up as you are."

My pack thumped against my lower back as I followed them through the deserted gate and into the terminal. We passed around security between bleary-eyed nightshift workers, and I looked ahead to where my escorts were leading me.

Alas, this is where we'd need to part ways.

"Ah," a husky voice purred. "You found my assistant."

Me?

I glanced back, my feet following, and found myself face to face with a gigantic caribou.

Inside the airport. What the hell was this?

"This is your assistant? She came on the flight for you?" the female guard asked the large animal.

I caught her slight blanch. Apparently this fae wasn't someone to piss off.

Which wasn't ideal for me.

The caribou lifted a hoof and set it down, then raised its head. My eyes shifted to its majestic antlers and the creamy white hair covering its thick muscled neck.

"Correct. Might we proceed? I have already cleared her paperwork with security." His voice rumbled strangely through the animal.

The fae was either a shapeshifter or a fae controlling this animal from afar. The latter would be easier to escape from.

The guards weren't convinced, and I tensed to bolt.

The soft, ringing chime of a harp seemed to flow from the caribou, and all five humans gained a glazed expression, their mouths going suspiciously slack.

I slanted a look at the caribou, who returned it with purpose, jerking his head to get me moving.

Just behind him, I walked beneath the banner reading 'Fairbanks Welcomes You!', through the automatic doors, and into the crisp air beyond the terminal.

"Should I say thank you?" I asked him lightly.

"Most likely," the hoofed animal answered as it strode along. "You looked like you were in a . . . how do humans phrase it? A pickle."

No idea on that front. Despite being half human, I'd spent little time around them since I was a child, and even then that was just me and my mom. "Can I know the name of my rescuer?"

He chuffed a soft laugh. "We both know a powerful fae like yourself didn't really require rescue, but I do prefer the tidy way of doing things whenever possible."

Me? A powerful fae? I wasn't a complete weakling, and I made sure to shore up any weaknesses when they came to my attention, but my magic wasn't anything to get excited about. Still, I wasn't about to enlighten him.

The caribou stopped by a silver SUV. "My name is Rubezahl. Like all of us who live here, I am an outcast fae. I sent this creature to attend a meeting as my vessel with a Seelie ambassador, but when I caught wind that a young fae woman was running from Unimak, I postponed my meeting to help you."

Hearing about a runaway fae had been enough to sidetrack him from his meeting?

Given that talking animals were no longer rare in the human world, the humans' response to his avatar indicated either he or his contacts were important and well known. If this man had sent a vessel to meet with a Seelie fae of high status, then he was certainly someone to be wary of.

"Thank you for the help, Rubezahl." I dipped my head. "I, too, prefer the tidy path."

Which was unfortunate, because I was about to steal a car. To figure this thing out, I needed to examine what remained of the entrance to Underhill. Of course, the entrance wasn't there anymore since Underhill itself was gone, but it was the logical starting point being the weakest part of the veil between the human and fae realms.

There was just one problem.

Usually, all a fae would need to do to find the gate was follow the threads of power as they thickened and amassed.

Those threads had almost certainly faded away with Underhill

. . . and we'd never been told exactly where we were going on the way to and from training there. Never been allowed to see the way.

I opened my mouth.

"Do you require further assistance, fae of Unimak?" the caribou inquired politely.

That was a definite yes, but should I trust this Rubezahl? His canceled meeting could have been with my father. Or Adair. For all I knew, he'd already met with them, and they were the ones who'd told him I was running.

If he knew about me making a run for it, then he had contacts back in Unimak.

Though he didn't really seem to care why I'd snuck onto a plane—he hadn't even asked . . . And he'd said he was an outcast himself—a fae exiled by one of the two courts.

That's what I was now. "I'm looking for the entrance to Underhill, actually."

"You mean the previous entrance to Underhill?" he replied in a mild tone.

He knows. How, though? Because he'd discussed it with King Aleksandr or because all fae had likely felt the fae realm shatter?

"Could you tell me where it is?" I did a quick check for company. We were still alone.

"Even better. I can show you in person. You would need to drive to meet me. This avatar doesn't care for vehicles."

That was a big, fat *no.* "Sounds great," I lied. "Where should

I meet you?"

"We'll meet close to the gate," he answered easily. "Drive south on Parks Highway—Alaska Route 3. Stop at Healy. Ask for me."

Close to the gate. Something told me he'd purposefully withheld the exact location. Which meant he was smart . . . and also that he wanted something from me.

I'd make my way to this place and figure out the next step from there. "Why are you helping me, Rubezahl?"

The caribou eyed me. What did this guy look like in person? Big floppy lips and sad hazel doe eyes?

"Ruby will do, young one," he said. "And I don't want anything from you, but your power does interest me."

It was the second time he'd mentioned my power. I really didn't have more *oomph* than the average fae. And I had to work five times as hard because my human side kept butting in every two seconds. "I don't know what you're seeing, but it's not power beyond measure."

His large golden gaze riveted on me. "Beyond measure. An interesting phrase to use. Perhaps in this moment, I might describe it as unusual. Regardless, your power is something I'd like see in action. Would you humor an old fae? I would be happy to tell you what I know of what's passed in my territory in the last few days in exchange."

The knot of caution unwound somewhat at his words. Not fully, however. "That sounds like a fair trade, but I warn you now that you'll be disappointed."

The caribou peered up at the night sky. "I should think not."

Okay, then. No sacrifice on my part if this was all he wanted in return.

"I suggest you get into the car soon," he said ominously. "I feel like rain and sleet."

I frowned. *He* felt like rain and sleet? Or the air did? I eyed the vehicle in front of me. "Yeah, I'm on that."

Sort of. How best to break in?

"This vehicle contains a map, and we leave it here for any newly outcast fae, so you may take it without concern. The key is in the ignition." As soon as the words left his mouth, the caribou let out an earthy groan and shuddered.

I shook my head in bemusement as I watched the animal sprint off through the parking lot.

No sooner had I turned toward the silver Subaru Outback than a fat drop of rain landed on my nose. I put my hand to the door and it opened smoothly. A quick look inside showed me a set of keys dangling from the ignition, a pair of miniature katana blades hanging from it. I snorted. Tracker blades, as if that subspecies of supernatural was real.

I settled into the seat and opened the glovebox.

Sure enough, a thick map titled *Milepost* sat inside.

Yeah, maybe that guy didn't give off a dangerous vibe, but his power level was a warning I'd be foolish to ignore. It made me wonder how the hell he'd ended up in the Triangle of all places.

Shaking my head once more, I focused on the task at

hand. Mastering human technology was part of our training in Underhill, and after acquainting myself with the controls, I reversed out without too much trouble.

Healy.

Parks Highway.

My grip tightened on the wheel and I took a breath. "Underhill, here I come."

Whatever remained of it anyway.

CHAPTER 9

The highway to Healy was blessedly deserted, only a few vehicles passing me during the first hour.

Radio turned low, I drummed my fingers on the steering wheel as I drove, mind working overtime. I'd escaped Unimak with little effort, found help from an older fae at the airport, and taken a car just waiting there for me. Free and clear.

It had all come together too easily considering what I'd done—or supposedly done—and that made me nervous as hell. Anxiety jangling through me, I focused on the road and fiddled with the radio, trying to find something that was soothing. White static crackled between the stations, and I found myself pausing there. What had I just heard?

Because it had sounded *a lot* like a voice whispering my name.

Goosebumps pebbled up and down my arms, and I turned the radio up a little, the static scratching against my ears as bits and pieces of words came through.

"*What the hell, Alli?*" Hyacinth's voice snapped through the radio.

I jerked the wheel to one side, nearly driving off the road. A car passing the other direction honked, and the driver gave me a one-fingered salute.

Heart hammering, I didn't know if I should talk back or . . . "Cinth?"

"*I can't hear you if you're talking to me,*" she said. Her voice cut in and out of the static. "*But I promised Jackson meals for a week if he told me how to contact you. He said this is how orders get passed to the Storm Wardens sent out to the Triangle, which is apparently where you are, you nincompoop! Have you lost your damn mind and decided to throw your entire life away?*" She was yelling, but I could also hear the edge of raw emotion in her voice.

I'd hurt her by leaving without saying goodbye.

If I'd told her about Underhill and the Oracle, she might not be saying this stuff, but I hadn't wanted to do that because—

"*—I'm on my way,*" Cinth said. "*Jackson knows the pilots and they told him they saw you. So he got me a flight out, and I'll be in Fairbanks at noon on the fifth. You better be there, because I'm not doing the human thumb thing to hitch a ride.*"

I looked at the time, jerked the wheel hard to the left and spun the SUV around, sliding across the road. The message repeated every few minutes, and I left it on as I sped back the way I'd come. "Dammit, Cinth."

Part of me knew it was stupid to go back to the scene of the crime—yes, we watched cop shows on Unimak too—but I wasn't leaving Cinth high and dry.

I had never intended for her to become embroiled in this mess. Then again, I hadn't intended for there to *be* a mess.

Goddess above and below, she must have moved fast to be so close behind me. I had less than an hour to get back to her. My heart warmed even though I knew she'd do some serious yelling when we saw each other.

The airport came into view, and there she was on the sidewalk with two pieces of luggage and a long, dark green cloak trimmed in fur that swirled around her legs.

I blinked.

She was wearing pants. Jeans, to be exact, which was . . . well, I wasn't sure I'd ever seen her out of a skirt or dress before.

Probably not the most important thing to think about right now.

Shoving aside her unusual appearance, I pulled up and flung open the door. She glared at me—*eek*—and tossed the two bags onto the back seat before sliding into the passenger's seat.

She didn't bother with the seat belt, and I felt relating car crash statistics might not be appreciated right now.

I pulled back out onto the road and got going—again.

When I was younger and waiting for Cinth to give me shit for something I'd done, or not done depending on the situation, I would worry at the inside of my cheek.

Now, I just let out a heavy sigh. "Why did you follow me? I didn't want you getting yourself cast out, Cinth. You worked too damn hard to get to where you are in the royal kitchens."

"Not your choice, Kallik." Her voice was sharp and the use of my full name told me just how pissed she was. "You're the sister of my damn heart, and I don't walk away from my family. I thought we both knew that."

Ouch, that was a shot and a half straight to the gut. "I didn't walk away from you," I said, and then grinned. "I ran like my ass was on fire and my clothes were catching."

Her gaze slanted my way, and I saw a glimmer of amusement there. "You shouldn't run when you're on fire—you should stop, drop, and roll, and let the people around you help put it out. For future reference."

I burst out laughing. "You would say that. Cinth, I . . ." I tightened my hold on the steering wheel, and whatever plastic material it was made of cracked under my grip. The brief mirth between us was crushed beneath the weight of reality. "You know that Underhill was . . . destroyed?"

She sucked in a little breath. "Yeah, like I told you the other day, I'd heard rumors something happened. So it's true?"

I nodded.

Cinth reached over and placed a hand on my forearm. "Was

this a ruse to send you to fix it again? Is that it? I *knew* you were the best of all those trainees. I knew it! Oh, that'll rub Faolan's face in it too! You, the one to be the hero! We can fix Underhill together and go back to Unimak as heroes, the both of us. Lugh's little left pinky finger. Jackson is going to be so—"

"I destroyed it." Those three little words cut short the fantasy she was spinning, which I'd interrupted for fear I would get caught up in it too.

The air temperature was dropping, and the rain coming down against the windshield had started to splat, thick and partially frozen, against the glass. Cinth was silent as the rain continued its transformation to snow, and soon we were driving through a whiteout. Late February in Alaska was in full swing.

Minutes ticked by while I waited for her to speak, and each second cost me another ounce of my belief that she would stand by me. I couldn't *not* tell her my secret. She was right, we were sisters by choice—far more than friends, and in many ways closer than sisters tied by blood. I darted a glance at her. She was staring out the window, her fingers pressed against the side glass.

"Cinth?"

"On purpose?" she whispered her question.

"Goddess, no," I yelped. "I didn't . . . it happened during the oath ceremony. I spoke the pledge, and the Oracle took my blood and then drove the crystal knife into the ground. Everything just . . . shit, it just shattered." I didn't dare take a hand off the steering wheel, but I wanted badly to run my fingers through my hair, an old tic from childhood.

"So what are you . . . do you think you can fix it?" Cinth pulled herself together, and I didn't like that she seemed to shrink from me in the same movement.

Underhill was sacred to the fae. It was the source of our strength, our magic, and it was the one place that no human could walk. Don't get me wrong, humans could walk through the Alaska Triangle—if they dared like Gary and Gord—but they couldn't actually access the fae realm.

"Cinth, I have no choice. I need to fix it or I'll never live a free life. They'll always hunt me. Besides, I want to make this right— it's our realm, for Lugh's sake. I didn't do it on purpose, I didn't even . . ." I struggled to find the right words. "Queen Consort Adair knows, and I'm sure Bres is the one who told her. The Oracle knows too. I don't think anyone else does. Yet." *Except for maybe my father.*

The back end of the SUV skidded in the thin layer of white, and I adjusted accordingly while Cinth squeaked. We drifted sideways for a bit before I got us straightened out. Another look at Cinth showed her clinging to the handle of the door, eyes squinched shut.

"I hate these metal boxes. I don't feel safe with all this iron around me," she whispered.

I nodded. "Less iron, more plastic now, but we're all good, Cinth. They made us practice driving as part of our training for those of us who might want to be guards for ambassadors."

Like what I'd blurted out as my chosen vocation.

Already, that felt like another life. An impossibility.

She cracked one eye open and stared at the snow. "So where are we going and how are we going to fix Underhill?"

"*We* aren't doing anything, I am," I said. "I don't want you cast out for good. Even now, you could go back. You could have a life, marry Jackson, and—"

"Yeah. That isn't going to happen. He helped me out of guilt more than anything else, and with the hope I'd forget what he did."

I shot her a look. "What did he do?"

"You know that he trapped me in a Dutch oven, right?" She let go of the door handle to reach over and grip my forearm.

"Dutch oven?" I repeated dumbly, my mind stalling at the unfamiliar words.

"Yes, he let out a fart, then jammed the blankets over my head and said, 'Breathe deeply baby, and it'll go faster.'" She mimicked Jackson's deep voice, and I couldn't help but laugh.

"What? You didn't like getting to know him on a *deeper* level?" I teased.

She made a gagging noise. "Please. That is the last thing I wanted to get to know, and stop changing the subject."

Pretty sure she was the one who'd brought it up.

"How are we fixing things so we can both go back to Unimak?" she continued.

"You believe that I didn't do it on purpose?" I ventured.

Hyacinth was quiet for a beat. "I've known you since the king's guards dropped you off at the orphanage, five years old with tears frozen to your frostbitten cheeks. You aren't destructive, Alli. Not then, and not now. Whatever happened, well, I guess the fates decided you were meant to leave Unimak, and they made a move to ensure it happened. And where you go, I go. You know that."

I looked over at her, my throat tightening in a way it hadn't in over eight years. "I love you, Cinth."

"Love you too, brat. Now, keep your eyes on the road, I don't want to test the limits of this plastic and iron contraption."

"ONE HUNDRED PERCENT. I think the Oracle did it and used you for cover."

I'd just finished a much more detailed account of what had happened in the Trials. Cinth settled deeper into her seat, arms crossed over her big boobs, which only pushed her formidable cleavage higher. Her look and posture indicated she'd made up her mind and no earthly being could change it. "I don't know why, but I'd lay money on her. She's always been an odd duck, and Merc"—Merc was the head chef in the royal kitchens and had been for over seventy years—"he said something once about her. She'd come through the kitchens asking for tea, and after she left, he called her a distortionist."

I frowned. "What the hell is a distortionist?"

She shrugged. "Don't know, but the way he said it made me

think it was nothing good. I mean it has the word 'distort' in it. Maybe it's a clue." Her expression brightened. "Oh, this is like those human books, Nancy Dew Drop or Trixie Belt In." She clapped her hands together. "We get to solve a mystery!"

I wasn't nearly as excited as she was, mostly because it was my head on the chopping block, and hers might get chopped *because* of me.

Glancing at the map, my chest tightened. "We're a few minutes out from Healy."

"Wait, why here?"

I filled her in on the assist I'd gotten from Rubezahl, and his request that I meet him near the gate.

"And you're just telling me now after two hours in the car?" Her eyes widened. "Who is this guy that he can control a meese?"

"I don't think that's the singular of moose," I said. "Maybe meese is plural for moose though? But he wasn't a moose. He was a caribou."

"Whatever," she waved a hand in the air, "but seriously, you think you can trust him?"

Her question wasn't unwarranted. "I don't have a choice right now." Ahead, snow had covered a bridge. The human-made construction spanned a rushing river full to the brim with ice-cold water, which flowed heavily with the start of a spring melt.

To one side of us was the rusted ruins of what had to be the original bridge.

I shuddered and struggled to swallow.

Across the bridge we drove, and as we made the crossing I could feel the immense, raw power of the elemental force beneath us. I could feel the pull of the water, to an extent, but I couldn't control my fear that the river would spill up and over the bridge. There was a splash to my right, and a small wave did just that.

Heartbeat picking up, I pressed the gas pedal down more despite the risk of slipping and sliding on the road. Making it off the bridge was the only goal—before nature washed it away.

A sigh of relief slipped from me as we made it across.

"Still don't like water?" Cinth asked gently. "I wondered if they would get you through that with training."

I shook my head. "Nope, training did not help with the water issue." She wouldn't bring up my childhood trauma of nearly drowning unless I did, and I wasn't about to rehash that particular memory again.

On one side of the road was a big red-brown building with a simple sign. Ruby hadn't said where to meet him in Healy, but the town wasn't exactly huge.

My stomach rumbled as if it had finally remembered I'd hardly eaten anything in the last twelve hours. I hadn't slept much either. Lack of sleep could lead to bad decisions . . . or, in my case, worse ones.

There was only one hotel in town—a sad-looking two-story number.

Cinth eyed the place. "Not exactly high end."

"We're in the middle of nowhere. Just be glad it isn't a tent.

And it has a restaurant." I parked the SUV and tucked the key fob into my pocket.

I stepped out into the sharp Alaskan wind, and it sucked the air right out of my lungs. Cinth gave a squeak as she rushed for the main door of the hotel, and I followed her at a more sedate pace so I could take the place in.

Not because it was anything special—it wasn't—but because there was a feeling to the air that I didn't like.

The itch spreading along my back and up my neck had me executing a slow turn.

I couldn't see anyone out in the snowstorm, and that's what doubled down the uncomfortable prickling. There could have been twenty fae watching me from less than a hundred feet away, and I wouldn't have seen them.

I was being watched. Of that I had no doubt.

Smiling, I bowed in all four directions, following up with a friendly wave. "Let Rubezahl know I've arrived. I'll wait for him in the restaurant for two hours." Long enough to eat. Long enough to figure out my next step.

Sleep would need to wait, however risky it was to put it off.

I felt a multitude of gazes boring into my back now, but I tamped down the urge to spin around again and hunt my pursuers and instead strode to the restaurant door.

A rush of warm air engulfed me, melting the snowflakes that had landed in my hair and on my long, dark lashes.

I blinked up at a blue-skinned bartender who wiped down

the long wooden strip of bar in front of him. He looked fairly human if I didn't count his skin color and physical size.

He had to be over seven feet and was heavily muscled, and had piercings in his lip and ears.

"Um. Hello?" I'd heard about ogres but never met one. They could be violent and mean and liked only two things in life. Fucking and fighting.

My fingers twitched for my knife. *Just in case.*

He shot me a wide, easy grin. "Name is Dox, ma'am. Welcome to Healy. What can I get you?"

I looked around for Cinth and found her at a table surrounded by four men. *Four.* In under four minutes. That had to be a record.

Her ovaries must double as a male homing beacon or something.

I sighed. "Something strong enough to take the edge off, please, and a menu."

Dox grinned and slid a menu across the bar. "I'll bring you some of my home brew. Just warning you . . . it could knock you on your ass."

"I'm fae. It'll take a lot to knock me on my ass." I took the menu, not responding to his grin. He didn't throw off a bad vibe, but I wasn't here to make friends.

"Ogre beer it is," he said. "Don't say I didn't warn you."

CHAPTER 10

Fuck.

I unstuck my tongue from the roof of my mouth and groaned, clutching my head. The slight contraction of my forehead muscles sent a spear of churning nausea up my parched throat.

"What happened?" I said hoarsely.

Hyacinth's soft chuckle was my reply. "What *didn't* happen? I thought I'd seen you drunk before. Consider me proven wrong."

Reality slapped me with the force of a kraken squeezing my guts. "Ogre home brew. Damn."

"Correct. Thank you, by the way. If I hadn't seen how you reacted first, I might have sampled that myself." She laughed again, the sound vibrating against my skull.

I willed my eyelids open, and they creaked, actually creaked, in protest. "I remember starting on the first drink. How many did I have?"

Hyacinth sat at a small table by a window with bars slanted across the glass. The curtains, probably white in a past life, were drawn back. The gold and blue bedspread clashed aggressively with the silver and red carpet. Purple and bronze wallpaper didn't help matters any. Goddess above and below, whoever had decorated this place had *not* considered potential hungover guests. Although we could be on the moon for all I knew, I had to assume we'd nabbed a room at the only motel in Healy.

My friend chuckled again. "That's all you had."

Really? One drink. "He did warn me." I remembered that much.

I inched my way up to sit on the edge of the lumpy bed.

"Rubezahl came, by the way," she said conversationally.

My stomach dropped out my ass. *Shit.* "He did? Tell me what he said."

"I told him it wasn't the best time. He didn't seem to be in a rush. Had a peek through the window and caught on pretty quickly to your state—you'd started a karaoke night event, and only you attended."

I regarded her through bleary eyes. One thing about a hangover this bad, it was hard to feel embarrassed at the same time. "Through the window?"

"Yeah, *Rubezahl*—though I find Ruby much easier to say,

personally—he's a giant. Like, the ground shakes when he moves, and the snow cleared with just a flick of his hand, then he looked through the window and smiled. Oh, and he carries a harp."

I recalled the soft twang of the harp that had made the airport security glaze over. "That's him." *Dammit, Alli.* I'd had one fucking job to do—wait for this guy to appear and not get drunk.

Cinth passed over a glass of water, and I sipped it with caution. *Note to self: never drink ogre brew again.*

"Ruby is meeting you in two hours at . . . where was it again? He did say." She riffled through some papers on the table.

I swayed on the edge of the bed, holding my head in my hands as I listened to her babble for a time.

She sat upright, triumphantly waving a post-it note through the air. "The last river crossing before the Usibelli Coal Mine! I looked it up. It's about a fifteen-minute drive from here."

I needed to get my crap together before I met this guy for real. I'd only heard of one giant ever—the protector of the Strays—and I had a feeling he and Rubezahl were one and the same. Just my luck seeing as giants weren't known for being particularly smart, or easy to deal with. Fingers crossed he was in the same bracket for giants as Dox was for ogres. A one-off. "I'll be in the shower if you need me."

"Okay, I should probably—"

I closed the door on my friend. Sue me, I was a miserable hungover person.

Leaning into the tiny shower stall, I turned the temperature to cold and shucked my clothes and weapons. When I stepped in a few seconds later, I gasped and almost turned the temperature up.

But the cold water achieved its purpose—the worst of the hangover subsided.

I spent time washing my long hair and scrubbing off the chaos of the last day—two days and two nights. We were on the second day since the night of the dinner.

By the time I stepped out, I felt more in control of my mind and body.

I'd leave Hyacinth here (whether she wanted to stay or not), meet with this Ruby guy, and inspect what remained of the entrance to Underhill to see where that led me.

Wrapping up in a threadbare towel that would have served better as a hand towel, I wrenched open the bathroom door.

"Alli," Cinth muttered.

At her odd tone, I glanced up and stared directly into dark eyes that were most certainly not hers.

Faolan stared hard at me. "Orphan."

I'd left my damn knife back in the bathroom. "What are you doing here?"

A slow grin spread across his full lips, and his eyes darkened. "I told you last night. Right before you danced in front of me for an hour."

My mouth fell open, and I shot a glare at Cinth. *This* should have been filed under 'tell Alli the moment she wakes up.' Had Faolan tracked me down, or was he here for the same reason I was?

It wasn't often the Seelie and Unseelie worked together, more like working parallel with a similar goal, but it wasn't *unheard* of. He could be part of a joint effort to bring me in.

Hyacinth widened her eyes and then stared pointedly down.

I looked down and died inwardly at the sight of my pink nipple poking through a hole in the fucking towel. Thanks to the cold shower, it had never looked more capable of stabbing someone in the eye.

I shifted the towel, and Hyacinth made an alarmed noise.

Peering down again, I saw that the entirety of my upper thighs and what sat between them was on display. I must have had nine lives, because I died all over again.

Faolan's rich voice filled the musty room. "I'd give up if I were you. That sad excuse for a towel can only cover so much. Don't worry, I'm not looking. You aren't my type, not even close."

Mutt. Orphan. Half-breed. Unspoken words, but I heard them anyway and my back stiffened.

I forced myself to meet his gaze and frowned at the rainbow swirl there, just barely visible in the dark depths. His eyes hooded as he dragged them over my frame, contrary to what he'd just said.

"Faolan, tell me why you're here. I'm not in the mood to play your stupid games," I said, feeling water from my hair drip in small rivulets down my arms.

He stepped farther into the room and held up a bag. "As a small peace offering, I brought breakfast."

I growled.

"And," he stressed, cocking one brow, "as I told you last night, I'm here with a group of Unseelie investigating what happened to Underhill. It would be easier if you told me what you know. What happened when you and the other Untried made your oaths. It would give us a starting point."

"Oh, yeah?" I said carefully. "What does this investigation of yours entail?"

"Underhill must be restored. You've heard the rumors of what can happen to us without it." He held out the bag of food to me as he spoke. I didn't touch the offering.

Hyacinth's gaze darted between us, one hand drifting to her chest. "I thought it was just something the royals said to keep us in line."

I absorbed the fear and pain in her voice before she took the breakfast bag from Faolan and strode past the bed to the tiny kitchenette.

"Are you implying fae really do go manic without Underhill?" I asked.

He shrugged, and I couldn't help skimming a glance at his hugging black leather uniform. A perfect crescent moon rendered in red decorated the space over his heart—a sign of the Unseelie court.

"We'd be foolish to dismiss the possibility."

I pursed my lips, thinking out loud. "What if Underhill has slowly been deteriorating for years or even decades? Maybe fae have been going manic for longer than anyone realized."

It would explain the situation with Hyacinth's parents. Their actions didn't fit the parents she remembered.

Silence thrummed between us, and when Faolan's attention dipped down again, I jolted but refused to back away. "I'm sure you have places to be. Thanks for breakfast and sorry for . . . well, for whatever happened last night."

Goddess help me that I hadn't kissed his other eye.

"What are you sorry about exactly? Did you do something you shouldn't have?"

I wasn't sure if he was talking about last night or something else. Like my role in Underhill's demise. I hadn't been drunk enough to spill the beans, had I?

I forced myself not to move, twitch, or even swallow.

"Getting shitfaced is a luxury not many of us have, Orphan. Despite the oath you made, you've ultimately chosen exile," he said softly, a thread of threat there in the undercurrent. "That makes you . . . unpredictable."

As a descendant of the Seelie fae hero Lugh who had surprised everyone when he was sorted into the *Un*seelie court, Faolan probably did envy that fact. He was and always would be held to a higher standard, no matter where he went.

My cheeks warmed as I picked up my bag in an awkward way designed to limit the amount of ass I flashed at him.

I had one foot in the bathroom when he spoke again. "Put your clothes on, Orphan. I'll be here when you get out, and you can tell me why you very conveniently happen to be at the entrance of Underhill too." His voice lowered. "I'm sure you have a solid reason."

"Fuck," I muttered under my breath.

He'd only mentioned being part of an Unseelie investigation, but there wasn't any way the Seelie weren't around for the same reason. Somehow I'd neglected to consider that in my haste to clear my name. And I was willing to bet the Seelie contingent was also looking for me.

I pulled on fur-lined leather tights and a fresh woodland green tunic, then tugged free a hooded cloak for later. Sheathing my weapons, I considered what angle to take with Faolan, secure in the knowledge that Hyacinth—despite her cheery disposition—was more than smart enough to evade his questioning and keep things vague.

Leaving my hair loose to dry, I re-entered the bedroom.

"Well?" He'd lowered into the seat Cinth had vacated.

I sat down opposite him and accepted a bagel smothered in cream cheese from my friend. Her face was flushed, and her eyes distracted, distant. My remark earlier had sent her thoughts spiraling toward her parents no doubt.

Purpose throbbed within me. If their fate really had been set in motion by the unwinding of Underhill, I intended to clear their names.

"I'm waiting, Orphan," Faolan said with a slight snap in his voice.

I took a large bite of my bagel and chewed it, making the

handsome bastard wait.

If I'd expected him to get angry, he surprised me. I detected a tiny hint of amusement in the dark depths of his eyes. Defiance turned him on, did it? Interesting. Not that I cared.

I lifted a shoulder. "Simple story, really. I cast myself out."

He leaned back in his chair and folded his arms over his chest. Shit, I could tell he was seeing through my lies. "Really? I find that hard to believe."

Suddenly, I found it hard to look up from my bagel. "I cast myself out," I repeated.

Faolan leaned forward, elbows on his knees now, hands lowered. "Why would you do that, Orphan? You emerged from training with Elite status. You had your pick of everything. Seems awfully strange to throw it all away. Unless you had another reason to run?"

Fuck, fuck, fuck.

"Nothing felt right," I blurted. "The home they gave me didn't feel right. The area of further training I picked didn't feel right. Being around the Seelie fae of high status didn't feel right. So I left. That was a choice too, even if it wasn't one obviously offered."

There, that was more than half true. I took another bite of my bagel, feeling his gaze riveted to my face. Reading me. Trying to untangle what I'd said and pull lies from truth.

"It can be an adjustment coming out of the training in Underhill, from what I understand," he said at last. "But here of all places? You want to live in the Triangle, where there is nothing but the worst our world has to offer?"

I glanced up at that. "It can't be so bad."

For the first time, I saw real traces of anger on his face. "It is worse than you think, Orphan," he said shortly.

My eyes narrowed. "What do you mean by that?"

He continued to study me, and I got the sense he was deliberating what to say. He shook his head and leaned closer. "Humans are going missing here. I'm not talking one or two. Over the decades, our sources say upward of thirty-five thousand. The humans believe it's more like sixteen thousand. The area has always had a Bermuda Triangle superstition to it, and that used to be enough to placate the higher-ups in the human world. But the number of human disappearances has increased in recent years. The government officials know fae outcasts are in this area, and now those officials want answers from the courts. Answers neither court has."

Shit, he really had the ear of the queen if he knew that much.

I swore softly. "I didn't know." That many deaths . . . I knew loss and grief all too well, I could only imagine the people who'd lost parents, children, siblings. My throat tightened, empathy rolling through me.

This was bad. Big-time bad. On top of the obvious horror of the deaths, angry humans were not good for our kind. There were just too many of them for us to take on. Our magic would only get us so far.

Faolan grabbed my chair and pulled me close enough that

he could lower his voice, his body and face filling my vision. "The courts have already been investigating certain outcasts with the help of some of the friendlier Strays."

Rubezahl. That's why he'd been heading to a meeting; maybe he'd even been headed to Unimak. "Do you think it's all linked? Maybe the human disappearances have to do with what happened to Underhill."

He didn't answer. "This is not a good place for you to be, Orphan, especially if you are here as an outcast in truth."

No, it wasn't. I didn't want to get caught in the crossfire of any action the courts took against the outcasts, but there was literally no other place for me to go.

"You should return to Unimak," Faolan said. "Go back to safety, where you won't put yourself and others in danger."

Pompous ass.

"I can handle myself, Lan," I snapped.

"I doubt that very much." He stared hard at me. "You aren't a very good liar, Orphan. And you're not going to get only yourself killed."

His gaze shot to where Hyacinth quietly hummed in the small kitchenette, pretending to give us a privacy the small space didn't really allow. He lowered his voice. "Because of you *she* is here. Can she take care of herself? You think you can protect her too? You can't. You're still that little girl in the orphanage."

I swallowed the urge to punch him in the nose. "She followed me here. I want her to go back, but she won't. Because we're both adults and can do as we please."

His jaw flexed, and he slowly nodded.

"A Seelie group is also investigating Underhill," he said, keeping his tone low. "I suppose she could join them as a cook. It might protect—"

"Protect who?" Cinth's voice whipped over our heads.

Grinning, I rested back on the wooden chair. "Faolan is trying to fob you off on someone else. Thinks I'm bad for you."

His dark eyes flicked between us. "It's for your own good. You know as well as I do that you're no fighter. At least the Orphan has some experience looking after herself. Even if it won't be enough for these parts."

Hyacinth drew herself up taller. "What's good for her is having me around. Just *try* to separate us. Just try. You'll see who she sides with. You may have a dick, but I can cook. Dicks go limp over time; good cooking is forever."

His jaw snapped shut, and I struggled not to laugh. Leave it to Cinth to put Faolan in his place with a penis metaphor.

I cleared my throat. "Cinth stays with me. I choose the, uh, cook." Because I wasn't so sure she'd be safer with the Seelie. They knew we were close, and if they found her here, they'd interrogate her about my whereabouts.

"So what's your plan then, just run off into the woods?" he asked, clearly mocking me.

My plan. My plan, such as it was, was complicated by the presence of both courts within the Triangle, and even more so by my new suspicions about the outcast fae.

I'd do well to keep an eye on everything, but I sure as shit wasn't going to lay out my cards for him. "I have to stay here. I've exiled myself, so there's no other option for me now. I'll contact the other outcast fae as soon as possible, but if they're under investigation, I'll need to be careful. So thanks for that heads-up." I paused. "Guess I'll run off into the woods and build a log cabin if worse comes to worst."

Right.

Hyacinth shot me a look, then carefully resumed directing her angry simmer at Faolan. Yeah, she knew the tone of voice I was using and what it meant.

I was about to lie to Faolan again—just a little—something that made me feel weirdly guilty.

For me, it had been eight years. For him and Hyacinth, it had only been four. Still, four years was a long time, and people changed. He'd changed the day he'd said goodbye to me in the orphanage.

Whatever bits of softness I'd seen in him back then had dissipated. I'd do well to remember that. He wasn't my hero anymore.

I hesitated. "Is there any way you could give me a further heads-up if a raid or something is going down? I don't want to end up fighting you and hurting your pretty face. If that happened, I'm sure the Unseelie women would put a bounty on my head."

He surprised me by standing and smiling down at me, his

eyes locking on mine in a way that I couldn't look away from. "Orphan, I'd like to see you try."

A challenge was not the way to get me to back down. I stood and faced him, our noses almost touching.

"Don't tempt me, Lanny." I purred his nickname, and the colors in his eyes swirled a little faster.

For just a second, a split second, I thought he might do something truly stupid—like kiss me.

Someone cleared their throat.

I blinked twice, suddenly and fiercely aware of Cinth's perusal. Given how absorbed she looked, all she needed was some crackled corn to complete her viewing experience.

Faolan recovered first. He stepped back, his eyes flicking between us. "I'll be checking in on you. On both of you." So much for getting him to tell us when the raids would happen. Instead we were going to have to watch our backs for both him and the Seelie looking for me.

"If you can find me." I tipped my chin up and found myself drinking in his face, tracing my eyes over his high cheekbones and the almost blue tinge to his black hair.

His smile was sharp and more than a little predatory. "I've never had trouble finding you. You should keep that in mind."

What did *that* mean?

He opened the door and frigid air blasted in. Looking back, he studied me for a beat. "Be careful, Orphan. You aren't in Unimak anymore."

Hyacinth crossed to the door. "She could kick your Unseelie ass, Lan. Get out of here before I sic her on you."

Not sure I could actually back up her words on that front, but I appreciated the vote of confidence.

Lan frowned at her, but it smoothed away as he looked at me again, that slight twitch of his mouth an almost smile.

"Give Rubezahl my regards."

CHAPTER 11

I stared at the closed door for all of two seconds before I ran to it and jerked it open, fully expecting to see Faolan smirking at me over his shoulder. But an undisturbed layer of snow stretched out in front of me, bearing not a single footprint.

"He's gone," I said thickly, my mind spinning like the snow still falling from the sky. Ghosting, the ability to disappear, was an Unseelie trick. Seeing it in action, I immediately wanted it for my own. But though some Seelie could *cloak*, we couldn't master the trick of going completely invisible. It took the kind of power that was tied to death, not life.

The wooden railing from which Faolan had pulled energy to work his ghosting magic had rotted and blackened, and there was a mass of dead and newly shriveled weeds between the pavers. Death was a sure sign Unseelie magic had been unleashed. "Shit, Cinth. That's a trick I need to learn."

I shut the door and turned back to my friend.

She fussed in the small kitchen and flashed me a quick look. "That was intense. I can't tell if he hates you or wants to angry bang you. Maybe both?"

I rolled my eyes. With Hyacinth everything was either about food or fucking—maybe both, which I didn't want to know about. Really, my friend wasn't all that different from an ogre. I smiled at the thought.

She flashed me a grin, misinterpreting the direction of my amusement. "So you *do* still want to get in his pants? Oh, Alli, he's hot, I'll give him that, even if he is a total and utter ass. I still wish my aim had been better with that rolling pin. He could use some humbling." She wiped her hands on her jeans and lowered into one of the chairs at the small table.

I held up both hands in mock surrender. "I don't want to get in his pants. Eight years, Cinth. People change a hell of a lot in eight years. And even if only four years passed for you and for Lan, I had a whole lot of growing up time. I don't want a bad boy. They don't . . . they don't make good partners."

Her eyes narrowed. "What aren't you telling me?"

A single childish mistake with Yarrow in Underhill had been enough to cure me of wanting a bad boy ever again . . . not that I felt like admitting that. I cleared my throat. "Let's go to this mine.

Usibelli Coal Mine, right? I want to get there ahead of ol' Ruby and scope it out."

I grabbed my coat and slid it on, pulled on knee-high, fur-lined boots, and then checked my weapons over. I touched each one to make sure it was in its place; a short curved blade holstered on each outer thigh, a hand-held collapsible crossbow with sights strapped across my chest, and twenty crossbow bolts on two belts slung low over each hip.

Just to be on the safe side, I tucked a four-inch dagger into my right boot. Just in case.

"What about me?" Cinth said. "Should I bring a weapon?"

I peered around the room, and my eyes settled on the chef's knife on the cutting board. "You're comfortable with that, so it would be the best choice."

If she could run around a hectic kitchen with that thing while chefs were yelling at her, then I didn't need to worry she'd impale herself on it.

She grabbed it and looked at me. "What do I hide it in?"

I took the chef's knife and wrapped it in a kitchen towel. "Tuck it under your arm like this." I put the wrapped blade under my arm so the handle just stuck out. "Easy access."

She did as I said. It felt strange to be leading the way. I was used to Cinth being older, but now we were the same age, and I was the one in charge. Not that my leadership had gotten us anywhere good so far.

"Hey, Cinth?" I murmured.

"Mmm?"

I searched for the right words. "Are you okay? That conversation had to bring up some feelings about your parents and their madness."

She stilled, and after a long pause, sighed heavily. "I've always wondered if I'd end up like them one day, so yeah, the fact that Underhill is gone makes me afraid I'll succumb sooner. That I've inherited my parents' . . . weakness, I suppose."

Resting a hand on her shoulder, I said solemnly. "I will never let that happen to you."

Tears glimmered in her eyes, one trickling over the burns on her face. "Promise?"

I wasn't sure how to keep such a promise, but I'd figure it the hell out if it meant saving my friend. "I swear it. Your mind isn't going anywhere. Not without me."

She sniffed and nodded. "Thanks, Alli."

"You got it. Now pull your shit together, we've got a giant to meet."

Cinth laughed, and we both hustled to the car through the cold. I pulled the SUV out onto the road, following GPS directions to Usibelli Coal Mine. Fifteen minutes in good weather, but I'd take it slow because of the snow.

Out in the car, Cinth fiddled with the radio, flicking through the channels. "Jackson said he'd try to reach me if he could."

His voice didn't come through the radio.

Nope.

The scratching white static hissed and buzzed before *multiple* voices, men and women, whispered over the line in unison. Not in English, but in Tlingit, the language of my mother. A language I could still speak fluently, although I had no one to speak it to anymore.

"Death is rising amongst us, Kallik. Stop the children of the moon before they destroy us all. The spirits are angry, but they will guide you."

My throat tightened along with my hands on the wheel as the radio went back to hissing static and white noise.

Cinth leaned forward, forcing me to look at her. "What the hell was that? I thought I heard your name. Did you understand any of it?"

I shook my head. "Just noise, Cinth. It's just noise through the radio."

I cleared my throat, thinking of the crescent moon on Faolan's chest, the emblem of the Unseelie. Is that what the voices meant by "children of the moon"? From the snatches of conversation I'd overheard, Queen Elisavana hadn't sounded like she knew what was going on with Underhill, but that could be a ruse.

How had the spirits known to use the radio to contact me? Or even when I'd be listening? Most importantly, how the hell did they know I'd understand that language?

Shivers worked their way up my spine.

I didn't have much time to dwell on it because the Usibelli Coal Mine suddenly came into view.

With the snow covering the mine, the peaks looked like their own miniature mountain range. The valleys where the humans had been digging had been rendered pristine by the fresh snow, which hid most of the deep gouges in the earth.

I grimaced. Humans loved to massacre nature. Why the hell would Rubezahl want to meet here, a place that was a virtual graveyard to the fae?

I pulled the SUV over and got out. The sharp bite of the wind smacked me in the face, and I tugged the hood of my coat up over my head. When Cinth popped her head out, I motioned for her to stay in the vehicle.

"I'm just going to take a look around," I said. "No point in both of us getting perky nipples."

She ducked back in. I didn't blame her, the cold out here was something else, digging into me like an animal burrowing into the ground for warmth.

I walked down a slope to the bottom of one section of the coal mine. A few machines were parked there. They stood out, bright yellow and orange, against the snow. Why weren't humans working here? It was the middle of the week, wasn't it? Sure, the weather had been brutal, but it was often like that around here.

As if on cue, a guy stumbled out of a portable building, yanking his coat on as he ran up the slope.

"Hey, are you okay?" I hollered to him. His face was about as pale as the snow.

He stumbled. "Lady, what in tarnation are you doing out

here? There's been an evacuation order. We gotta get outta here!"

Evacuation order, huh.

"What happened?" I let my feet take me closer to him, trying for all my worth to put on some fae charm.

Ten feet away, I could see that the human was shaking too hard to zip his coat. I closed the distance and gently moved his hands away to fasten the jacket. As I did, I let my indigo magic loose. This close, it was easy to pour energy into the charm, a kind of magic that wasn't my strong point. But with a human, I should be able to manage.

"What happened?" I asked the question softly. "Why is everyone evacuating?"

"Giants," he whispered. "The giants are coming. We have drones up to keep an eye on things. Last time they were here . . . they . . . they killed the entire crew." His lower lip trembled, and a tear formed in the corner of one eye. A grown man moved to tears because he was so afraid. Of the fae. Damn it.

Should I be afraid too? Ruby was a big guy—a giant according to Cinth. Shit, was his whole crew of giants coming to collect me?

I patted the human on the shoulder. "You'd better go then."

"What about you?" His concern touched me, and I winked.

"I'm right behind you. You go on."

He turned and ran, not once looking back. Which was probably for the best. While Unseelie magic left death in its tracks, Seelie magic did the opposite. Snow drop flowers burst out of the ground in his footprints, as white as snow and visible only for their thin green stalks.

I made my way to the center of the mining pit and glanced over my shoulder at the SUV, giving Cinth a double thumbs up. She smiled, but her smile faded as her attention diverted over my shoulder.

I didn't have to look to know what was behind me.

The ground trembled under my feet like an earthquake. Branches and rocks cracked like jolting claps of thunder.

The giants were here.

I motioned for Cinth to get down, and she bobbed down on her seat again. Turning back, I got my first real look at the giants of Alaska.

"Motherfuckers," I whispered. I mean, there was no good word for these ... creatures.

Ten of them approached, exiting through the trees easily, as if they walked through brush and not out of a huge, old growth forest. They were twelve feet tall, maybe more, and each of them held what looked like a section of tree trunk that had been smoothed out and turned into a club, branches for spikes.

So that wasn't ominous at all.

They wore clothing dyed in natural colors, and their long, tangled hair represented all shades from the brightest blond to a deep, dull black. If not for the way they'd zeroed in on me, I might have taken them for trees.

If all that wasn't enough, their squared off and blunt teeth cracked as they ground their jaws back and forth, the sound crawling up and down my spine. Their heads wobbled from side to side with the rhythm of their steps, as if they couldn't help the motion.

I had to play this carefully.

I didn't move, didn't flex my fingers toward my knives. Quick movements only drew a predator's eyes. My heart picked up speed, and I stared at the one in the lead, making solid eye contact with him.

Voice pitched to neutral, I called out, "I'm here to speak with Rubezahl. Is that one of you?"

The one in the lead, male if what dangled out of a hole in his britches was any indication, let out a wordless roar and rushed me.

So much for being careful.

I took hold of the two short swords strapped to my thighs, waiting. He thundered toward me, and I pulled both swords at the last second.

I dove between his legs, dodging the dangling piece, spun on my knees, and slashed out at his hamstrings.

A roaring scream ripped out of him, turning into a squeal as high-pitched as that of any pig at slaughter as his legs gave way and he crashed face first into the ground.

He had started it, but I would finish it. Another of Bres's teachings.

"I'm here to speak to Ruby. Either you play nice and tell me where he is, or things are going to get tense." I held the tip of my sword to the back of the fallen giant's neck. I'd kill him if I had to, but only as a last resort.

The others circled me, teeth grinding, homemade clubs raised in the air. Careful not to slice myself with the wicked edge of my second blade seeing as I wasn't putting either sword down if I didn't have to, I inched a hand toward the crossbow slung across my chest. A flick of one finger snapped it out, and drawing blue threads of energy from the snow, I slid a spear of my indigo magic into the weapon, listening as it clicked into place, preparing the crossbow for use. Wildflowers popped up through the snow, never looking more out of place, but I did nothing more than send them an automatic thank you as I watched the giants for movement.

I'd thought the standoff would last longer, but boy was I wrong.

The giants moved en masse, charging me in a single heartbeat. I drove the sword into the neck of the one on the ground, then rolled and came up with the crossbow and bolts ready to go.

I fired twice, hitting two of the remaining nine giants, both in the left eye. They fell back, howling, but not dead.

How were they not dead? That'd sure kill *me* and any other fae I knew.

Sidestepping the big fuckers and wishing, not for the first time, that I had one of Lugh's legendary weapons on hand, I kept firing.

They weren't going down. The one on the ground, I'd literally sliced through his neck, but yeah, he'd had enough of his nap and was *getting up*.

"Lugh help me," I whispered.

But it wasn't Lugh I got.

CHAPTER 12

"What are you doing here?" I said angrily, grunting as I dodged a swinging club and cut through the Achilles of the nearest giant.

A tight smile was my only answer as Faolan spun from the reaching, greedy grasp of another giant and kicked out his—or her—knees. The giant of questionable gender crashed to the ground and bellowed in fury, flailing on their back like an overturned turtle.

"How the hell did you piss off *giants* within thirty minutes of me last seeing you?" he shot at me rather than answer my question.

I dodged between thick legs, barely missing getting clunked in the head with the giant's *third* leg. Whirling, I leaped onto the fae's back, scanning for a weak spot. Every fae had a secret weakness. I just had to find it—and quick—these giants weren't getting any more dead.

"They attacked me," I panted unnecessarily, my human mind taking over for the time being. "I didn't do anything."

"Uh-huh. Giants don't just attack people, Orphan," he growled while dodging another blow.

"They do if they've lost their damn minds, you jerk face."

There was a brief pause as Faolan and I shared a moment of dawning understanding.

Right.

Maybe they *had* lost their minds. But at this particular moment, it didn't matter. Whatever their motivations, or lack thereof, they clearly intended to kill both of us. "Don't suppose you know anything actually useful to help stop them?" I kicked off the giant's back right before another brought his club down on his friend with a brutal *crack*.

Ouch.

The first turned and lunged for the other giant with a wordless snarl, and I scrambled clear as they wrestled, forgetting us for the moment.

"Turn them on each other," I called to Faolan. "Unless you've got a better plan?"

"Their brains are small and located at the base of their skulls. The rest of their heads are bone. Only a direct injury to their brain will injure or kill them. Everything else regenerates at an extraordinary rate."

Huh. That *was* useful.

Just how small of a brain were we talking? We weren't sure whether they were addled, so killing them didn't feel right. I mean, Underhill was supposedly gone because of me—even if my role was unintentional. And I knew through Hyacinth how difficult it was to lose people to such circumstances.

Whether because of that or because he didn't want giant brains on his boots, Faolan didn't strike to kill either.

He baited another creature and slid smoothly out of the way when her club connected with two others. The trio of huge fae began to fight, and when one of them careened backward into another two, a *real* brawl began.

Gasping, I put distance between me and the ten furious giants tearing at one another in a tangle of limbs. I winced as a fistful of long hair was ripped from the scalp of the smallest creature in the mix.

Faolan gripped my arm. "Injured?"

"No. You?"

"I'm fine," he said curtly. "How did this happen?"

Nope. My turn. "Why are you here? Are you following me?"

His jaw clenched. "What I'm doing is investigating an evacuation call put out by the coal mine. They reported a giant sighting." Faolan swore. "I need to get my team here to keep the giants away from the more heavily human populated areas. The Storm Wardens are busy in Juneau, dealing with tourist season starting up."

I'd wager about half of that was true. He'd definitely been following me. And I hadn't noticed a thing, dammit.

He rounded on me, but whatever asshole comment he'd no doubt intended to make was interrupted by a ground shaking that put the effect of ten giants to shame.

The giants in question fell apart as if in response to the new threat.

I crouched low to keep my feet and fixed my eyes on the bordering forest. If we were looking at any more than five newcomers, we'd need to bail until the appointed time Rubezahl had set.

But it was only one joining us.

My jaw dropped as a giant bordering on twenty feet tall exited the tree line. His gray beard was scraggly to the extreme and reached his knees. Where the smaller giants were thick-thighed and muscular, he was lean, knee joints knobbly, and possessed an air of fragility that I'd be remiss to put any stock in.

Basically, he was old as dirt.

A thick, brown, woolen, and long-sleeved tunic extended below his knees and a dark blue overlay rested atop of it, belted at the middle with a woven vine. His thick leggings and boots faded to the background when set against the gleaming gold harp fastened to his hip—around half my body in size—and the gnarled staff that extended from his shoulder to the ground.

Rubezahl.

The giant swept his blue gaze over us, then focused on the giants, still frozen mid-fight.

"Did they attack you?" Ruby asked mildly.

Even if Hyacinth hadn't given me the heads-up, I would have recognized his voice. It was the one the caribou had used at the airport. "They did. Unprovoked."

I did not want to pick a fight with this fella.

He nodded as if unsurprised.

The largest of the fighting giants growled at Rubezahl, mouthing nonsense words, hands flailing into the air. He simply unhooked his harp and strummed a few notes.

A calming melody hung in the air, and though the magical intent wasn't aimed in my direction, I felt the drifting residue nevertheless, my adrenaline crashing and my breaths slowing.

The largest giant blinked a few times and then stared at the fae around him. "Ruby?"

Groans filled the air as the sprawled creatures struggled to their feet.

"Do you remember what happened?" Rubezahl asked them.

All ten shook their heads, and I exchanged a loaded look with Faolan. This had to be related to Underhill.

Fastening his harp back in place, Rubezahl spoke softly to the giants in what sounded like German or Dutch—I really wasn't up to date on my human languages.

When the battered creatures made to walk off into the trees, Faolan stepped forward. "Rubezahl, I'll need to speak with these fae before they leave."

"You may speak with them once they've tended to their wounds and regained their composure, grandson of Lugh."

Faolan flinched at the title.

I stepped forward. "Can I take your interference to mean that you didn't send those giants to kill me, Rubezahl?"

He stepped farther into the snow-covered clearing, now spattered with blood. The protector of outcasts glanced around the coal mine, and though his expression didn't change, the small tension in his shoulders indicated he wasn't a fan of what humans had done to the area.

I could second that.

"Yes, you may, Kallik of No House," he replied. "I am glad my arrival was timely. The demise of Underhill has affected us all, far faster than I would have thought possible."

"How many have shown similar symptoms in the last week?" Faolan asked. "What about during the last year?"

Rubezahl faced him, and for the first time, a flicker of irritation showed on his features. A mist began to creep over the thick floor of snow. Was this what Hyacinth had meant about Ruby affecting the weather? "You may relay to your queen that if she desires information from me, she needs to go through the appropriate channels. As always, I am available to help Seelie and Unseelie alike, but my people come first—as both the king and queen are well aware."

I expected Faolan to keep going, but he stood back and

nodded once. "I will pass on that information."

Had he expected Ruby's answer? If so, why ask? To push the boundary of what was allowable. Ass.

And this was why I refused to go for bad boys anymore. My life was complex enough without having to constantly question someone else's motives. Give me a carefree, sweet guy with an easy smile and no ulterior motives.

"Kallik, we had a prior appointment. Unless you are otherwise engaged now, my time is shorter than I'd like in this current climate." Rubezahl inclined his head, and from the corner of my eye, I noted Faolan's sudden frown.

I lifted my chin. "I'm not."

Faolan reached for my arm, his fingers wrapping around my wrist. "Orphan—"

But I didn't give him the chance to finish. I freed myself with a sharp jerk, crossing to the giant.

Rubezahl glanced back the way I'd come. "I will know if you follow us, grandson of Lugh. She will not come to harm while she is with me."

"She's less likely to get herself killed in your company," was the sharp reply.

I gritted my teeth and glared over my shoulder. "You're welcome to pull your disappearing act at any point, grandson of Lugh."

As soon as we got into the trees, I called upward. "Will the giants return to the coal mine?"

Rubezahl glanced down at me, one of his strides worth five of mine. "Your friend in the car is safe."

Of course he'd known Hyacinth was there, because there was no doubt he referred to her and not Faolan. This guy seemed to know more than either the Seelie or Unseelie rulers. "Are you leader of the outcasts then?" I couldn't help myself from asking.

"Protector." He gently guided a tree limb out of his path. "I have never sought to lead."

Which just made him smart in my book.

He halted in a large meadow, and I glanced at the black bear picking its way through berries on the opposite side. Rubezahl lowered himself to lean against a huge pine, and I took the hint, perching on a log close by.

"Do you remember why I was particularly interested in meeting you, Kallik of No House?" he rumbled, looking at me with clear blue eyes.

A wrinkle formed between my brows because, in all honesty, I'd forgotten until that very moment. "You said my magic was unusual."

"Unusual," he hummed. "A good word for you."

Cool. Thanks? "Do you remember why I was particularly interested in meeting *you?*" I prompted.

The ghost of a smile hovered on his lips, just visible amidst his unkempt beard and moustache. "You, like many others in recent days, would like to inspect the entrance to Underhill. The previous entrance to Underhill, I suppose. I thought it prudent, given the nature of your arrival in Fairbanks, that we meet farther from the entrance than initially intended."

It was prudent. Did that mean I trusted this guy? No.

"When can we go to the entrance? Is it constantly watched?" Shit, that could be a problem. And if the Seelie and Unseelie teams had trampled all over the place, they might've ruined any hints and clues by now.

I curled my hands to fists.

"The teams will leave soon. We can go after dark. Which gives us time to speak of your power."

I had bigger priorities right now. "If the teams are leaving soon, I'd prefer to leave now to reach the entrance as quickly as possible."

Rubezahl regarded me with crisp blue eyes. "I do not know why you are truly in the Triangle, Kallik. Nor will I ask you. That is something I would never demand of the fae who choose to make their home here. We seek out this place for a range of reasons, each of us on our own journey. What the years *have* shown me is that our journeys are often linked to our magic. By understanding our magic better, we are better able to understand ourselves and what led us to this wondrous place. You wish to see the entrance to Underhill, urgently, I can assume. So I ask you a question now." His face softened. "Do you believe that your magic is tied to the reason you're in the Triangle?"

I stilled.

Since that day, plain ol' denial hadn't wanted me to admit this could *actually* be my fault. I mean, the blade the Oracle had plunged into the ground had my blood on it, and blood was a conductor of magic. Obviously, *something* magical shattered Underhill.

But *my* magic?

I'd wanted the reason to be something like coincidental timing—maybe Underhill was just ready to go and chose that moment. I'd considered the possibility the Oracle did something dodgy and used me as the scapegoat, or even that the trainers were in on a plot cooked up by Queen Consort Adair, who'd decided to get rid of me once and for all.

Entertaining that I'd played a larger role, a magical role, wouldn't bring any shock with it, perhaps, yet the concept *did* fill me with dread.

Though if I'd caused it, then maybe whatever I'd done could be undone. At the very least, I should pursue this trail alongside my other investigations.

"And if it was?" I replied stiffly.

Rubezahl smiled kindly. "Then I would ask my second question. Would you like help understanding your magic? Guidance of that type is a passion of mine, but it does not need to be me. There are many in the Stray network who could help you find the answers you seek, as well as those who could help you to settle in this area. We are well versed in housing new arrivals, and in providing them with employ."

He was the first person who hadn't tried to convince me to go back to Unimak.

Instead, Rubezahl had offered me mentorship, housing, and a job within an hour. On the one hand, that was kind of his job as protector of outcasts. On the other, that kind of thing didn't usually come without strings. Invisible strings, likely, but still strings.

What I *did* know was that the outcasts were under investigation, and I couldn't fully align with them if they were camped out on a sinking ship.

Spurning their help could bite me in the ass if I couldn't return to Unimak. The thought shook me. I had to go back. Despite what I'd said to Faolan, the thought of never returning to my mother's homeland filled me with a strange sadness.

I took a breath. "I'm not ready to settle here, but I would like help with my magic. And I'd prefer if that came from you, if your offer was sincerely meant."

The giant placed a hand over his heart in an old fae custom I'd rarely seen in my lifetime. "My words were sincere, young one. I will assist you and gladly."

He seemed to mean it, so I decided to take a chance and ask him about something that had played on my mind since Underhill shattered. "I don't suppose you know where the Oracle lives? I'd like to discuss something with her."

To put it very lightly. The old hag owed me some answers.

The giant raised a brow. "The Oracle comes and goes as she pleases, young one. I'm not aware of anyone who knows her location."

That was about what I'd expected. And I wasn't going to

fleece this realm for her in a fool's search unless I had no other lead. I suspected she would show herself when she was ready, as was her wont.

Rubezahl spoke again. "If you change your mind about joining us, you need only ask. We protect our own. We always have. You're also welcome to remain with us as a guest until you make a choice regarding your future."

This guy really did seem invested in helping outcast fae, and regardless of whatever agenda he might have—because everyone had an agenda—he had more information than any other fae I'd come across to this point, and I'd be stupid to turn away from that.

He was the one to stick to.

So stick to him I would.

CHAPTER 13

Rubezahl stood and motioned for me to follow him. He led me back to the edge of the coal mine. "Here I must leave you, young one. But not alone." He turned his head over his shoulder and let out a high-pitched whistle that sounded distinctly like the scream of a hawk. The sound echoed over the trees and seemed to be carried by the wind itself.

I stood there, patiently waiting. Another lesson I'd learned from Underhill was the value of keeping your mouth shut. Not that I always remembered that little lesson, but I tried.

My patience was rewarded. A few moments later, a figure dressed in camo ghosted through the trees to our side, a single weapon hanging from his hip. Not a sword, but a gun, and a decent sized one at that.

I tensed, hands going to my weapons.

"Easy," Rubezahl said. "He's with me."

Since Rubezahl seemed to know the gun-toting human—

The human took his balaclava off, stopping me mid-thought. A tangle of chestnut hair stood up in all directions, outlining a sharp nose that had been broken at least once. The stubble on his face was a new addition, but . . . I *knew* him.

I stared, open-mouthed. "Drake? You—I mean, you're here?" Sure, I'd known he was somewhere in the Triangle, but I hadn't expect to run into him. We hadn't talked to each other much during our Underhill training. He'd been expelled and punished only a few months into it. There had been a lot of kids in the beginning, but his good looks had kind of made him stand out. That, and what they'd done to him.

He frowned and shook his head. "Do I know you?"

Had I changed that much over the course of training? I guess his answer said it all. "Kallik. We were in Underhill together for a while before . . ."

I made myself not look at the stump where his left hand had been.

His deep green eyes swept over me. "You made it all the way through training."

"Barely." I gave him a nod. "Yarrow kept trying to get me booted out."

Drake's entire body stiffened, but Rubezahl tapped the ground with his foot. "Children, I must attend other matters. Drake, do see that Kallik and her friend get settled in at the house. They are our guests for the foreseeable future." The giant turned and strode away, disappearing into the trees with ground-shaking force.

I lifted my hand in a wave. "Thanks."

Rubezahl continued on as if I hadn't spoken. Drake, however, was another matter altogether.

"What the actual fuck are you doing here? If you finished training, why didn't you take a job?" Drake asked. "I mean, that's the goal usually, isn't it?"

I took his measure. We'd started out the same age, but I was now almost four years older than him. From the look of him, he had just a splash of human blood, barely enough to be stuffed into training in Underhill versus in the Seelie court.

I sighed. "I cast myself out."

"You . . ." He blinked a few times and then shook his head. "That can't be right. I remember you now. You were intense right out of the gate. And scrawny with no boobs." He grinned suddenly, flashing bright white teeth. "Mind you, I also thought you were going to die in the first week, so there's that."

He stepped out of the tree line, and I fell in beside him, again doing my best not to look at the stumped end of the arm closest to me. "Is it too much to hope Yarrow's dead?"

"I thought you two were friends?" I asked. "I mean, everyone wanted to be friends with him in the beginning." Including yours truly, much as I hated to admit it now.

Drake tossed a glance my way. "Yeah, not so much." He held his left arm up. "This is his fault. He pinned everything on me. He was the one who stole the healing balm."

My jaw dropped. "Yarrow stole . . ."

Fuck, of course he did. What a slimy fake bastard. "I'm sorry, Drake. No one deserves what they did to you. You were only sixteen. And it's about five hundred times worse that you were punished for something you didn't do. That's complete and utter shit."

He tucked his right hand around the gun handle. "It's in the past. I'm trying to move on. Ruby . . . he's a good guy, Kallik. He's looked out for me more than my own people ever did. He's helped me figure out what I want in life, and how to go for it even with this." He tapped his stump with his good hand.

I frowned. "You speak of him like he's a different species. He's fae too, just like us."

"Yes and no," Drake said and didn't elaborate. He got us back to the coal mine where the big divots in the ground were the only evidence of the wrestling match between giants.

"That your car?" Drake pointed at the SUV.

"For now. My friend is waiting inside." I hoped. Outside of cooking, Hyacinth wasn't the patient type.

"You brought your boyfriend with you?" He snorted.

"My girlfriend," I said.

"Didn't think you swung that way, not with how you mooned after Yarrow," Drake said. There was nothing mean about how he'd said it—the comment was just plain honest. He wasn't wrong, and the reminder of my stupidity back then, which I had thankfully grown out of, still stung all these years later.

"Look." I put a hand out against his chest, stopping him, but also copping a feel of his human weapon. Plastic carrier? So that's how he managed to hold it close even though there had to be bits of iron in its inner workings. "Yarrow tried to kill me in Underhill, so he and I are hardly on what I would call speaking terms. Given the chance, I'd take him out like that." I snapped my fingers in the air.

Drake gave me a grin. "I think we'll get on just fine then. Even if you don't swing for my team."

There'd been some misunderstanding, but I just shook my head and let him lead the way down to the SUV, where Cinth peeked out of the window to check out the sound. As soon as she saw me, she threw the car door open and ran to me, dropping her knife in the process. So much for using it as protection.

Boobs and ass bouncing, she grabbed me in a damn bear hug and lifted me off the ground.

"Damn it, Alli! You can't do that. My poor heart can't take it. Giants flinging themselves around, you and Faolan fighting them like devils in the flesh." She put me down and then gave me a weak punch to the stomach.

I doubled over and fake gasped. "No more. Don't hurt me no more!"

She slapped me on the back of the head for good measure as if Drake weren't standing there gawping.

I straightened slowly. "Drake, this is my sister, Cinth."

The words popped out—we'd called each other sister before but not out loud around others.

Hyacinth gave me a look before shifting her attention back to a bemused Drake. "Hyacinth, if you please."

I cleared my throat in the silence afterward as he tried not to stare at her burn, and she tried not to stare at his stump. "Let's get going, shall we?"

"And where, exactly, are we going?" Cinth asked.

Drake grunted. "Ruby's house."

My brows climbed. His actual house? I supposed that made sense, what with him assessing my magic and all, but this arrangement would keep me a fair sight closer to him than what I'd envisioned.

We climbed into the SUV, and following Drake's directions, I got us headed east—moving deeper into the Triangle.

"How much longer?" I took the next left hand turn at Drake's request and stole a glance at the chestnut-haired man stretched out and comfortable in the passenger seat beside me. Yup, nice eye candy, I'd give him that.

"Just under an hour by car. Shorter as the crow flies, but there's plenty of bush and snow to get through," Drake said.

Looked like I wasn't getting to the entrance to Underhill today. Frustration bubbled up, but I forced it back down. I really needed to inspect things in the light anyway.

In under two minutes, Drake was turned around and chatting away with Cinth as if they'd been besties for years. Between that and the way he kept trying to look further down her cleavage, I considered jabbing him in the ribs every time I came to an intersection, just to make it stop.

The hour passed quickly as they talked and I drove, and soon enough we rounded a final curving hill, and the 'house' came into view.

I'd expected it to be big—Ruby was twenty feet tall, after all—but I hadn't expected *this*. It was a massive damn castle made of beautiful polished timber. The doorway was large enough to accommodate a giant of Ruby's size, and upon closer inspection, I saw that while the left wing of the massive building was a single story big enough for Rubezahl or any other oversized fae, the other side appeared to be three stories of average-sized housing.

Plenty of room for any random fae who showed up.

"Holy beetroot tickles," Cinth breathed out as I parked the car off to the side of the building. "I bet the kitchen in there is amazing. *Please* tell me it's amazing. I could have an orgasm right here if it's got marble countertops."

Drake smiled at us both, laughing at her. "Come on, I'll give you the tour. I don't know anything about kitchens, so you'll have to be the judge on that."

The kitchens didn't interest me as much as the sheer fact that this place existed—and I hadn't heard about it until this very moment.

How had the humans not found it?

Did the courts know about this?

Why hadn't I heard any whispers about it?

If I'd thought the building impressive outside, it was even more so once we entered through the main door. The wood-panel walls, covered in intricate carvings of wolves, ravens, orcas, and eagles, reminded me of the longhouses of my mother's people. Some of the doorways were formed of whales' rib cages, and the timber throughout the house had been polished to a high red-brown sheen. Here and there, the windows were bubbled from having been made by hand. None of these materials had been bought from the hardware store.

What caught my attention most was how much iron was around the place; wrought iron hinges that had been hammered by hand, the dents in the metal giving the building even more character.

I couldn't resist. I brushed a finger along one of the hinges and let out a low hiss of pain.

"We had locals help us with that," Drake said. "It's a reminder that we aren't immortal or infallible. An issue that Ruby says has brought fae to this low point in our history. Too much pride."

"Yeah?" I murmured. On Unimak there wasn't iron anywhere, and if there was it was wrapped in plastic or some other substance to keep it away from our skin. Like the gun that Drake carried.

Here, iron was everywhere I looked.

Part of me was impressed. Okay, a lot of me was impressed. It was a bold move. Risky.

"Well," Drake said. "Maybe he's right. Maybe not. All I know is that things happen for a reason. There has to be an explanation for why Underhill collapsed, right?"

Uh-huh, and he was looking at it.

"Agreed," I said softly, staring at the surrounding iron once more and thinking of how it burned at even the slightest touch.

Pride and iron. Both destructive to the fae in ways I knew all too well.

CHAPTER 14

"I'm a guest here, remember?" I said, tossing and catching the keys back and forth.

Drake strode beside me toward the SUV—at least that's where I was headed. Ol' chestnut locks seemed to think I should go back inside.

But to my reasoning, it would soon be dawn.

Which meant light.

Which meant I was getting to this entrance to Underhill whether he wanted to take me or not.

"Rubezahl would want to accompany you," Drake repeated.

"And I want a cherry and beetroot tickle," I replied.

He cut off whatever he'd been about to say. "Huh?"

My face slackened. "We're discussing wants, weren't we? I'd also like a chai latte if we're rolling with this. Full fat, none of that skim milk shit."

Drake rolled his eyes, a corner of his mouth lifting in a half smile that . . . interested me. There was no denying Drake was easy on the eyes, and it looked like he might be in my life for a while. He hated Yarrow, which showed sound judgment.

Of course, this was the absolute worst time for me to be interested in anyone, so I shoved those thoughts aside as I opened the SUV door.

Drake planted his right hand on the cool metal, promptly shutting it. Sliding my gaze from his hand to his stubbled face, I cocked a brow. "Is this where you tell me I'm really a prisoner and the guest routine was a ruse?"

Something sparked in his eyes, and his lips twitched. "Not unless you want to play that game, Kallik."

Well, he wasn't short in the confidence department. "Get out of my way and stay here, or get out of my way and join me. It's up to you," I said.

I'd already wheedled the location of the entrance out of him last night with only a little bit of help.

Cinth may or may not have brought a couple of bottles of the ogre's home brew with us, and I may or may not have spiked Drake's drink.

I'd never tell, and Cinth was still sleeping off the amount she'd downed—and yes, I'd put a little bit of the ogre brew in her drink too to keep her sleeping while I investigated.

Drake groaned and took me up on my second offer. Brushing against me, he moved around the car to take the passenger seat.

"I'm glad we could work out an arrangement," I said demurely as we both got inside.

He glared at me, but it quickly turned to a rueful laugh. "You're going to get me in trouble, I can see it clear as day."

Uh-huh. "And unless you want me to begin seriously contemplating that Rubezahl has set me up and you're actually my prison guard, you better get explaining," I said.

Reversing between two trees, I spun the wheel and headed back the way we'd come the night before, bouncing down the rough track. We were closer to the entrance now than yesterday, and I struggled to keep my fingers from drumming with anticipation. It wasn't far at all. Which did somewhat muffle the cautionary whispers telling me I'd unintentionally drawn too close to the outcasts too quickly.

No doubt Rubezahl really did intend to accompany me to the entrance later.

Going myself felt like I was erecting a clear boundary.

He wasn't *my* guide or protector, even if by now I truly believed he embraced that role for the other outcast fae. He and I had made no agreements other than his offer of magical training.

Drake sprawled in the passenger seat as he'd done the day before, widening his thighs and rubbing at his face with his hand. Yeah, that hangover was the real deal. "Look, you know

I've been assigned to help you settle in, which means you are my responsibility at the moment. Ruby may be the fatherly type, but he isn't fond of a job badly done, so unless he says otherwise, then I'll interpret his request to mean that I should follow you to the entrance. Not that you'll need my protection," he muttered. "You have enough weapons to take care of yourself."

There was some bitterness in his voice, and I could wager his thoughts had turned to the future Yarrow had stolen from him. "Sometimes it's nice to have an extra body around. You know, if it's one hundred against one."

"What happens if there are only ninety-nine?" People so rarely flirted with me that I almost missed the teasing lilt to his voice. In truth, if I hadn't borne witness to the literal hundreds of pickup lines directed at Hyacinth, then I might not have registered that that was what Drake was doing.

It was actually kind of nice.

I looked him up and down. "If there's ninety-nine, don't worry about stepping in. Doesn't make sense for both of us to work up a sweat."

He laughed, a warm and rich sound. "Well, not unless that's what we want."

Was he referring to sweaty sex? Sounded like a sweaty sex comment to me. And I was surprised how much it tempted me. "Before we get sweaty together, tell me a bit about yourself."

Drake glanced at me, a bright interest in those green eyes. What? He hadn't expected me to take him up on the offer? Wasn't sure if I would yet, but I honestly couldn't recall the last time I'd enjoyed flirting like this. I'd been so set on Faolan when I was young, and then I'd closed myself off to anything that might interfere with training after my crappy judgment call with Yarrow.

Maybe sowing some oats wasn't such a bad idea.

"This left," he said. After I took the turn, he continued, "Not much more to say. You know I went to training. I couldn't go back to the Louisiana faction after what happened, so I fled here minus a hand. Ruby took me in as a stray. Proud to be one, to be honest. It's a simple life—and peaceful. We help each other out and work together, keep to ourselves. Maybe not the life I'd aspired to live, but now I wouldn't have it any other way."

Did he realize how attractive his uncomplicated life sounded? I'd never aspired to more than a stable roof over my head. His situation sounded perfect. Other than the unjust hand amputation, of course. "You don't ever miss your court?"

He shrugged a shoulder. "Less bullshit here. The people are just better. We're too busy surviving to play games."

The sky was a deep gray between night and day, and as I surveyed the thin stand of trees, I mulled over his words.

There was a lot of dancing around in the court—in both courts, I'd imagine—but not all the people involved in it were bad. And though I might roll my eyes at the posturing of some of the higher status fae, I didn't think they were beyond redemption either. Adair was another story, of course.

Something I remembered the orphan matron saying flowed

from my mouth. "Power tends to corrupt, and absolute power corrupts absolutely. Great men and women are almost always bad."

Drake shot me a look. "Pretty deep."

"That's me, I got layers." I smiled over at him, even as those words rattled around in my head.

"What about you, Alli?" Drake asked in a low voice. "Tell me about you."

"We're on nickname basis now?"

"You object?"

I pursed my lips. "I'll let you know."

"You do that. In the meantime, pull down this road a bit. We'll park here and hike the rest of the way—assuming you'd like privacy for whatever you want to do here."

I tensed, trying not to let it show. "What would make you think that?"

He gave me a side-eyed look. "Just your general vibe. Suspicious, wound up, and mysterious."

I snorted, parking the SUV out of sight of the main road. "Oh yeah?"

"Never said it was a bad thing. Most newcomers are like that for a bit. The Triangle doesn't have the best reputation and the fae that come here, well, they're usually out of options."

"No kidding. I hear the human disappearances are off the charts. Is that true?"

He frowned. "It's an isolated area—and hostile even to those who've grown up here. Full of unpredictable weather and creatures that will win fights against humans. People aren't always smart, and even if they are, nature can still drag them down."

I considered that, following Drake into the trees, hunching my shoulders against the bitter cold that already curled through my layers. "You think all those missing people were taken down by nature? I've heard the humans put it down to Bermuda Triangle stuff."

He sighed. "They would. Always looking for a cover for their own stupidity."

Whoa. "Not a fan of humans?"

Drake peered back, coloring slightly. "Sorry. That's just the bitterness talking. I didn't always want to be here, remember? It's not easy being confined to certain areas of the world. I . . . didn't handle that well for a time, and it's easy to slip into old habits now Underhill is gone."

"Sure, I get that. Must make the trapped feeling worse, knowing you can't escape into the fae realm anymore." Even if Underhill was as apt to kill us as be kind to us, at least it was a place for all fae. Outcasts included.

He resumed walking, shoulders tensing as he hunkered against the cold. A beat went by before he replied, "Guess so."

I studied his back. *Okay.* "What's the update on the entrance then?"

"This area has been pretty flooded by both courts checking things out. They're all searching for answers."

And the odds of me finding anything new were minimal.

"What's your take on what happened to Underhill?"

Drake slowed his steps, and I crouched beside him a moment later in a mass of trees surrounding a clearing. *The* clearing. Black charring coated much of the grass. This was where it had all gone down.

His throat worked as he faced me in the cold dawn. "That's a question for Rubezahl."

"Why?"

"Because he'll decide when you're worthy of our trust."

Shit. It sounded like he knew something. Did that mean I had nothing to do with this after all?

As the thought spun in my mind, Drake jerked his head toward the clearing. "But that is straightforward. A few days back, the ground shook so hard, we felt it from the house. We followed the vibrations to the clearing, and the way to Underhill was gone. Now it's hard like ice. You know what I mean?"

I'd been through the entrance twice. Any humans who'd wandered over it wouldn't have noticed anything out of the ordinary—just a solid, grassy surface—but for a fae it was like entering an ocean. Those with magic merely had to wade in until they were submerged. The world then tipped upside down, jolted a bit, and presto: we were in our native realm. The passage was an area where the magical threads on Earth congregated, matched on the other side by a nexus of magic in Underhill. I guess because there was such a collection of power in both realms at the same location, it weakened the natural barriers.

I scanned the area, listening hard for unwanted company.

Faolan could literally be lurking in the middle of the charred remains of the entrance, and I wouldn't know. Maybe skipping out on Rubezahl hadn't been a great idea.

Too late.

"Stay here." Without waiting for his answer, I strode out. First things first . . .

I knew the answer, but couldn't help testing it out for myself. I walked across the former entrance.

Drake's description was perfect. *Hard like ice.*

It felt like normal ground, in other words—in Alaska, frozen ground.

I began to inspect the entire clearing in quadrants, searching for anything out of the ordinary. Nothing popped, not that I was surprised. The investigation teams would have taken away anything useful by now.

Except certain evidence could not be cleared or removed. Magic always left a mark.

Moving to the middle, I closed my eyes and stretched my fingers outward, at the same time opening myself to the magic inside of me. Starting with the area around my feet—the deepest part of the closed entrance—I slowly scanned outward to the tree line. Drake appeared as a mass of vibrant blue threads—almost like a human-shaped knitting ball.

The trees weren't giving off the lush, verdant magic I'd expect given their isolation and age. In fact, the color was all wrong—

yellow-green where it should be green.

The trees closest to the entrance were weakest—their threads almost wisp-like—while the trees farther away were in a better state.

I pushed my senses out as far as possible, trying to gauge the extent of the problem, and the yellow-green taint went as far as my senses could reach.

In contrast, the ground underfoot had *nothing* to it. It was a magical black hole. The sheer mass of magic that had once resided here had, for all intents and purposes, been extinguished like a cigarette.

I'm so sorry this happened to you. I couldn't help sending out a useless apology to the depleted area. The lack of magic here just felt so . . . abhorrent.

Magic didn't just *go*. There was a solid reason why Seelie and Unseelie had to coexist. When Seelie used magic, they created life. When Unseelie used magic, they drained it. The magical equation was balanced when we inhabited the same places. Which was why the two courts always resided in an area together.

That thought brought me back to the question at hand.

Magic could be balanced or unbalanced, but it didn't *eat* itself in this way, not without leaving a trace, and it didn't just blow up either. If the magic wasn't here, then it had to be somewhere else. But if someone had moved it, they'd done it without leaving a trail—something that should have been impossible.

I crouched and pushed my fingertips into the black ground

made mushy after the snow yesterday.

Had I done this?

Had I *eaten* the magic somehow?

I shook my head.

"Any luck?" Drake called over.

Luck. If he meant answers, then no.

I had more questions, if anything, but that wasn't a bad thing. "Nope. Do you feel how strange the residual magic is here?"

People had varying abilities with magic. Some were better at sensing it than practicing it, and others excelled at honing it into useful skills like the Unseelie ability to disappear. Drake may not see what I was seeing, and if that was the case, I didn't want to give away the information.

He nodded. "The area seems drained of life, don't you think?"

I tapped into my magical sight again. Drained was an excellent word for it. It was like Underhill had pulled in as much magic as possible before closing. "How far out does the damage to the trees go?"

"To Healy."

I couldn't help my small gasp. We'd driven for an hour from Healy yesterday. "That far?"

"In all directions."

There was a muted thud in the distance, and both of us tensed. I'd barely cast my magic out when Drake beat me to the punch.

"Seelie," he growled as he twisted around, eyes squinting.

"They've not seen us yet."

If I concentrated, I could see their magic—a fierce mixture of blues, greens, and bright golds—which meant they'd see my deep indigo if they chose to look.

"Quickly. Into the trees," he urged.

Didn't need to tell me twice. I joined him, and he lost no time swinging me into his arms like I was some damsel in distress.

I opened my mouth to point out that I didn't need saving, but he closed his eyes and a foreign warmth slipped over my head, sliding down to the tips of my toes.

My gaze flew to his, and I studied his broad chest—looking for the magical underlay. "Where's your magic?"

"Masked. I masked yours too. Needed body contact."

I cast him a doubtful look—because, really? But he'd never appeared more serious. On quiet feet, Drake moved us back the way we'd come.

Voices reached us from the far right.

"We've already searched here. What's the point of coming back?" someone grumbled.

I froze and so did Drake.

Yarrow.

There was no mistaking that voice. Drake's head whipped right so fast I wondered if it would bounce off into the trees. His breathing turned shallow and rapid. Gone was the carefree version of him—a wild light had entered his eyes.

One that spoke of future mistakes. "Get it together, Drake.

Not the time. There will be a group of them." I kept my voice low and calm and tightened a hand on his.

Those fae out there, they'd all be Elite or Middling at the lowest possible level. Not a good fight to pick with just the two of us.

Drake didn't appear to have heard. I sighed and reached around his torso. Working under his thick layers of clothing, I rested my freezing hand on his lower back.

His inhale stuttered, and his attention slammed to me. "What was that for?"

"That kind of anger doesn't lead to good things. Stay on task," I whispered.

Cold murder shimmered in the depths of his eyes. "I haven't seen him since . . . "

I extracted my hand from his clothing and squeezed his arm. "I know. And when the time is right, you may get your chance at him. But it would be a mistake to try today."

He blinked a few times and heaved an exhale.

"Back to the car," I said quietly.

Back to Rubezahl's house.

Because he'd been right. The answer to this riddle was certainly buried in magic, but I had a feeling my magic was just one piece of the puzzle.

CHAPTER 15

We took one step into Rubezahl's house, and I sighed in contentment as a warm, glorious scent washed away the questions rolling through my head. At least for the moment. "Cinth is baking. Come on!"

I grabbed Drake's arm and dragged him through the house, following my nose. Because if I was smelling right, she was baking pixie bread and some sort of berry jam to go with it, and I wasn't missing out on a single slice.

I didn't have to drag him for long. "Glorious Lugh, is that what I think it is?"

He glanced at me, and then we were both running full tilt like kids, straight into the kitchen.

Cinth was not alone. She was—shockingly—in the center of a group of fae men who were in various stages of complete adoration.

Seriously. How did they find her so fast?

"Listen boys, I told you that I had to keep at least some for my little sis. This is her favorite, and she's had a rough few days." Cinth looked up as Drake and I fought to reach the kitchen bench.

The food really smelled that good. Some things were worth killing for, and Cinth's pixie bread was surely one of them.

I barely glanced around, but even that quick look told me Cinth would be in culinary heaven. Everything was high end, finished in oil-rubbed wood and marble—freaking marble!—and the pots and pans were bright copper, polished to a high sheen. I wasn't a baker or a cook, but I could appreciate that this place rivaled the castle kitchens in Unimak, and Cinth didn't have two hundred other chefs to work around. The previous cook—a fellow who made nothing but beans and wieners for the crew— had gladly given up his spot to her.

"Pretty please." I gave her a goofy, strained smile that never failed to crack her up.

Laughing, she pushed a plate of sliced pixie bread over to me. Already layered in butter and a bright orange-red jam. I eyed Drake as he took a piece.

Bastard had better only have one.

The bread was made in layers—a simple bread dough, a pixie dust and sugar mixture, and melted butter, all rolled into a loaf which had to be baked at a precise temperature. The bread was decadent and lush even before the addition of the sweet and tart fresh jam.

"That's huckleberry jam. Damn little berries were so small." Cinth pinched her fingers together. "I was getting so few of them the boys here offered to help. Worth it, though, don't you think?"

She smiled, oblivious to the mooning expressions being tossed her way. Hell, I'd moon at her for another slice or two. Maybe I wouldn't drool like the big blond fella, though.

"Amazing," I mumbled, then stuffed another slice in my mouth. I hadn't eaten breakfast, and it was after lunch already.

Having a high metabolism was great and all, but it meant that not eating wasn't an option. I barely refrained from licking my fingers.

A soft knock on the door disrupted the content rumbling in the kitchen. A slight woman, smaller even than me, stood quietly in the opening. "Rubezahl is here, and he would like to speak to you, Kallik of No House."

I washed my hands off quickly and glanced at Cinth. She nodded and threw me a wink, happy in her kitchen surrounded by adoring men.

Following the woman, I took her in. She stood barely to my shoulder, but her long white hair hung nearly to the ground in soft waves. Her ears were tipped, pointed like only one species of fae I knew of.

A species that was no longer supposed to exist.

Manners kept me from blurting out the question, but I saw her shoulders tense as if she'd guessed what lingered on the tip of my tongue.

Actually, that was probably exactly what had happened. The mystica fae were mind readers, which was the reason the fae Elite had killed them off in the last war. Or at least that's what we'd been taught in school.

I swallowed hard and focused my thoughts. *I love her hair, it's so beautiful.*

Then, before I could change my mind, I stepped up next to her and glanced down. Her cheeks were pink, but there was a soft smile on her face. She looked at me, her cheeks flushing a deeper shade of pink as she waved to the massive, twenty-foot-tall door straight ahead. "He waits for you there."

"Thanks." I picked up my pace. Not that I was afraid of her, but . . . a mind reader was not the ideal person to have around when you had secrets.

I clamped down on my wayward thoughts, thinking of pixie bread until the woman was out of sight. She hadn't even introduced herself, which was fine by me, seeing as I was going to have to avoid her ass like the plague.

One stray thought about my potential involvement in the destruction of Underhill, and I'd be done. "Fuck me sideways, Lugh," I muttered as I rapped a knuckle on the door.

"Enter." Rubezahl's voice echoed through the thick wood. I blinked and stared at the door, my eyes landing on the carvings etched into it with an expert hand.

On one side was the crescent moon of the Unseelie court, encircled by nocturnal animals. Bats, wolves, cougars, and owls, to name a few. And on the other side, the sunburst of the Seelie court was surrounded by bears, birds, deer, and eagles. I traced a finger over both court symbols, a distinct pang reverberating through my heart as thoughts of Unimak hit me. I'd barely missed the island during training—aside from Cinth and thoughts of my mother—but I was realizing that was because I'd always expected to return.

Now, I might never get back there. Not that the life of the fae in the Triangle didn't call to me on some level, but I didn't want to abandon my long-held dreams either.

A place of my own had been the only thing keeping me going for the last eight years.

Sighing, I let myself into Rubezahl's office.

He sat on a tree stump carved into a massive chair. The ground was just that—dirt. There was no floor, and my boots made no sound on the hardpack. A roaring fire inside a square-shaped river rock fireplace that was as tall as me kept the cold at bay.

Cool.

"Young one, I see you went to the entrance of Underhill on your own." There was no rebuke in his voice—he was just stating the facts.

"I did." I nodded tightly as I settled into my training stance. Feet shoulder-width apart, hands tucked behind my back—one hand clasping the other wrist—I focused straight ahead.

"You may be at ease, Kallik. I am neither your master nor your liege. I wished only to go with you so that I might see your reaction to the damage done to Underhill." He leaned back in his chair and pulled a pipe from somewhere under his clothes. "What did you see?"

This was where things got tricky. I needed his help, but I couldn't spill all my damn secrets. "Drake said it felt drained in the area, and I agree."

"He has told me his impressions. I'd like to know yours. What did you see and feel?"

I frowned and stared at him. Curls of smoke rolled from his pipe as he watched me over it. "It felt empty," I said. "As if there was never any magic there at all."

He puffed a few times, inscrutable eyes never leaving my face. "Interesting."

There was that word again.

"The Seelie troops arrived, so I didn't get to stay as long as I would have liked." Frustration leaked into my words.

"You thought you could solve the issue of Underhill in a day?" He laughed—softly for him, I supposed, but to me it was an impressive rumble. "Young ones, they never change."

He motioned for me to sit across from him, and I moved closer to the rough human-sized wooden bench by the fire. Heat rose from a stone cup resting on the wood, and he motioned at it with his pipe. "That is nothing more than hot tea infused with herbs and honey. I have a penchant for herbals. I'd like your thoughts on the combination."

Well, that was an abrupt change of subject. I picked up the cup and took a sip. The flavors coated my tongue and throat, warming me almost like a sweet liquor on a cold night. My muscles relaxed, and my first thought was that this would be a damn good nightcap. "Nice. I like the touch of maple in there. It offsets the chamomile."

He smiled. "You have spent a day with us, Kallik of No House. Have you thought more about my offer to join us? You could train our people to protect themselves, and in exchange, I will help you deepen your understanding of your magic. An area I can see has not been overly developed."

I took another sip. "And Hyacinth?"

His grin widened. "I believe the fae here have already fallen under her spell and would revolt if I so much as suggested she leave."

I laughed, spilling some tea on my pants. I brushed it off. "She has a way about her."

"That she does." He sucked on his pipe a few times. "What do you say of my offer?"

I knew what I should do: ask for more time. Put him off for as long as possible without making a firm commitment. Because I had it on good authority the Strays were being watched, and I didn't want to get picked up in a raid.

But that wasn't what I said.

"Hyacinth will need to make her own choice, but I accept." The words popped out of me before I could catch them. I clenched my fingers around the stone cup, the warmth soothing me. This felt like the best choice. And it wasn't like I really had another option. Hyacinth would likely choose to stay, too, and after talking to Drake . . . well, he was right. There just wasn't any bullshit here. My heart felt heavy at the thought of losing Unimak, of leaving Mom's grave behind, but the things I wanted most—a house, freedom—I could have them here eventually.

Rubezahl leaned forward and held out his hand. I put my palm against his and felt a distinct tingle between us. Not in a sexual way, more like his magic was meeting mine. Our gazes locked and held.

"We will help each other," he said. "Like family."

Throat tightening, I stood swiftly. Family was no small thing to me, so he'd be waiting a while for me to say those words back—perhaps forever. "Thanks, Ruby."

He nodded. "Rest, young one. We will meet again soon. I'm afraid there is much that requires our attention."

CHAPTER 16

I woke in pitch black to the sound of wood squeaking lightly on wood. The squeak came again, a flush of cold night air seeping in with the sound.

I didn't move, didn't change my slow, long breaths as I faked sleep. A floorboard creaked on the left side of the bed as another cool brush of air swept in from the window.

I shot a leg out, satisfied with a deep *oof* as I caught the intruder in the thigh. Rolling up to my knees, I grabbed him around the neck in a death hold. At least that was the plan. Would have gone off without a hitch with anyone else but *him*.

Faolan's eyes gleamed in the thin moonlight as he ducked out of my arms, twisted me around, and pinned me back down to the bed. I locked my legs around his body and nearly managed to reverse our situation, but he pushed his hips down and pinned my wrists above my head.

"What in the name of Lugh's left nut are you doing here?" I hissed at him as though he weren't the one in control.

He grimaced, no doubt at the reference to his grandfather. "Recon."

"And you just happened to find *my* window?" I snapped my head forward, trying to catch him in a head butt. He moved out of the danger zone, easily avoiding me.

Damn it, I was one of the best fighters in our training group. Why was he constantly besting me? "How about you let me out of this cute hold, and we make this a real fight?"

"I'm not that stupid, and I told you, Orphan, I can find you anywhere." He peered down at me, and I glared at him, trying not to notice the rainbow flecks in his eyes, which seemed to glitter even in the dark. Trying not to think about how much I'd like to see him like this, poised over me, under very different circumstances.

"Again, *why* are you here?" I growled, squirming under him, trying to find a way to flip him off me.

His gaze narrowed as I bounced and the bedsprings squeaked. "Getting a layout of the house."

That didn't seem to have any connection to an investigation into the disappearance of the fae realm.

I froze. "You aren't here for Underhill, are you?"

He didn't look away, but his jaw tightened. "The Strays need to be brought in and dealt with before they cause more chaos."

Dealt with. I knew exactly what that meant. Killed or put into servitude. If the courts had decided to close in on the outcast fae, they must believe Ruby and his crew were the cause of Underhill's downfall.

Instead of trying to get him off of me, I changed strategy. In a sharp, liquid-fast move, I wrapped my legs around his middle, and snugged him tightly to me. His eyes widened, and I laughed. "Don't flatter yourself, Lan."

I squeezed his middle tight, and he tried to suck in a breath. Tried and failed. Big strong human thigh muscles, for the win. I may not have been the fastest in my training group, but strength and endurance were always my fortes.

He reached with one hand to free himself—mistake. The move gave me a hand back. I drove my elbow into his clavicle, and he snarled, rolling us to the floor with a massive thump.

I didn't let go, and neither did he.

Faolan jerked my other hand down, sliding what felt like a leather wrap around it. My jaw dropped as he *tied my hand to his belt.*

At least this time when I tried to head butt him, he couldn't get away. I slammed my forehead into his and saw stars.

No, not stars. My magic had flared unexpectedly, thin ribbons of color shooting from me to wrap around Faolan. His magic responded, coiling around me and snuffing out the light.

I sucked in a breath as his thoughts filled my mind.

Why are you here? What are you doing with the Strays? What had made you run so far from everything you ever wanted?

"What the fuck—?" I tried to pull away from him but our magics kept . . . wrapping around each other, prodding, until there was a burst of light and a scene ripped through my head.

A memory from my recent past, one I'd been replaying again and again.

The Oracle stood before me as I spoke the words of my oath—my happiness and satisfaction burned a hole in every bad thing that had happened in my life. The last word of the pledge left my lips, and the Oracle coated my blood on the crystal blade, driving it into the ground.

Underhill exploded, and I cried out with the others.

"*Underhill is no more, Kallik of No House,*" the Oracle's voice rang in my mind. "*You have destroyed it.*"

I gasped, and Faolan grunted, our magic finally untangling.

I scrambled away from him, or *tried* to. Still tied to his waist, I only made it to my shaking knees. Faolan rose to his, too, wordlessly staring at me.

"*You* . . . you were the one who destroyed Underhill." In another situation, I might have been amused to see such shock and horror from a guy who didn't emote. But not here, not when my life was on the line.

I shook my head frantically. "I didn't . . . I don't know what happened. The Oracle does, maybe, but she disappeared, and no one knows how to find her."

He wouldn't believe me. He worked for the Unseelie queen and was one of her favored soldiers. He'd fucking string me up and march me right back to my death.

I couldn't allow that to happen.

I made myself look him square in the face. "I won't go easy, Lan. I won't. I'll fight you every step if you try to take me back. I'm here to . . . to figure out what happened. I have to fix this."

His eyes swept over me, and he took a step back, dragging me with him. "*Fuck.*"

That about summed it up.

"What in the name of the goddess am I supposed to do with you now?" He scowled at me.

With that question hanging between us, the side door burst open. Hyacinth, who was staying in the adjoining room, stuck her head in, eyes still mostly closed. "If you and Drake are boning, can you keep it down? A girl needs her beauty sleep."

The door shut, and she disappeared.

I closed my eyes, groaning inwardly.

As soon as I opened them, I saw Faolan smirking at me.

"I'm not . . . oh my goddess. That's not what it sounded like." I wanted to curl up in a corner and die.

Maybe I should just let him take me back to Unimak, because I was pretty sure that's what waited for me.

Faolan ran a hand through his raven hair. "Orphan, you are in a far bigger mess than I could have ever imagined."

Yep.

I leaned against the wall, and he joined me. "You aren't telling me anything I don't already know. But the question is, do you believe me or are you going to haul me off to an early grave?"

"Option C," Faolan replied, untying me, his fingers flinging the knot open in seconds.

Blood pumped in my ears. Because maybe I could escape Faolan. *Maybe.* But he had tricks I didn't. And he'd already found my new 'home,' snuck in, and somehow pulled the truth out of me with magic, something I'd never heard of before. "What's option C? And what did you just do with your magic to pull that memory from me?"

Shadows cloaked his face. "What did *you* do?"

"Me? I didn't do anything. That's never happened to me before." I glared at him.

He was quiet. "Option C means that you work with me to figure out the Underhill entrance situation."

That was the best-case scenario for me, but I wouldn't let him know that. "Depends. What's in it for me?"

"I don't drag your ass in to the Unseelie queen, and you get to be close to me. Something I know you want."

"Oh, please," I scoffed. "You've changed, and so have I. Eight years is a long time, Lan."

He pushed off the wall and faced me. "Keep fooling yourself, Orphan. What's 'in it' for you is that I don't—what was it?—'haul you off to an early grave.' Given our history, I'm willing to allow you time to prove your innocence, maybe even help you, but I'll need a little something in exchange."

I crossed my arms. "And what's that?"

In the dark, I caught the twitch of his lips. "The Strays you're staying with. I want a few details about them. That's the deal."

About Rubezahl and Drake and Hyacinth's kitchen harem?

This would complicate things, but the foolish human notion that fae couldn't lie was just that. I could string Faolan along for a week or two. It wouldn't last forever, but it didn't need to. "I just arrived here. I don't know anything about them, and they won't hand me information on a platter—they don't trust me any more than you do."

"And you'll try your best to give me insignificant details to lead me along." He waved an impatient hand.

Okay, maybe a week or two was stretching it.

He neared. "I'm serious, Orphan. The good stuff, that's what I'm bargaining for. If you can't provide that, then we know the alternative."

Part of me wanted to ask if he'd really cart me away, but I already knew he wouldn't break his oath to the Unseelie queen for me. And I'd never ask that of anyone.

I took a breath. "You have a deal. In return, you keep the memory you stole from me to your damn self."

"I didn't steal a thing, Orphan."

Confusion filled me. "Then what *was* that?"

Faolan stepped closer, and my gaze flew to his as he cupped my jaw. His dark eyes darted over my face, and he leaned in.

Goddess. It was happening.

A small breath escaped me as I tilted my head, closing my eyes on reflex.

He was going to kiss me. He—

Faolan's lips connected with my left eyelid, and then his hand slid from my face. My jaw dropped to the floor as I stared at him in disbelief, wiping the moisture of his kiss from my *eye.*

"Knew you wanted me," he said smugly, already striding for the window.

I spluttered. "You kissed my eye!"

"I hope it haunts you, too, Orphan." He swung a leg through, and I stormed after him, fists bunched by my sides.

"You are completely misunderstanding what just happened."

He glanced back at me. "Then why are you so flustered? I'll be back. Don't forget our deal."

"I dislike you immensely," I hissed after him as he dropped out of sight into the cold, dark night.

His infuriating chuckle floated through the air.

Cheeks aflame, I slammed the window shut, narrowly missing a red crossbill.

"What are you doing up, little guy?" I cooed.

A deep voice echoed from the tiny bird. "Our visitor has departed, Kallik. It is nearly dawn. I would like to meet you for your first training session if this is a convenient time for you."

Rubezahl. And he knew about Faolan's visit. Of course he did. What else did he know? Because Ruby wasn't someone to piss off, and he wouldn't be pleased with the deal I'd just made to save my hide.

"Sure," I told the avatar.

It shuddered and chirped, and I opened the window so it could zip out again.

Sleep would have eluded me after Faolan's visit anyway. Dressing in light trousers, I belted them at the waist over a tight, long-sleeved woolen top, then pulled my hair up into a high ponytail.

I assumed Rubezahl meant the magical kind of training. With those knobby knees of his, I doubted we were going for an early morning run.

Not long afterward, I knocked on the enormous door to his sitting room and entered at his direction.

"Good morning," he said from his chair.

I was glad for the fire. Had he moved since last night? His pipe was nowhere to be seen, but his harp now rested on his lap.

I moved to the bench. "Morning."

His blue eyes rested on me. "I trust the grandson of Lugh did you no harm?"

"Nothing more than a fright to find him in my room. I didn't ask him to come here."

Rubezahl dipped his head. "I had gathered. I thought it best to let him in and see what the Unseelie queen is up to."

Here it was.

The test of loyalty. I would have preferred to keep this

to myself, but maybe this could work in my favor. "He's got something on me, unfortunately. I made a deal with him to stop him from carting me back to his queen for questioning. The courts are watching you all—the Strays—and they're about to pin the demise of Underhill on the fae in the Triangle. Faolan wants information on you all. I'd planned to string him along, but he's smart and he knows me. It will be easier if you can help me feed him important-sounding but still useless information."

A soft smile curved the giant's lips, and I knew I'd passed the test. "A sound solution. Thank you for telling me."

Yeah, well, I enjoyed my head remaining on top of my neck. "You aren't surprised to hear what the courts are planning."

"They circle us more as our numbers grow. Alas, it is not the first time in our history that innocents have been used as scapegoats to cover the actions of the powerful."

I frowned at that. "Why would they do that, unless . . ." My mouth dried as the pieces clicked together inside my head. "You believe the courts had something to do with the demise of Underhill."

He hummed and the walls vibrated. He dipped his head toward me ever so slightly. "Yes and no, young one. I think we can discover the answer ourselves. To begin, let us speak of your magic. Tell me of it."

The change of direction pulled me up short. Tell him what about it? I frowned and spoke haltingly. "Seelie magic. Deep indigo in color. I'm only half fae, so . . ." I shrugged a shoulder.

He'd know what that meant. I was weaker with my magic, which was why I'd worked so hard with my other training.

"So your eventual understanding of magic will be far greater than that of most full-blooded fae," Rubezahl replied. At my silence, he added, "Where there is no incentive to understand, most do not strive to do so. Natural ability does not equate to excellence."

I'd never thought of it that way. "I'm willing to work on my weaknesses, although I don't know how much good it will do."

His gaze softened. "I can see that you are willing, young one, if full of doubt. Let us take a closer look at your energy."

Tapping into my magical senses, I blinked to adjust as the carved walls came alive with an influx of colors. *Wow.* Ruby's home was even more beautiful this way. Threads of magic and energy cocooned us, woven with an expertise equal to that of the ornate carvings visible to the non-magical eye. No wonder he'd detected Faolan so easily.

Turning both palms up, I turned on my mental tap and let wisps of my indigo essence flow into my hand.

"Purple. It is a beautiful color," the giant rumbled. "Tell me. What comes most naturally to you when you use your magic?"

I considered that. "Nothing. I can safely say that every magical task I've learned has taken me a while to master. Learning to warm my skin in cold temperatures took just as long as connecting to nature and asking for its help. A few of my classmates took far longer than I did to grasp tasks initially, but over the years their speed improved and mine did not."

He nodded a few times. "In my experience, there is always an element of magic that is subconscious. For instance, you are very quick to access your magic."

He was right, I hardly needed to think about it. But there were some who didn't need to 'tap into' their energy at all—it was a constant overlay on their human vision. "I suppose. It's the using it part that takes practice and focus."

"Or at least using it in the way you were taught. Like the human schooling system, the courts are fond of forcing stars through triangle spaces."

"I don't understand," I said plainly. "I always use my magic with intention."

"An experiment, perhaps," Rubezahl suggested.

At the very minimum, I was intrigued to see what exactly he meant. "Okay?"

He carefully set his harp against the leg of his massive chair and extracted his pipe from the pocket of his tunic. Holding it out, he smiled. "Do you agree that this is a pipe?"

I searched his expression, then reached out to touch the wooden pipe. "Yes. It's a pipe." My magic only found a small pulse of green energy, a remnant of what had once been part of a tree.

Rubezahl closed his eyes, and I sucked in a breath, staring at the object in his hands.

"Do you agree that this is a goblet?" he asked me next.

A metal goblet now rested where the pipe had been a second

A COURT of HONEY and ASH

prior. "It appears to be a goblet."

I didn't know anyone who could alter one material to another. A wooden pipe could become a wooden goblet. Plant or animal fibers could become clothing. But to change the essence of one substance to another? That was abhorrent. "It has the appearance of a goblet," I repeated, nonplussed.

"The appearance, yes. Look closer."

He clearly intended for me to look at the magic, so I squinted and straightened. "The essence is still the same."

Metals in the ground often gave off a silver-blue energy. For this to be a metal goblet, it should show signs of the same color. But it still carried the same subtle green energy of the wooden pipe. "It's an *illusion*."

"It is. I wonder what might happen when your magic meets it."

Meets it. I hadn't heard that phrase before. "All right."

It was nothing to send tentative indigo threads out to meet the metal goblet. I didn't expect anything to happen, but an ear-splitting shriek rent the air, and the goblet instantly morphed back to a pipe.

The illusion shattered.

I stared at the pipe in his palm. "Why did it do that?"

The giant didn't answer, lost in thought as he regarded the pipe too.

"Ruby?" I asked quietly.

He blinked and looked across at me. "Why? That is a big question, young one, and a question we must figure out together.

However, we do know that your magic just dispelled an illusion, naturally and without conscious effort on your part. Or, put another way, it destroyed a *lie* with no effort on your part."

Huh. "I never knew."

"I suppose you didn't until, oh, say a week ago."

A week ago? My mind didn't immediately switch gears, still caught up on what had happened with the pipe. When it did, I stilled and glanced up.

A week ago, I'd destroyed Underhill.

Blood rushed in my ears.

"Sometimes, the powerful like to use the innocent as scapegoats," he repeated his earlier comment.

I bolted to my feet.

I hadn't destroyed Underhill after all.

"I destroyed the *illusion* of it," I said aloud, eyes rounded.

Rubezahl dipped his great head. "Underhill has been gone for far longer than any of us realized. Years longer, in fact."

The blood left my face. "The king and queen know all this?"

"They know, yes. And they guard the secret closely. Very closely. It was mere chance that I discovered the ruse," Rubezahl said. "Not only that, but if my assumption is correct, they were the ones to create an illusion of the false Underhill to placate our kind and maintain peace while they figured out how to restore access to the true fae realm. I made a point of tracking their movements. The king and queen leave Unimak more often than they'd like their subjects to believe—together—and they only ever visit one location."

"The entrance," I whispered, my gut churning.

He dipped his head. "Topping up the magical stores at the entrance to maintain their illusion, no doubt. And concealing their work so thoroughly that I've been unable to find a trace afterward. Their mastery over magic is undeniable, but they failed to factor in one thing, Kallik of No House."

I'd take one guess. They hadn't foreseen that a half fae "orphan" would accidentally shatter their lie. But now that I had, they had a convenient scapegoat to pacify their people and the human government.

This was bad.

Really bad.

It wasn't a matter of clearing my name anymore. They knew I was innocent, and that was far more dangerous to my future longevity. "What can I do?"

The giant sighed. "What can *we* do, young one? You are not the only one they are coming for by any means. My interest, as always, lies in protecting the fae in the Triangle from outward threats. You saw what happened to the infants of my kind when the madness took them."

My brows shot up. "Those were babies?"

"They were toddlers at best."

Some of them had had beards . . . but okay. "They lost their minds," I offered.

"I was able to stabilize them, but you are correct. This, as you may know, is the effect of not entering the fae realm for too long. Or, in their case, ever."

"I'd heard the rumors."

"Underhill must be restored," he said gravely. "But the trail is now so very cold—years dead, not days or hours—that I do not know where to start."

No wonder I hadn't been able to trace magic from the grove. This could have happened decades ago. The courts had been given plenty of opportunities to scrub away evidence of their lies.

"I have no idea where to start either," I said honestly. "Maybe it's best for me and Hyacinth to go into hiding." Even as the words left my lips, I knew that would never happen. I couldn't outrun a problem this big. Not when both the Seelie and Unseelie were involved. "I mean, it was an accident to start, but I wasn't exiled by the king. I made an oath and then broke it to come here. If they catch me, I don't want them to bind my magic."

"You swore upon a fake Underhill. You made no magical oath that day, young one, because your magic shattered their illusion. You have no liege."

I didn't? Really? "But when I returned to Unimak, I spoke the oath again to the king."

The giant pursed his lips. "I see. And did he present you with any orders?"

"No."

"Then you have not yet broken your oath to the court. Unless the pledge has changed since I last heard it, then I believe young fae only swear to obey the king or queen's orders, nothing more. Unless you interact directly with the king in the future and refuse his command, then he has no basis to bind your magic."

It seemed like a very weak technicality to me. I couldn't imagine my father seeing it in the same light. And I'd still chosen to go on the run . . . "I don't know what to do, Ruby."

"Sometimes, in times such as these," he murmured, "it is best not to look for a solution, but to assess who may have the most to lose."

"Me. Specifically, my head from my shoulders." I grimaced and touched my fingers to the pulse points in the sides of my neck.

He smiled slightly. "Yes, it is in our best interest for it to stay there. I refer to the courts. We only have our lives to protect, but they have an image to maintain. That image is what gives them power, so they can imagine no worse fate than for it to crumble."

"You think they'll make a move?"

"I think that they are already desperate, and they'll soon act with something akin to panic. What has experience taught you about those who panic?"

I blew out a breath. "Their decisions aren't particularly great."

"No," he said, picking up his harp. "They are not. I would expect there will come a time when the courts overplay their hands. If not, it may become prudent for us to apply some pressure."

CHAPTER 17

R uby's words rumbled through my head with a buzz akin to one of those human recording machines as I left his sitting room.

Apply some pressure.

What in the name of Lugh kind of pressure did he want to apply? And how?

He hadn't offered anything more, and I hadn't asked—Drake's words about earning trust hadn't failed to make an impression.

So I'd listened rather than spoken. And when Ruby offered me a map, rendered on thick, homemade paper, I took it. The oversized timber castle sat at the center, and to the north were three lakes connected by rivers. That's where I was to meet the

Strays he wanted me to train, whom he'd summoned via avatar.

I popped into the kitchen first. Hyacinth bobbed and danced to a tune only she seemed to hear as she worked on some sort of multilayered pastry.

"Cinth, I'm going to go train the Strays."

She blew me a floury kiss. "Don't be too hard on them. They're scared of you."

I laughed, but she didn't appear to be joking. "Seriously?"

"You trained in Underhill, and they're not sure they can trust you even if Ruby does." She folded egg whites into the mixture, sprinkling something pale pink and glittering over the top. "Look, just be mindful that many of them have been here a long time and they don't trust outsiders. And you're a woman."

I grimaced. "You're a woman and they trust you, because—"

She glared as I cupped my hands out in front of my chest. "Because *food* is the way to every man's heart whether or not he'll admit it. So if you need help, let me know." She did laugh then. "Look at me, helping you train the boys."

I rolled my eyes, grabbed an empty flour sack, and stuffed it with the first batch of the tarts she was still baking. "Hint taken. Bribery it is."

"Those are for lunch!"

I kissed her on the cheek and ran from the kitchen, dodging her attempt to grab the sack of fresh tarts. "Thanks, Cinth."

I'd never trained anyone else. None of the trainers had ever shown me favor in Underhill. Yarrow had helped with training on occasion, and I'd hated those days the most.

Cringing, I stepped out of the castle and eyed the surrounding forest for the trail that would lead me to the first lake.

I had a few ideas to get started, and I grinned, relishing the thought that others would suffer today instead of me. So much for making nice with the tarts.

Maybe I'd keep them all to myself.

As I walked through the towering green trees, I considered what Ruby had shown me. If the Underhill I'd known had only been a placeholder, a construct, then where was the real deal? Hidden? Broken? Closed off?

I didn't know.

I didn't think Ruby knew either, which left a knot of worry grumbling in my gut. Or maybe I was just hungry, there was that too . . .

The snow crunched under my boots as I strode down the narrow path between the dark pine trees. In another time and place, the crisp air and smell of bursting sap might have been enough to wash away my concerns. Nature was good to fae, bringing us peace and solace in times of uncertainty.

On some level, I believed it did the same for humans.

But today it couldn't entirely rid me of the stress bearing down on me.

My ears twitched at the softest crunch of snow.

I dropped my flour bag of tarts, spun and pulled my two short swords, pressing the points into the belly of the guy right behind me.

Drake had his hands—pardon me, *hand* and arm—up in the air, his green eyes wide. "Jeez, Alli. Remind me to call your name next time. You okay?"

I blew out a breath. "Yes. And no. You want a tart?" I picked up the bag and offered him one. Slightly squashed but still warm.

Drake accepted the tart and walked beside me despite the narrow path. Had he purposely done that so his shoulder would keep bumping mine?

"You want to talk about it?" he asked.

"It's nothing. Just a bit concerned about training the stra— guys." *Nice catch there, Alli, nice catch. Dumbass.*

"They want to learn." He licked his fingers, and I found myself watching his mouth a little too closely. "They won't be hard to train."

"How long were you with us in Underhill?" I asked him. "Three months?"

"Four. Why?"

I sighed, and my breath fogged out around my face. "There was something of a purge at month five. The training ramped up, and those who couldn't keep up were sent home. More than half of the trainees left after that."

From the corner of my eye I saw him frown. "So?"

"I'm going to use the same method of testing. It will tell me whether they have mettle. Whether I can actually train them."

Drake slowed and put his hand on my arm, stopping me.

"Why push them so hard out of the gate? Even the trainers in Underhill eased us in. They *want* to learn. You could break them in easy, over weeks, and gain their trust."

It wasn't my place to tell him that a fight was coming, that the Seelie and Unseelie courts wanted to pin their own mistakes on the Strays. That if we didn't prepare for the storm on the horizon, we'd all be speared with lightning and drenched with rain.

I lifted a shoulder. "I . . . already discussed it with Ruby. He agrees this way is best."

"Then why did you bring the tarts?" Drake's frown deepened.

"I'm not going to be their friend, Drake. I'm going to be their trainer. If they don't respect me, if they don't put their all into this, I won't be able to work with them. Anyone who can't hack it can find another vocation with Ruby." I pulled my arm out of his hand. "And that includes you."

I felt him stiffen beside me. Yup, making friends wherever I went. But he had to believe I'd drawn a hard line in the snow if this was going to work. They all did.

Drake said nothing else as we came to the end of the trail.

The path opened onto a stunning vista with a frozen lake, a stark mountain peak sitting behind it. Ice glittered in the bright late winter sunshine, making my eyes water. I lowered the flour bag to the snow.

Aside from the natural view, I took in the men I was to train. Thirty-five? Against how many trained Seelie and Unseelie warriors? Goddess, this was no fair fight.

It would be a damn slaughter.

Steeling myself, I approached them. "Rubezahl has asked me to train you. I've recently completed my training in Underhill, and was assigned as an Elite fae." I paused and let that sink in before I went on. "I want to see what you're made of before we commence. First, I need to know that you will do as I tell you even if you don't understand why. That you won't argue with me when I give a command. That you will follow orders in the heat of battle." Yes, it was repetitive, but it was also important. And it was what Bres had said to me and the other Untried he'd been assigned before he started working with us.

The men exchanged looks before shifting their gazes back to me. A few nodded, the rest just waited quietly, faces unreadable.

I swallowed hard and lifted my chin. "We need that ice opened up. Thirty feet by thirty feet, as fast as you can. No magic."

Shock filtered through the crowd. They didn't move. I wrapped indigo magic around my throat and lifted my eyebrows. "Now!" I bellowed with the force of a cannon. *Oops*, they'd probably felt that one down to their bones.

But it got them moving.

Some had weapons, and some had tools, but they all went to work on the four-inch-thick ice, Drake included.

I stood at attention, arms behind my back, legs shoulder-width apart as I watched them. The swing of the black-haired man's sword was sloppy, the guy next to him had something wrong with the right half of his body, and the one with the shaved head could barely hold the hammer he was using to chip at the ice. Goddess, this was . . . this was worse than I'd thought. I kept watching, though. Hoping for some standouts to emerge.

The guy with the hood over his face had potential. He swung a pickaxe in a smooth motion that suggested his body was in relatively good shape. That could be developed into swinging a weapon with the right training.

The man next to him puffed hard, his cheeks scarlet red with cold and exertion, his belly protruding out of his too-tight tunic.

I forgot the cold as I watched them, cataloguing their strengths or lack thereof. The first five feet by thirty they carved out of the ice wasn't too bad seeing as their feet didn't get wet. But the next five . . . they were in the icy water now, up to their mid-calves, whether they liked it or not.

I remembered how merciless the water had felt on my skin and muscles. It didn't escape me that I could end their suffering, and yet it was the only way for them to learn. We didn't have time. Before we knew it, both courts would be bearing down on us. There could be no babying, no coddling.

They began to slow.

"I want you moving like your ass is on fire and your hair is catching! We need that ice block opened up *now*." I didn't move from where I stood. Five of the thirty-five were stumbling hard, bodies shaking with cold and fatigue as they flopped back toward the shore.

They'd been working for less than thirty minutes.

Was Faolan watching me right now? He would be, if he'd been sent to keep an eye on the Strays. He was probably feeling pretty good about his chances. I should ask Ruby how to detect his presence, seeing as he'd known the second Lan had come into the house.

My money was on a spell that was woven into the walls that would have been tripped when someone not welcome crossed the boundary.

Those in front lined up shoulder to shoulder under Drake's direction, and they kept at it, chopping concrete ice away inch by inch. Another foot, then another and another. Five more feet in, they were halfway to their goal.

Seven more men dropped back, shaking so hard their teeth chattered loudly enough to be heard from shore. Their tools and weapons slid from their blue-tinged fingers, and they gave up.

As each minute ticked by, more of them buckled under the harshness of the task. I knew it was hard, and that was kind of the point, but there was no, well . . . it was like they had no heart in them. Weak, I could work with, but no heart? No grit?

"Can we start a fire?" The man with the sloppy sword swing approached me. He'd been one of the first out. "We're freezing out here."

I locked eyes with him, keeping my face a careful blank. "When the task is done, you can all have a fire and what remains of the food."

"Bitch," he bit out.

And there it was. Bres would never have allowed anyone to backtalk him. I felt everyone pause in their exertions to see how this played out.

He picked up his sword. "You're a power-hungry bitch, and I'll say it even if the others won't. Should be Drake training us, not you."

I could back down and walk away. I could tattle to Ruby and let him handle it. Or I could teach this piece of work a lesson about being rude to strong women. I gave him a slow, deliberate smile.

"You have no idea what a bitch I can be when I'm pushed." My two swords were out before I finished speaking, and I swung them one after the other against the blade of his sword, snapping it in half with a shriek of metal breaking metal.

He stumbled, and I slammed the hilt of my left blade against his hand, forcing him to drop the stump of a blade.

With a roar he came at me, bare-handed—Balor's balls, he'd been faking the whole exhaustion act, had he?

I spun under his arms as he reached for me and, aiming the swords I still clutched away from him, punched him in the back, right over the kidneys. He went to his knees, and I placed the tip of one sword at his neck, the other in the middle of his spine. "Yield."

He struggled to breathe. I hadn't even broken a sweat.

"Never to a woman and an outsider." He spat to one side, blood flecking the snow.

I stepped back and studied the surrounding men, seeing anger in their eyes. Distrust.

And here I'd thought they could be a new family to me. This was a stark contrast to the welcome and help I'd received from the Strays so far.

I hadn't realized how badly I'd wanted that until this moment, when it became obvious it wasn't to be. That once more I wouldn't fit in. An outcast amongst outcasts. My heart cracked, old wounds seeping open.

Jaw tight, I sheathed both swords and shook my head. "I will not train anyone who can't respect that a woman can fight as well as any man." I paused, not wanting to disappoint Ruby. "Leave now. Any who will not take my lead. Leave."

The man at my feet stumbled to standing, cursing me in several languages. "Come on, you lot. We don't need her. Come on, boys."

Only . . . no one else moved.

Not a soul.

"Come on, Ivan," another man called. "You're stirring trouble, not the other way around."

My slowly breaking heart healed a fraction. Maybe the distrust wasn't for me. Maybe it was for this asshat.

Slumpy sword guy, aka Ivan, snarled and stepped back. One step. Then another and another. "You'll pay for this."

"Says the man whom I beat in under thirty seconds," I said softly. "Go. Before I change my mind and finish the job."

He strode away, and I kept my back to him. He wasn't worth worrying about.

I lifted my eyebrows. "That ice won't clear itself."

Drake's jaw dropped, along with a few others, but I didn't have to repeat myself.

More than that, the remaining men—even those who'd already abandoned the task—went back into the water. They finished the last fifteen feet while I built a roaring fire.

Maybe there *was* some grit in them. Maybe they hadn't forgotten what it meant to have heart and honor.

As soon as they finished the big chop, the men stumbled from the frigid water and peeled their clothes off. It was the right thing to do to keep from going totally hypothermic, but I couldn't stop myself from checking out Drake's naked, chiseled chest— and watching with interest as the hooded guy to his right, the one with the good pickaxe swing, started to peel back his cloak.

Oh fuck.

I froze, staring into Faolan's dark eyes as the cloak dropped to the ground. He slowly peeled his shirt up and over his head, revealing not only his bare torso and muscles that made Drake look like a schoolboy, but one hell of a tattoo on his right pec and ribcage. Celtic in design, it showed a man wielding a fiery spear in one hand and a gleaming sword in the other. The figure was surrounded by woven bands that crossed at the bottom, forming vicious wolves' heads.

Drake cleared his throat, drawing my eyes back to him. "This here's the new guy, forgot to tell you about him. Goes by Lan."

Sure he did.

Sure he fucking well did.

Bastard.

I pulled myself together with some difficulty. "I know him, Drake, though I'm surprised to see him here." I paused and handed out the tarts. They were cold, but damn, Cinth's cooking held up.

I stared hard at Faolan. "You still with Pete and Adonis, or did you break up with them before they kicked you off Unimak? Because I heard they weren't happy once they found out you didn't have any balls."

His eyes narrowed at the stream of lies, but I kept my smile in place. Take that, Unseelie Guardsman. If he wanted to play this game, then play it I would.

One count for Kallik of No House. Zero for Lugh's grandson.

CHAPTER 18

I stormed back toward the house after instructing the—for the most part—sorry excuse for warriors to gather at the same time the next day for the *real* training to begin. They straggled out behind me, their groans and moans filling the crisp air.

Kudos to Cinth. They'd been far more amenable after eating her tarts.

"Where are you running off to so quickly?" a low voice reached my ears.

I didn't spare a glance for the jackass—aka Lan. "Anywhere you're not."

"And after I snuck into the Strays' ranks to be close to you."

I'm sure that was the reason, only not the way he was implying it. "Go away, Lan."

"Have you forgotten our little deal, Orphan? You owe me information."

I snorted. "In the few hours since I last saw you, I've assembled an in-depth dossier. It includes evidence of the outcasts' involvement in the demise of Underhill. Pictures. Hair samples. Everything. I'll have it on your desk by six a.m. tomorrow morning."

His fingers closed around my wrist. Instead of pushing back, I pulled, darting a leg out.

Faolan stumbled forward.

Didn't fall—the agile fucker. But not gonna lie, it felt good to crack that ever-sure step of his.

His eyes narrowed as he turned to face me on the narrow path. "What has you so worked up?"

My ire rose as the question left his lips. The guy clearly didn't speak female. "Couldn't be the asshole using me to gather information for the Unseelie court just threw me another curve ball. I mean, if I were guessing."

Faolan's expression chilled. "The asshole who chose not to turn you in, that who you mean?"

I stared hard into those dark eyes of his. "Because he saw an opportunity, not out of the goodness of his heart. We aren't friends, Lan. I'm not that big of a fool."

He stepped closer, and not to be outdone, I did the same. We stood nose to nose.

His jaw clenched. "What would you have me do? I took an oath to obey and serve my queen."

I smiled without an ounce of humor. "I've learned that trying to control what others do is pointless. I can only control how I react."

Faolan stiffened. "What does that mean, Orphan?"

"It means I liked you a whole lot better before you were sorted. Before you said goodbye and ran away to the Unseelie court to be held up as their poster boy."

Before he called me useless.

For the first time since my return to Unimak, I saw true anger flood his features.

"The *Unseelie* court?" He laughed shortly, pacing away from me before whirling back. "You speak of things you know nothing about."

The words cut into me. "There has to be a reason you've become this," I waved a hand at him because I couldn't even pinpoint it. He'd gone from quiet and brooding to . . . hard and unreadable. "If not the Unseelie court, then what?"

His lips twisted in a cruel smile. Faolan spread his arms wide. "This is who I always was. You chose to see what you wanted. Everyone did. And when they finally saw the truth, well, *then* I found out who my real friends were."

Was he speaking of being sorted into the Unseelie court? I opened my mouth.

He lowered his arms. "I thought you might be different from

the rest, I'll admit. Funny. I guess we were both wrong."

Faolan strode off, and I watched him go until he disappeared from view, a curious mixture of defiance and guilt churning in my gut. If he wanted me to treat him differently than 'the rest,' then he should give me something to go on. Some measure of honesty.

Even so, the pain that resided in me sensed a fellow sufferer in him. That didn't fail to make an impression.

"Alli?"

I jumped and looked up as Drake reached my side. "Hey."

"Lost in thought again?" he asked as I resumed walking to the house.

I shook my head.

"No, I didn't think so. I sometimes stop in my tracks in the middle of the forest for no reason too," he replied.

I shot him a glare.

His lips twitched.

I sighed. "Okay, yes, I was thinking of some stuff."

"Anything I can help with?"

"Nah. Nothing I can't handle."

Drake was silent for a moment, the two of us walking side by side. "Then at least allow me to distract you. Consider me proven wrong. The men needed their asses kicked today. You separated out the bad blood, and in doing so, showed most of us just how ill-equipped we'd be against the courts' warriors."

The knot in my chest loosened slightly. "I'm glad they received the message as intended. I felt the change when they grasped the seriousness of the situation."

Drake nodded. "So did I. So what's the verdict?"

They didn't stand a chance. Not with the numbers so stacked against them. "We have work to do."

I felt his gaze land on me for a second before he roared with laughter. "That's putting it nicely, Alli."

My lips cracked into a small grin. "Perhaps."

The forest cleared, and Rubezahl's home came into view.

"*Definitely*," Drake said, still laughing.

I chuckled with him, but said, "It's important for everyone to understand the gravity of the situation, but I don't want them to be defeated before training has even begun."

He sobered. "I understand. Don't worry. This is just between us. You looked . . ."

"Wound up?" I said dryly, borrowing his description of me from yesterday.

"Stressed."

And then some.

Drake winked. "But you're still stunning."

I arched a brow at him. "So I look stressed and stunning?"

He rubbed the back of his head. "Not my best compliment."

"Oh, that's what it was?"

"Supposed to be. I thought I'd take a stab in the dark after the way you checked me out earlier. You might have lost interest if the pants came off—that water was fucking cold."

I grinned as we entered the house. "It wasn't the worst view

I've ever seen. The top half, that is. I won't speak for the lower half."

"Thank you. He should receive a fair trial—in a setting with a lukewarm temperature at the minimum, and perhaps in the company of a beautiful woman."

Laughter spilled from my lips again. "Well, let's get Cinth then. She can provide both."

Drake took a breath, ignoring my comment. "I noticed you looking at Lan too. I wasn't sure if he'd caught your fancy, if I'm being honest."

I nearly gave myself whiplash turning to stare at him. "No. He didn't. Not at all."

Damn. That sounded defensive.

Drake, however, just dipped his head closer. "Glad to hear it. He's a hard one to read."

My focus darted between his green eyes. *Okay,* maybe I could admit the truth to myself. With Faolan, there was history. There was an old attraction that I wasn't sure I'd ever shake. When I was with him, I always felt an unspoken *something.* From the first time I'd seen him at the edge of the boundary, before I'd known what fae were, there had been something about him I couldn't put my finger on.

And that was exactly the issue.

In ten minutes, Faolan had made me mad enough to spit rocks. In the ten minutes afterward, Drake had made me laugh more than I'd laughed in a week. He'd lessened my worries.

He was what I aspired to be.

Free and happy.

Drake may see me as the prize, but he couldn't possibly know how alluring I found his honest personality—as well as the obvious physical perks.

Lowering my lashes, I seized the moment to take stock of those perks. Heat stirred under my ribs.

Definite perks.

Nearing him, I tilted my head up.

He sucked in a breath, and I smirked, gripping the front of his half-dried tunic.

"Is this about to be my lucky day?" he whispered.

I hummed. "Could be."

Pushing onto tiptoes, I dragged his head to mine and softly brushed my mouth against his.

He moaned into my mouth, and I deepened the kiss. Drake had nice, smooth, warm lips. He quickly caught the rhythm of my movements and brought our bodies flush, wrapping one hand around my waist; the other arm he pressed into my upper back.

Looping my arms around his neck, I gave in to the kiss, letting my blood heat in a way I hadn't allowed it to for a *long* time and never in this way.

This was not an unrequited crush.

It wasn't a shameful mistake like I'd made with Yarrow.

This was two adults enjoying a blip in time.

That felt wondrous, maybe even more so than the kiss itself.

I broke off, and remained close, watching Drake catch his

breath. His green orbs were hooded, eyes dilated, and I would have guessed his mood to be in the vicinity of greatly turned on even without the firm outline of an erection against my thigh.

"That was . . ." He smiled widely.

I patted his chest and walked away down the hall.

He called after me, "Where are you going?"

Ignoring the question, I instead replied, "You passed the trial. The setting was lukewarm enough for you, right?"

Kind of jubilant at having pulled off that sexy encounter, saucy parting remark and all, I pushed into the kitchen.

"How'd it go today?" Cinth murmured, drizzling purple icing down the sides of a three-tier cake.

My stomach rumbled, and I stole a still-warm cheese twist off the counter. "It'll be a bit of work. One guy pulled a fit, and I sent him packing."

"Do I need to beat him to death with my rolling pin?" Her eyes never left her task.

I wouldn't put it past her, actually. "Should be okay. Your tarts went down well."

"Naturally."

She wasn't even bragging. The woman just knew her worth. I still wanted to be her when I grew up. "Hey, so I wanted to quickly warn you that Lan is sniffing around."

"Your junk? Or just in general?"

I rolled my eyes and lowered my voice. "In general. He figured out what I did to Underhill, and to stop him from dragging me back to the queen, I agreed to give him information on the Strays."

Cinth stilled and finally looked at me. "Is that wise?"

"Nope. That's why I told Ruby. He'll tell me what to pass on to our snooping friend."

Her brow cleared. "That's my girl."

"Lan also snuck into training."

Cinth's confusion about equaled my own. "Why?"

"He said it was to keep an eye on me. I guess to make sure I make good on our deal." Or maybe because he didn't trust me to pass on good info.

She hummed. "That's going above and beyond, I'd say."

That's what I thought too. "He has another angle."

"I know you're not going to buy this, but could it be *you*?" Her eyes flicked to me, then back to her decorating. I swiped a bit of icing and stuck the sweetened paste into my mouth. Honey and rosemary lit up my tongue as I considered her question.

Could it be? I had no idea. I shouldn't *discount* the possibility, but . . . "He . . . I'm not getting that vibe. All I'm worried about right now is convincing Rubezahl that we are on his side. I'm not sure how Faolan got into training, but he should know."

Her hands moved swiftly as she put together a series of rose petals for the top of the cake. "Good plan. Let's not piss off the enormous giant. You have no idea how much more I get done being the only one in this kitchen. I like it here."

I could tell. "On my way to find him now."

"Then take a cheese twist with you. Butter him up some."

Swiping two, I nibbled on one as I pushed out the other side of the kitchen. Drake hadn't appeared, and I grinned at the thought of what he might be doing. Given the way I'd left him, some solo time might have been in order.

Chewing my last bite, I knocked on the doors to Ruby's section of the house.

"Enter," he rumbled.

This time, he was standing before the rustic wooden bookshelf that occupied most of the right wall.

He glanced down at me. "Kallik. How can I help you?"

"Cinth made this for you." I held the tiny pastry out to him. Maybe I should've brought the guy a few.

Rubezahl carefully took the cheese twist and devoured it in one bite. "My thanks. Hyacinth brings forgotten warmth to our home."

Yep. And it was a magic no one else could replicate. "Something came up at training today," I said.

Rubezahl carried a book that was quite possibly half my size back to his chair and sat. "You refer to the presence of our Unseelie friend?"

My eyes popped. "Uh, yeah. You already knew?"

"He approached an ogre acquaintance of mine in Healy with a cover story. I thought it prudent to go along with the story to see what he might do."

An ogre. "The ogre with the wicked knock-you-on-your-ass home brew?"

"The same." The giant's blue eyes twinkled.

I sat on the bench opposite him. "Do you expect Faolan to give something away? Wouldn't it make sense to keep him at a distance?"

"What worries you about his presence?"

What *didn't* worry me about his presence? "He's smart, Rubezahl. His loyalties and fighting skill make him dangerous. He'll take what he learns here back to the Unseelie queen. He's not someone I want to turn my back on, put it that way. And if he's around, won't it be harder for me to feed him believable fake information?"

Rubezahl heard me out without interruption. "You have exceptional instincts, Kallik. That seems to be the crux of your hesitation over Faolan, yet that is why I have allowed him to infiltrate our ranks. Your instincts are a match for his. It is a risk, I am well aware of that, but some risks must be ventured for us to survive the coming months. I would prefer to keep an eye on the Unseelie queen through her vessel. The alternative is to be blind to what may come."

I considered that. "Okay. I can understand that. And if he becomes a problem?"

"Then we will reconsider our stance, certainly." He hesitated. "I have been considering another course of action. One that may be agreeable to you. I believe it prudent for those fae in the Triangle to gather. Though we prefer to spread ourselves out, we will be stronger together if there is to be an attack."

He was not wrong about that.

"The other benefit being that it would become harder for our Unseelie guest to report to his people. The appointed leaders of our flock already have a location in mind and will bring their people in from the various parts of the Triangle. Getting there would take some time, but I wondered if this might be the perfect opportunity to train your force on the road. I would need to spread order as we travel, but I'd check in to continue our magic lessons whenever possible."

Leaving this area would help keep Hyacinth and me safe, and a greater number of Strays boded well for our protection too.

Isolating Faolan from his Unseelie buddies was just the cherry on top.

Benefits to me aside, my training squad would get a chance to really know their comrades' weaknesses and strengths, and that was a crucial part of any solid fighting force.

"I like it." I smiled. "I like it a lot. When do we leave?"

CHAPTER 19

"There is one other thing before we actually leave," Ruby said softly, the skin around his eye wrinkling with concern.

I tensed, sensing a bomb was about to be dropped. "What's that?"

"The spring equinox is coming." He looked up at me, the smoke from his pipe just a thin trail now, even the smell fading from the room.

I frowned. "Okay, I know. Late March as always." The equinox was about two weeks away.

Ruby bowed his head. "The Seelie king has sent a missive that if Underhill is not restored by the spring equinox, he will send his army to wipe out those who live in the Triangle."

I struggled to find words. "So we aren't just gathering everyone, we're making a run for it?"

"The Unseelie queen has sent a similar missive. The two courts will join forces to carry out the threat." He lifted his eyes. "So yes, we are running. To a place that I am not sure either court knows about. A place that must remain secret from them. I have already asked Drake to inform the others, and they will be packing as we speak."

It was my turn to frown. "How can that happen if Faolan is with us?"

"We will come to a point of no return, a crossroads for several different paths. It is there that Faolan will no longer be welcome in our ranks." He stretched to his full height, bones creaking and popping. The glimmer of his golden harp caught my eye, attached to his back but visible underneath his long cloak.

"What—"

"You will have several days to consider how best to deal with him before we reach that crossroads." He strode past me. "But for now, pack, and let us begone from this place."

More than a little stunned, I made my way to my assigned room.

My bag was as small as it had been the week before. Tossing in the few items around the room, I threw it over my back and went to help Cinth in the next room over.

"How in the name of the goddess above and below am I

supposed to fit all my stuff in one bag?" She gave her suitcase an experimental kick and then jumped around, cursing at the pain in her soft toes. She still had icing on her hands from her decorating.

I sighed. "You act like we won't be taking vehicles."

She shot me a sharp look. "You didn't hear? We're *walking* the whole way. In *March*, in freaking kill-me-now-my-tits-are-frozen, *Alaska*." She shivered as if already feeling the bite of the air.

A knock on the door turned us around, and Drake poked his head in. "We have a wagon, you can bring both of your bags, Hyacinth." He grinned. "Trust me, none of us wants you unhappy."

"Praise be!" She threw her hands in the air and finished stuffing her suitcases full, handing one to me. I mock-slumped under the weight. "What you got in here, bricks?"

Her scathing retort made Drake laugh, and she followed him out of the room and down the stairs. I trailed after them, lost to my thoughts.

The two courts were coming after the Strays by the spring equinox, and I had to find a way to make Faolan leave the group—in a matter of days.

Fuck me sideways, I could break down under this kind of stress.

We stepped into the icy night air, and a burst of yelling erupted. Two of the men from this morning's training were on top of each other, rolling in the snow, their fists flying hard.

The one on top was, shocker I know, Ivan. The trouble maker in the unreasonably small shirt.

A glint of a blade had me moving fast, and I booted the blade out of Belly Shirt's—aka Ivan's—hand. He turned on me, face twisted with a rage so hot his skin had turned a brilliant red.

He launched at me, but I deflected his blows easily, staying just out of range. He'd tire far more quickly than I would . . . or would he? It occurred to me that madness might be involved. The fae guy seemed unreasonably furious.

"Drake," I hollered, blocking another sloppy punch, "get Rubezahl, I need him to calm this one."

A guttural roar bellowed out of Belly Shirt, and he went to his knees, clutching his head as words poured from his mouth. Words in Tlingit.

"The spirits . . . they will come for you on the night of the full moon. Be ready."

His mouth snapped shut, and he fell to the side, convulsions wracking his body. I dropped to his side and held him so that he wouldn't bite his tongue.

A large hand reached over my shoulder and rested on Ivan's upper body. "Easy, my friend, easy."

A few notes of the harp echoed, and the calm that flowed over the space was immediate. Ruby's eyes swept around us. "The madness continues to infiltrate our ranks. We must remain vigilant."

Only *now* I wasn't so sure it was fae madness alone that had taken this guy. He'd spoken Tlingit. Just like those words I'd overheard on the radio.

He'd spoken of spirits too.

Drake and a few others lifted the unconscious fae into one of two wagons. I blinked and took in the massive animals hitched to said wagons. Twice the size of normal draft horses with three sets of wings down their backs and tails that were smooth, muscular, and tipped with barbs, their coats were dappled pale blue and white as if frostbitten. Icicles clung to their manes, tinkling like bells with each shake of their massive heads.

From my vantage point, I could just see the fangs protruding from their long mouths.

"Land kelpies?" I breathed.

"Cast from the courts for being vicious. But they are not all bad." Ruby patted one on the butt, and the kelpie grunted and lifted a hind leg in an obvious warning that Ruby seemed oblivious to.

Most of the gear and bags were put into one wagon, and everyone started climbing into the other.

"Wait." I held up a hand. "Any who are training with me will be on the ground."

The men I'd had chopping ice just a few hours ago gave me incredulous looks.

A few muttered.

Lan wasn't with them, I noticed. Had he decided to split already? Or was he running back to his Unseelie friends to let them know what we were doing?

I shook the thoughts off and raised an eyebrow. "Here's the

game. If you catch me before our first stop, you can ride in the wagon the rest of the way."

Cinth winked. "My money is on her, boys. Extra tickles if you catch her." I wasn't sure she meant the treat either.

I tossed my bag to my friend, suddenly spotting the tremble in her hands that she hadn't managed to control. Damn. Seeing Ivan like that would've scared her. "It's okay. You're okay."

She leaned closer, darting a look at the others as she swallowed. "Ruby said madness is infiltrating our ranks, Alli."

He had. Dammit. "And you saw how easily he settled Ivan, right?"

Her brow cleared, and she flashed me a quick smile.

Ruby approached. "Can you pick out the little bear constellation, Kallik?"

Uh . . .

"Ursa Minor," he added.

Oh. I scanned the sky, nodding as I zeroed in on it. "I have it."

"Take that direction and you will come across our first campsite—a wide clearing and one you cannot miss."

"Got it. Thanks." Without another word, I broke into a run.

The hard-packed snow trail was easy enough to follow. Here and there the ground was cleared down to bare earth, and that was worse, soft and unsteady.

There weren't a lot of things I could do better than the other fae, but damned if I didn't have stamina for days. Running long distances—much as I hated it sometimes—was my jam.

Ahead of me was the first real challenge, a mountain covered in snow that went upward for what looked like a mile or so. *Perfect.*

I heard the crunch of feet on snow behind me. I had no doubt Drake would be at the front of the pack, and probably Faolan if he'd joined us on the road. But a quick glance back showed only Drake running hard to catch me.

I sprinted up the mountain, driving my feet into the snow, and all but leaping with each push off. The flow of the surrounding earth and snow slid through my veins, under my skin, and into my bones. The bits of ground that were solid rock, not slippery with snow or ice, lit up a brighter blue than the rest, and I took the help nature offered, thanking the magic for its aid as I rocketed ahead of the men I was training.

The mile flew by, faster than I'd ever moved even on flat ground, and at the top, I turned and looked down. Drake wasn't halfway yet, the others far behind him. I waited for him to reach the three-quarter mark of the mountain before I continued.

I hadn't thought through what it would mean to get to the campsite first, so when I burst into the clearing, breathing hard and with sweat freezing against my skin, it was with more than a little shock to see an encampment had already been set up. Men milled about, and the smell of several small campfires curled through the air.

I lifted a hand. "Front runner for Rubezahl."

The fae that assessed me were all male and noticeably rougher than Ruby's group. Hair hung off their heads and faces in tangles, with chunks of dirt, sticks and leaves everywhere. Their clothing was rough cut, hand sewn with leather and pieces of bone. But they held their weapons as if they knew how to use them. I made my way across the clearing. I was pretty sure I could take them, or most anyway, but as I walked more arrived. Twenty-two of them and just me. Damn. They had to be . . . wild. Wild fae.

Not what I would call legendary, more like infamous. Fae always did best in a strict society, bound by oaths so that their magic was contained. But once oaths were broken—or never made—the magic could take on a life of its own. Of course, like the madness that was spoken of, I'd assumed many wild fae tales were put together to keep people in line. But in front of me was the truth of what our magic could cause if we did not channel it toward following a leader.

Not a single one spoke to me as I set about putting together a fire. I didn't have flint or matches, but I located a weak tendril of red energy deep within the ground and encouraged it to the surface to aid me. I'd broken into a sweat when it finally broke through, lighting the branches and wood with a snapping crackle.

"Thank you," I murmured to the ground, smiling when the surrounding grass doubled in length.

I fed the flames more fuel and got myself settled on a log where I could stretch my legs to absorb the heat. Running in the middle of the night was no fun, but I needed to get in training wherever I could. And given we were so few and the courts had so many, running was a skill set the Strays absolutely had to master.

Over thirty minutes later, Drake jogged into camp, his eyes sweeping the area until he found me.

"Damn, how did you do that?" he asked in a steady voice.

"Run? Lots of practice," I said. "Training for eight years, remember?"

"No, up that hill . . . it was like you weren't touching the ground." He flopped down next to me on the log, putting his arm just behind my back. Was that so I could lean on him if I wanted to?

Before I could answer him, the two land kelpies dragged the oversized wagons into the area. Looked like they'd woven around the base of the hill rather than headed straight up and over it. I'd heard the creatures were fast, and they'd certainly lived up to that.

Ruby sat in back of one of the wagons, legs dangling in the snow. Cinth chatted away next to him, her hands fluttering about like birds as she explained some thing or another.

More runners arrived over the next hour, and I mentally catalogued their fitness as I helped set up the basic camp. We weren't planning to stay long.

"Eight hours and we leave. I suggest you get food and sleep in that order, my friends." Ruby's voice carried over the large clearing. "At each stop we'll pick up more of our family."

There was no muttering against his words. Everyone ate in silence.

No tents went up. We were all sleeping in the open and would be for the foreseeable portion of the trip.

Cinth was right. It would be a cold ten days until we reached the sanctuary.

I dragged my bedroll and Hyacinth's out of the wagon. "Here, go underneath."

"We'll get run over," she squawked.

I pushed her gently. "Go."

She ducked under the wagon, tall enough to form a low roof, and I followed her and flipped out our bedrolls. "At least if it starts to snow we'll have shelter."

Despite the cold, a hush quickly fell over the camp. A large portion of the men would be exhausted from the run, and I wasn't in a much better state. Everyone slept close together, not willing to use any spell for warmth in case we were being watched. While I thought it unlikely, I didn't argue.

I needed to sleep, *wanted* to sleep, but I lay there staring up at the dark wooden underside of the wagon, practically counting the minutes ticking by.

A feeling I couldn't put my finger on pushed at me, and after a solid twenty minutes of ignoring my gut, I finally listened to it.

Giving up on sleep, I slid from my bedroll and laid it over Cinth, who snuggled in deeper, making soft murmuring noises in her sleep. Probably cooing to her cupcakes or something.

Creeping out from beneath the shelter, I crouched and looked over the camp.

No movement that I could—

I froze, watching a dark figure slide between the trees on the far side of camp. The body was transparent but not quite invisible. The fae was just cloaking.

Seelie, then.

Before I could change my mind, I was moving, slicing through the darkness and creeping after the spy.

The dense trees helped me move undetected as I hurried after the cloaked figure. It paused once, and I ducked behind a giant fir, holding my breath as I waited fifteen seconds before peeking out.

The figure was already on the move again, faster now, as if it knew that someone was on its tail. We went a mile by my reckoning before the cloaked fae slid out of the trees and into a much smaller clearing.

"What have you found?" A voice crawled over me like thousands of insects.

Yarrow. Fucking Yarrow was here?

"They sleep," another voice, softer, replied.

My heart clenched as I identified that voice too. Bracken. She was working with him now? Damn it, had she been working with him all along? I doubted it, yet that pain of betrayal cut into me. I'd thought that Bracken was a friend. A brief flash of regret burst through me—I should never have given her that second coin.

I'd thought myself undetected by the Seelie court to this point. Or maybe they had no idea I was with the Strays just yet. Maybe they were just tracking Rubezahl and the others.

Either way, this was bad.

"Then that fool Ivan spoke the truth after all," Yarrow sneered.

"You expected him to lie?" she replied.

"Who knows with weak outcast scum. But no, he seemed angry enough to betray his kind. This was the path he said they would be on."

Bracken paused, then asked, "What now?"

"Now, we take them," Yarrow announced.

Fuck.

My hands went to my swords, but I didn't know how many Seelie guardsmen were close by. Too many for me to fight on my own?

Although sorely tempted to take care of Yarrow then and there, I turned and ran back to camp, moving so fast it made my climb up the hill look as though I'd been slogging through mud.

I burst into the big clearing and drew energy from a nearby shrub to fuel my indigo magic and amplify my words, pushing them at the sleeping Strays.

"Time to go, we've got Seelie coming to kill us in our sleep," I ordered.

Nothing like a death threat to wake everyone up.

CHAPTER 20

The camp erupted in a hushed flurry.

I strode through their midst, giving quiet orders as I shook the others awake. "Arm yourself. A Seelie contingency is ready to attack. Spread the word, clear the area. And keep it down!"

How many did they have?

Because every one of their fighters would be worth five of my measly training force, maybe more. I sincerely hoped the wild fae had some spectacular hidden talents.

I slipped between two bleary-eyed men from my training force, searching for one of them in particular.

"Alli!"

"Drake." I gripped his arm. We'd all gone to sleep fully dressed against the cold, but he was bright-eyed and armed to the teeth already, including his gun, which he cradled tightly. Good. "Get Cinth and those less able to fight in the middle. I want our men spread out around them. You're going to command the left flank, and I'll command the right. The order is to disarm and incapacitate or kill. We can't chance any of the Seelie escaping. Got it?"

He nodded tersely. "Got it."

I left him and approached Rubezahl, who'd had the good sense to keep still and not move about and shake the ground. Our frantic murmurs were likely reaching the Seelie through the forest anyway, but we may as well keep them off-kilter and unsure of themselves.

"What do you need?" I asked him.

His lips curved, and his blue eyes, usually warm, looked like the ice at the heart of a glacier. I'd always felt a hint of danger from him, purely because of his sheer power. No one in his company could miss that Rubezahl was only friendly and kind because he *chose* to be.

Tonight, it was clear, he'd made a different choice.

"Just space to move," he answered.

Perfect.

I took a moment to switch on my magical vision, blinking as threads of color sparked to life all around me. Blues, greens, indigos, oranges, reds, and yellows, and every shades in between.

But I was specifically interested in one thing . . .

Staring into the forest, in the direction I'd followed Bracken to Yarrow, I counted the shapes approaching us through the thick trees. Twenty-one. Eleven from the left. Ten from the right.

Shit.

As I watched, five of the magical signatures disappeared, cut off as though the fae they belonged to had been erased. Another seven disappeared in the coming seconds.

I knew exactly what that meant.

"Ruby, you know that cloaking thing Drake does? Can you see through it?"

"I can."

"Can you count the figures approaching through the trees, please?"

He turned his huge head and swept the forest clearing. "Twenty-nine."

Double shit.

Thanking him, I jogged back through the group, which was in some semblance of order thanks to Drake. "If you're capable of cloaking your magic, do so now," I whispered.

The word was passed around as I approached the wild fae standing at the front of their force. Every one of them had cloaked.

I took in the bows each of them held. "I'm guessing that's your strength?" I asked the man with straggly red hair.

He dipped his head.

Thinking quickly, I ordered, "I want five of you surrounding our weakest members at the center. The rest need to get up into the trees."

The male fae's eyes swept to where Rubezahl was finally getting to his feet. As though sensing the attention, the giant glanced our way and nodded once. "Follow her orders."

Needing no further encouragement, the wild fae spoke rapidly to his crew, who dispersed as I'd asked.

Just under half of our convoy had been cloaked by now. Better than nothing.

I approached the right half and studied my fighters. Goddess, they were a mess. Ignoring their alarm, I started rearranging the ring they'd formed around the perimeter of our clearing.

"You're a pair," I said to the two men on the end. Working around to the front, I kept pairing them off, then stood back. "You have partners now. Watch each other's backs from now on. Protect each other. The warriors coming are fast and well trained. Don't hold back for a second. If you do, you're dead."

Standing before them, I drew my swords and circled my wrists a few times. Adrenaline had pushed sleep and grogginess away, and my blood sang at the promise of a fight. This was like another day of Underhill training—well, Fake Underhill. But still. I'd spent days waiting for something to happen, and I *relished* the thought of letting go.

"Boss?" a blond guy hissed.

Was he speaking to me?"

"Boss Kallik," the man said louder.

Apparently so. "What, soldier?"

"A few of us have some magic tricks that could come in handy."

My interest was piqued. "As long as it's nothing that will harm our group, go for it."

The man nodded and smirked. He focused intently on the tree line for a moment, and—still tuned into my magic—I watched his red magic extend outward, leaving a trail of dead grass and wildflowers in its wake. Unseelie then, at least originally.

In response to his call, gnarled roots popped from the soil, twisting into a labyrinth that would snap the ankles of anyone idiotic enough to run into our campsite from the surrounding forest.

That *was* handy. "Good work."

A shout rocketed toward us from the thick trees. "Outcast fae. Surrender to the Seelie court in the name of King Aleksandr!"

Yarrow never failed to get my blood boiling, and I opened my mouth to retort, but Rubezahl beat me to the punch.

"What quarrel does the Seelie court have with us, peaceful fae of the Triangle?"

"You are harboring a criminal fae who is wanted for her crimes against Underhill."

I was guessing they weren't after Hyacinth for putting too much salt in the stew.

Gazes flittered to me before returning to their forest vigil.

Rubezahl spoke again. "There is none amongst us who has committed a crime against Underhill."

"We've seen the mutt with you," Yarrow roared.

Temper, temper.

"You refer to Kallik of No House? She has committed no crime that I am aware of. I assume you have irrefutable evidence of her involvement."

Yarrow's reply was closer this time. "Over fifty eyewitnesses. Try that, you oversized, filthy stray."

A growl left my lips, and I wasn't the only one.

Insulting Ruby was a big no-no. I'd wager he'd helped every single person here at one point or another.

Thunder clapped overhead. At the same moment, a mist rose steadily from the earth and spread outward from our tree archers toward our attackers. I peered at Ruby. His eyes weren't the only glacial things now. His face could've been carved from stone. He was after blood in a big way.

"Never piss off Rubezahl," someone said in awe.

The comment stole my attention. "Why?"

It was the chatty blond guy again. "Haven't you heard the stories? He's as benevolent as they come, but insult him at your peril. He can be as vengeful as he is kind."

I might not have agreed yesterday, but seeing him in this moment . . .

Lugh's left nut, Yarrow was in for it.

"This is your last chance to surrender," Yarrow boomed. "Our force of fifty has you surrounded."

Fifty, huh? Liar liar, pants on fire.

"Does this order come from King Aleksandr?" Rubezahl's voice was mild despite the icy expression frozen on his face. "He has made it known he values a strong relationship with the fae here, and with myself. Are you certain that you do not act too hastily, Yarrow of House Gold? It's possible that you will start something that you cannot finish and that will set much in motion. The outcasts have no quarrel with the courts."

My ears picked up low and unsettled murmurs from within the shadows of the trees.

"Mutts and weaklings are no friends of the Seelie court. You outlived your welcome in this realm and the next long ago," Yarrow bellowed.

There was no other exchange, only a furious roar before the two Seelie forces advanced.

"Disarm, incapacitate, or kill," I shouted across the clearing.

The sound of pounding footsteps alerted me that Yarrow and his troop were running through the mist. Part of me winced as the first Seelie reached the labyrinth of roots. Bones snapped like branches breaking, and screams quickly rent the air. Those in the back didn't stop to aid their comrades before leaping over the lattice to enter the clearing. I waited for half of them to get through.

"Loose," I boomed to the wild fae in the trees.

The twang of bowstrings was the only confirmation they'd listened. A Seelie reached me, and I extended my sword upward to parry what would have been a lethal blow. Kicking him in the gut, I whirled to slice through the upper thighs of the female behind him before launching after him again.

Rubezahl's words had surprised me—*we have no quarrel with the courts.* Strangely, I echoed the sentiment.

I didn't know this man who was just following the orders of an idiotic superior—he didn't deserve death if I could avoid it. Bringing down the hilt of my sword on his skull, I bounded up and entered the dance I loved.

Deadly and dangerous. Full of sharp edges and dire consequences.

I drew from the trees around me, as most of the other fae would soon do, if they hadn't already. Pulling tendrils of energy, I whispered for the threads to energize my muscles and fuel the power of my blows. Flowers burst into life throughout the small clearing.

I rained down a brutal blow on a man's crossed swords and he dropped them both, gaping at me. An arrow appeared in his back, and I moved onward, aiding my men whenever possible and doing my best to keep the Seelie scattered.

We were winning.

"Kallik," a soft female voice urged from behind me.

I immediately put distance between myself and Bracken. She was still in translucent form, barely visible and dodging blows with ease.

"Rubbing shoulders with Yarrow? Never thought I'd see the day," I spat at her feet, not breaking focus from my surroundings.

Her form shimmered as she stepped out of the path of an arrow. "He's gone rogue. He didn't consult the king before ordering this attack."

It didn't take a genius to guess that. Which was a crazy risk considering the oath Yarrow had made to the king and the consequences of breaking it. "So what?"

She followed me as I lunged to slice the calves of a female Seelie bearing down on one of my weaker fighters.

"He believes this is his chance to surge up the ranks before his time," she said. "He's consumed by it. You can't let him leave this fight alive."

I scoffed, dodging back from a wild swing that made it clear the Seelie wasn't an Elite fae by any means. I disarmed him easily and kicked him toward other fighters. "And I should trust you why?"

"Because it was bad luck that got me landed with Yarrow. I'm not strong enough to fight him and win. I tried to steal his radio to contact someone in Unimak, but he guards it too closely. I'm oath-bound to do what I can to uphold King Aleksandr's orders, and you're the only person I can think of with the skill to stop Yarrow."

I turned to answer, but only caught the faint gleam of her translucent cover as Bracken headed for the trees.

The battle was losing steam, but furious shouts swelled from the left flank. "Check for dead. Bind the unconscious," I ordered before sprinting toward the sounds of a brutal clash.

Ten fae lay at Rubezahl's feet as I passed, and I swallowed at the unnatural angles of their bodies, certain each of them was dead, but my focus was pulled to the clash between Yarrow and Drake, blades dancing wildly.

I barked my orders again at those looking on, and they scrambled to obey, keeping half an eye on the fight. Standing to the side, I remained on the balls of my feet, ready to intervene if necessary.

I had a big bone to pick with this asshole, sure, but Drake had the first claim.

"Miss your hand?" Yarrow sneered.

Fury thrummed deep in my veins.

Drake didn't answer, completely occupied with the task of killing the man who'd cost him everything. And it was a wise move. He was not the better fighter. He had only four months of training to Yarrow's eight years, and it was beginning to show.

Yarrow gained ground, directing Drake into a corner. "What's wrong, Drakey boy? I thought we were friends."

"You're a backstabbing bastard," Drake gritted out.

I edged closer, willing him not to take the bait. Yarrow wanted to get in his head, to force him to make a mistake.

"Perks of being a somebody," Yarrow answered. "You should try it sometime. It'll get you in with the girls." He blew me a kiss, the fucker.

Drake roared and abandoned the semblance of controlled footwork he'd maintained so far.

I knew the fight was over then, and so did Yarrow.

Sidestepping Drake, Yarrow swung his blade low and then reversed the trajectory, bringing the blade down directly over Drake's good arm.

"No!" I yelled, lunging to parry the blow that would take Drake's second hand. I grunted with the effort, my arm muscles protesting the crappy angle I forced them to take. My blade slid between them, and Yarrow's sword glanced off in my direction.

He spun and delivered a vicious backhanded blow across Drake's jaw. His green eyes rolled back, and he hit the deck.

For the first time, Yarrow looked around and seemed to realize he was severely outnumbered. Not a single one of his force remained standing, though it was hard to see with all the magical fallout. There must have been more Seelie than Unseelie in the battle because the clearing was overrun with native flowers and shrubs now, and the trees were far taller than they'd been twenty minutes ago.

Wild fae climbed down from the enlarged trees, and Yarrow paled as his gaze swept over them, the fae at my back, and then landed on Rubezahl.

"You fucked up, Yarrow," I said softly. "Big time. King Aleksandr didn't order this attack at all. You'll be executed for a mistake of this magnitude." I wasn't sure of that, but I wanted him to think it.

He didn't bother attempting to correct me.

Bracken's words rang in my ears. *You can't let him leave this fight alive.* She was probably right, not that it mattered. I could have cut him down in the heat of battle, but the battle was over. Yarrow, the clever slimeball, wasn't fighting.

Eight years in the company of the same people taught you a lot about them.

It had taught me that Yarrow was the worst kind of asshole because he was both intelligent and a coward. It had taught him, no doubt, that I had lines I wouldn't cross, a moral integrity I clung to even in the heat of battle.

"How many Seelie are in the Triangle?" I demanded.

His gaze narrowed. "Three hundred."

I nearly groaned. How daft did he think I was? The huge number he'd just spouted made me wonder if the *real* number wasn't somewhere far closer to zero.

But when the king heard Yarrow's account, he'd send more. And probably a far larger number than zero.

Dammit.

I glanced over his head at Rubezahl, who stepped forward.

"For one so ambitious, the worst penalty imaginable is admitting failure," the giant said.

Yarrow skittered back, glancing at the forest to his left. "Get away from me, abomination."

My brows shot up. "The only abomination here is you, Yarrow."

"Not what you thought eight years ago."

I smiled, letting my blade catch the light. "Would you like to settle the matter over swords?"

That would solve my problem, but Yarrow was, as always, smart enough to know when to fight and when to be spineless.

"Leave the Triangle," Rubezahl boomed. "Return to your king and tell him of the decision you made here today. If you are wise, then you will learn something."

"He's really not wise," I said in the giant's direction. Should I say more? Bracken wasn't the type to speak unless it was important . . .

But then I'd need to explain her presence here, and that I'd let her get away.

I swallowed the words back.

He shot me an amused look. "No, but everyone deserves a second chance, do they not? Return to Unimak, Yarrow of House Gold. And know this. I will send a missive to the king seven days hence detailing what happened here today—in case you need . . . extra incentive to confess the truth."

Yarrow was chalk white. "He won't believe you."

The giant lowered his head, his eyes never colder. "I have advised your king on important matters since long before your birth." His eyes flashed. "Leave now. Or face my wrath."

With the other Strays, I watched as Yarrow turned tail and sprinted for the trees.

CHAPTER 21

T he next three days of travel were blessedly free of incident other than the usual things that happen on extended camping trips in sub-zero temperatures. Some frostbite, some burns from the camp fires, the occasional argument that was settled with a pissing contest. Seriously, a person would think these guys had only just learned they could pee standing up given how much they flung their junk around drawing things in the snow.

Had to be a guy thing. Maybe if my bits swung low like that, I'd do the same.

Each day we camped, more and more of the Strays' 'family' joined us, until we were nearly a hundred strong. That many people . . . and all *men*. Of course, fae women were very rarely outcast—the numbers of fae children being born were too low for our leaders to allow that to happen. But on Unimak, there were plenty of both genders, so even though it made sense to see so many males, it was somewhat unsettling to be one of two females in the group.

Cinth and I stood out, but more her than me with her curves and bubbly personality. Each night, she cooked up some sort of stew with whatever game one of the designated hunters had brought down, and in under an hour start to finish it would be ready, along with bread she baked *in the fire*.

"I don't know how you do this," I mumbled around a mouthful of the bread I'd just dipped into the night's stew, thick with deer meat and spices that left a pleasant burn at the back of my throat and helped chase the cold away.

Hyacinth shrugged off the compliment. "This really isn't all that good, limited produce, limited spices. I wish I could do better!"

A chorus of protests rose, especially from the wild fae. The food was making serious inroads with them, and they'd started interacting with the rest of us. Hell, a few had even trimmed their hair and beards, making them look far more . . . well, normal, and not like fae who'd become lost in time and magic.

Training continued, and the men seemed more dedicated to it after the attack on our group. I ran every day ahead of those who trained under me, forcing them to find a new level of fitness whether they wanted to or not. A few newcomers had joined the original group of thirty-three, bringing us up to just over fifty trainees. At the end of the day, when they were exhausted, we practiced basic swordplay. *Parry, thrust, block, slash.* Over and over until Cinth called us to the massive copper pot that would be bubbling over the fire—fuel for the next day of training.

Bowl of too-hot stew in hand, I made my way to sit next to Rubezahl.

He glanced down as he smoked his pipe. "Young one, I can tell you wish to speak with me. Please, be at ease." He waved his hand, and I gaped as the wilderness disappeared, replaced by the interior of his office.

"An illusion?" I sat on the bench across from him. Felt pretty real to me, but then again, so did Underhill for eight years.

"Yes and no." He smiled. "But this will give us privacy. None will hear us speak."

That was good because he was right, I had things I needed to say. Things I needed to ask.

He paused and rolled his hand, producing a small teacup that sat in his palm. "Here, have some tea while you wait for your stew to cool. Tell me what you think of it. It's a new brew of mine."

I accepted the cup and sipped. "Huckleberry, I think. Something earthier in it too, like a truffle or mushroom?" He grinned, and I smiled back. It was a small thing to talk tea with him, but I enjoyed it.

I took another sip. "Lan hasn't come to me for more information, and . . . I don't know if he's even hanging around anymore. That worries me." What if he'd been hurt in the fight, and no one had noticed? I'd carefully looked for him each day in the camp and not seen him once. Not once.

"He's here," Ruby said, and my head jerked up, making him chuckle. "He is never far from you, watching you always. Are you certain, Kallik . . ." He paused. ". . . that he is here for the reason he said? Perhaps he stays now for a more . . . delicate reason?"

It wasn't the first time I'd been asked that question. I looked down into my bowl of stew, which had made the journey with me.

Cinth had made the same suggestion, but that wasn't . . . Just no. I pissed him off as much as he pissed me off. When I'd first returned, maybe there were a few moments strung together when something might've happened if we'd been different people. But no, who was I kidding? He was Unseelie. Nothing could have ever truly come from it.

We both knew that.

I changed the subject. "Yarrow will try something else. I know him. I trained with him for eight years and . . . he won't go quietly into the night. One of his . . . men who I know from training warned me. I believe him." I wouldn't throw Bracken to the wolves. Even if I wasn't entirely sure she was being honest, she was the closest thing to a friend I'd had in training.

Ruby drew a slow breath on his pipe, held it, and then exhaled in a steady stream. "What do you suggest?"

This was where it got tricky. "I've been thinking on how to deal with him. Yarrow knows me. He knows I'll come for him personally." I paused and then plowed on. "If I take a team of men with me, we could catch him by surprise. The sentries said they've picked up on movement during their sweeps at night. I assume that's him waiting for me to give chase." Ruby said nothing, so I continued. "If Lan is still here, I could take him with me long before the ten-day mark, which would separate him from this group and our destination."

I'd take Yarrow out, but then . . . what would I do? *Kill* Faolan?

Something in the region of my heart twisted at the thought. If we were discussing anyone else, I could maybe bring myself to do it to keep us all safe, especially *if* that person were the Unseelie equivalent of Yarrow. But . . . damn it, I didn't think I could kill Faolan.

The tea seemed to coat my mouth, going sour as the dark thoughts rolled through me.

"Sometimes steep prices must be paid," Ruby said softly. "The secret of where we are going must be kept safe. Even from him." His words resonated with me, and I knew them for truth.

A gush of air slid out of me. One life for many.

Damn Faolan. If he weren't so stubborn and perseverant, then I'd simply threaten him. And if he were a mite less intelligent, I'd simply cover my tracks, but he'd proven that he could find me in the middle of nowhere.

I stirred my stew as if I would find the answers within. On some level I knew what had to be done, but that didn't mean I'd actually be able to do it. This entire time I'd been spouting off to Cinth about how much Faolan and I had both changed, but suddenly it felt like we hadn't changed at all.

Because he *was* the handsome, rugged boy who'd held my hand through some hard times, when the orphanage had been too much, and I'd felt alone. Despite how he'd said goodbye when I was ten, there were five years before that when he'd visited me. When he'd read to me. When I'd seen a softer side of him as my friend.

"When will you go?" Ruby asked.

"Tomorrow morning, as everyone leaves," I replied. "I won't tell Cinth. She'd fight to come with me, and this isn't a journey for a cook, not even one in her league."

He laughed and then blanched. "She will be greatly angry with you. Maybe me. I doubt she'll make me anything to eat until you are back safe and sound."

Of course that would be his chief concern.

I cleared my throat. "What about Underhill? The whole reason I came here was to figure out what happened to it and get it back, but I feel like the entire world and everyone in it is pushing me away from seeking out the answer." Wow. I hadn't even realized I was feeling that way until the words tumbled out.

Rubezahl's eyebrows shot up. "You think you are being kept from seeking Underhill?"

I gave a short nod. "Yeah, I guess I do."

He tucked the stem of his pipe between his teeth. "Sometimes the world pushes us in a direction we think is wrong, because it is not of our choosing. That does not mean it is taking us to the wrong destination, just that the path is one we didn't foresee." He looked down at me, kindness in his twinkling blue eyes. "Take heart, Kallik of No House, I have faith in you and your purple magic. Underhill has waited this long—a few more days until we are all safe will not be end the world."

I grimaced. "Don't jinx us."

He snapped his fingers and the illusion faded around us like the smoke from his pipe. No one was obviously looking our way, but I could feel eyes on me.

I turned to see a hooded figure at the far side of the camp, closest to the river we'd set up next to. Clever of old Ruby. Faolan had been drawn out by our temporary disappearance.

No time like the present.

I strode across the space between Faolan and me, passing him and making a motion for him to follow.

He fell into step with me as I made my way to the river's edge. Here, the rushing water would help cover my words.

"You want info?" I still held my bowl of stew and made myself take a spoonful while I waited for him to speak. Dang, it was lukewarm now.

"I'm in the camp. I don't need your 'info' now." His tone was sharp and hard with more than a thread of anger cutting through it.

I shrugged. "Okay." I sat on a large riverside boulder and stared out across the dark space. Minutes ticked by without a single word from him or me.

Finally, he moved closer to my perch. "Tell me."

Hook, line, sinker. Just like ice fishing with Mom.

"He's sending me out to hunt Yarrow at dawn." I took another mouthful and spoke around it. "From there, we'll go straight to the hidden outcast stronghold that neither court knows about."

Faolan didn't so much as shiver, but his magic flared, the dark tendrils diving into the water to draw energy from it. The color of his magic had been mistaken for the deepest blue on the lighter end of the magical spectrum during his childhood. Because no one would believe that he'd be sorted into the Unseelie court, not Lugh's grandson. To me, the darkness of his magic didn't seem to have a color—or rather there were many of them, and they were ever changing. Like his eyes.

The river iced over in seconds in response to his magic, and he created a path across the raging water. "Do you trust me?"

Yes. But I did not trust the water. "No."

He held out his hand. I didn't take it. *Couldn't* take it. I was consumed by the memory of another river rushing over my head, of the current dragging me and my furs to the bottom of the river. Four. I'd been four years old and the memory left me sweating even now, unable to think about crossing the flow with him.

"What do you want me to do?" I said to distract him. "Run away with you?"

"This is too dangerous," he said, ignoring the implication of what I'd said. "You can't be here any longer. The Unseelie queen, I think . . . Orphan, I could convince her to hide you."

His words rocked me somewhat because it sounded like he was worried about me. As the humans would say, he was willing to go to bat for me. What flying rodents had to do with a show of commitment I'd never know. "I have a job to do, Lan. Yarrow isn't just a danger to the lives here, but to me personally. To anyone who crosses him."

He swore under his breath. "Then you and I will deal with him. Alone. There isn't anyone here capable of taking him on. You saw Drake, and he's the best of your crew. The best . . . a man with one hand and four months of training, who almost lost his other hand two minutes into a fight with Yarrow."

He saw that, did he?

I sighed and leaned over my bowl. "I know."

Lan turned his head, and I froze inside . . . damn it. Still sitting, I twisted to look over my shoulder.

Drake stood behind us, green eyes flat and the line of his mouth tight. "Rubezahl is calling everyone in."

"Drake—" I called after him, but he was already gone into the night. *Fuck.*

"He cares for you," Faolan said, his voice carefully neutral.

"I saved him from Yarrow. Now he doesn't know what to do with me." He'd mostly ignored me after the battle, but I knew the look of wounded pride and hadn't pushed. Still, emotions and past scars could fester, and my heart was heavy over the knowledge that Drake could just as easily decide to turn his back on whatever we had rather than pull me aside to talk it out.

The Unseelie who'd haunted more than one of my dreams laughed under his breath. "A woman who will kiss you and then save you in a battle is a rare thing. He should be grateful and hold you close, not push you away."

I snapped my mouth shut. He knew about the kiss too.

Goddess, Faolan really *was* watching me. Why?

He walked past me, his cloak brushing against my hands, giving me a distinct shiver. Gathering my thoughts, I followed him.

Back in camp, Ruby was playing his harp, calming the fae and lulling them to sleep. He'd done it every night since the Seelie attack. With the exception of the sentinels who took the night watch, we'd all soundly slept for a solid six hours. And if that had worried me the first night, I'd shoved away those concerns when I awoke feeling absolutely incredible the next morning.

Cinth saw me and waved, covering her yawn with the back of her hand even as she slumped down in a pile of furs and blankets. Gifts from the guys who adored her from afar. Though . . . I'd noticed that she never returned anyone's adoration. Jackson was the only guy she spoke about—and even then she was as likely to complain about him as compliment him. For the first time, I wondered if my bestie had some pent-up commitment issues. A lot of us orphans did. Hard not to when our parents were ripped away so young.

"You look comfortable," I grumbled.

I was still on a bedroll.

She nodded, now mostly asleep.

Gentle harp notes hung thick in the air as I contemplated borrowing one of her furs. Glancing over, I caught the dip of Rubezahl head toward me and then Lan. His voice carried across the sleeping occupants of camp. "The time is now, Kallik. Yarrow is west of us from the last report. I do believe you will find him at a small river town in that direction. Be safe, young one, and do not forget *all* that you must do."

Like killing Faolan?

I didn't grab my bag, didn't take anything but my weapons and what I was wearing. I paused and leaned over Hyacinth, who'd fallen soundly asleep during my brief exchange with Ruby, and kissed her on the cheek. "Sorry, my friend, not this time."

Faolan fell in beside me as we jogged west, away from the group, and we settled into a comfortable rhythm through the forest.

"How long can you go for?" I asked.

He grunted. "Longer than most."

Yup, my brain went straight to the gutter, and three little words popped out before I could catch them. "I meant running."

A laugh from him caught us both off guard. "Then at least as long as you."

Still wasn't sure that wasn't a double entendre. But if he could keep up, then I was going to push us hard.

Because Yarrow wasn't as fast as me, not by a long shot, and he had no stamina. I reached out to the surrounding trees and drew on their vibrant green energy, feeling Faolan do the same beside me, the same plants slumping in death.

Our magics tangled as they had that night in Rubezahl's house. Dark tendrils coursed through me, and my indigo threads sought him like a plant grows toward light. The twirling combination of our magic burst through the flora and fauna around us.

There was an undercurrent of warmth to his magic that surprised me. He grunted as if feeling something unexpected too. "Is this what happens when Seelie and Unseelie magic touches?" I breathed out as I hopped over a log.

The taste of honey coated my tongue and around us bits of ash fell from the trees, floating like gray snowflakes as the trees were eaten by Faolan's Unseelie magic, and then given life from my Seelie magic.

Balance.

The reason the courts had to depend on each other.

I felt as if I could run for hours, days, a week if asked to. The combined energy between us thrummed and danced, continuing to grow, and I suddenly wondered . . . what it would be like if our magic were cascading over our bare skin, whispering between us, teasing us both as we—

Faolan yanked his magic away, so hard and fast that I stumbled, my breath coming fast for a reason that had nothing to do with running. "What did you do that for?"

"Enough. It's forbidden for a reason," he growled.

It was. Every young fae was taught that an Unseelie and Seelie union was impossible because our opposing magics would battle for dominance until one of the fae was drained and dead. Thank Lugh, Faolan hadn't lost himself to those sensations too.

I peered ahead, trying to pick up on any colors up ahead that might signify Yarrow. The light had changed as we'd run. Time had slipped by in a blink, and that was worrying. How long had I been distracted?

A gold tendril floated by on the breeze—ha!—a perfect beacon.

Too perfect. "He knows we're after him."

"Clearly," Lan answered. "But we wiped out his troop, and he's still not cloaking his magic, so who the hell does he have with him?"

Lan wasn't wrong. Yarrow was a coward on a good day, never mind when he thought he had something to lose—like his life. He wouldn't make a target of himself unless he thought he would win.

Which meant we could assume he had help.

The two of us crouched low as we tracked Yarrow through the last of the forest, the ground a covering of old dead needles and small patches of snow. The trunks thinned and the sound of moving water tugged on my ears. We'd reached a wide river, dotted with piers. It wasn't bustling by any means, but it had the most activity of any place I'd been since Fairbanks.

Through the trees ahead of us, I could make out something gleaming and white on the water. Huge. The thing was *massive*, and it dominated my attention, though it took several minutes before I found the words for it.

It was one of those human cruise ships.

"What do you want to bet he's down there?" Lan pointed to the big ship and the faintest whisper of gold leading straight toward it.

That was moderately suspicious.

A dozen figures moved along the quiet docks, scuttling and darting to remain hidden in the shadows. The magic they gave off was both Seelie and Unseelie.

As if things couldn't get worse. The two courts had joined forces.

But there was something else going on here.

Yarrow's magic led directly into the *human* cruise ship. And that ship was surrounded by fae.

It was clearly a trap. And knowing that Yarrow prized nothing more than his position, I could guess he'd cooked up some solution to the ultimatum Rubezahl had forced on him.

Damn it, this was not how I wanted to start my day.

CHAPTER 22

"We could refuse to play his game." The words died on my lips as a fae began scaling the gleaming side of the cruise ship. Extracting a can from his cloak, the fae spray-painted words in a large red scrawl.

This Land Belongs To The STRAYS.
Leave Now!

Faolan nudged me. "Look over there."

I followed his line of sight to the front of the hull, where fae were tossing small barrels down to other fae on the first deck. One cracked against the railing, and a stream of purple poured out. A gasp left me. "That's Glimmer."

So named after a deadly plant brought out of Underhill that exploded upon contact with anything. Some brave fae soul had learned to stabilize the substance in powder form. It wouldn't blow without contact with fire. But . . .

"Yarrow's going to blow up the cruise ship and frame the Strays." My face numbed as I spoke.

Faolan glanced at me. "You seem surprised. Didn't you train with the guy for years?"

I had. And I *still* couldn't believe he'd go to such lengths. For that matter. . . "How did he convince so many Seelie and Unseelie to go along with him?"

"He's House Gold. How do you think?" Lan said.

House Gold meant he ranked well above anyone but actual royalty, despite his bastard status; he was still full-blooded fae. Not only that, but House Gold was known for their ability to charm other fae. No one would dare say no. Just like Bracken.

This couldn't happen. The Strays had nothing to do with this bullshit. I refused to stand by while Yarrow got away with murder *again*. "I shouldn't have let him go."

"No, you shouldn't have," Faolan said, his voice low and his words hard.

The reprisal stung, but only because it was true. "We need to get the humans off and secure the Glimmer. Then we deal with Yarrow."

With just the two of us that was going to be a monumental

task. Because it *was* just the two of us. The human police were a two-hour drive and a two-way radio call away. Not that they'd be much help in a situation like this anyway. We'd just be getting more humans in the line of fire.

"Let me speak to the Unseelie first," Lan said.

I considered that. "You think they'll listen?"

"The fae on my team aren't bad. Whether it's madness or lies that have led them to do this . . . Maybe I can talk reason to them. We need more hands. Wait here," he ordered. He slipped down the slope, descending toward the docks as the still lightening sky highlighted the world.

Wait here, huh?

Arrogance sure had its drawbacks. Maybe Lan would learn that one day. Really, by disobeying, I was helping him become a better person. Yes, I was going with that theory.

I waited until he'd disappeared into the cruise ship's enormous shadow before I started my own descent. Skidding between chickweed, I crouched at the base of the slope, scanning for company.

The fae were mixed so I didn't need to worry about letting my indigo magic flag fly—being seen was the bigger risk.

I tugged up my hood and strode into the shadows, then began to climb.

Pausing at the sound of voices on the first deck, I waited until they'd faded before peeking above the railing. The coast looked clear, to the visible eye anyway.

Hoisting myself onboard, I jogged to the hull and slowed to a creep as voices swelled ahead.

"The Strays were behind what happened to Underhill," a woman said. "The courts need to know. Especially since it seems you've gone rogue."

I honed in on the tone, unsurprised to see she was talking to Faolan.

He stood with his hood off, and the first rays of sun caught the sharp angles of his cheeks and jaw. "Soldier, you're not thinking clearly."

"You disappeared five days ago. Where have *you* been? We wondered if you'd ditched us to go begging the Seelie court to take you back."

Faolan flinched, and my mouth dried at his non-verbal response.

The Seelie treated him as an outcast because he was Lugh's grandson, and everyone had thought he belonged in our court. But I hadn't realized the Unseelie treated him like an outsider too.

The woman stepped closer to him. "Yarrow told us you've joined the Strays." Her eyes took on a wild gleam as she peered around and stiffened. "There are others here, aren't there?" She opened her mouth—

—Faolan's fist snapped out and connected with her jaw.

The woman crumpled at his feet, the sound nearly masking the soft curse he uttered. Grabbing her ankles, he dragged her out of sight.

I took stock.

There was a pile of Glimmer here, but they'd thrown up far more barrels than what I was seeing. I assumed that's where everyone was right now, moving more of the explosives. They'd left the single Unseelie woman to guard it.

Dodging forward, I picked up a barrel and carried it to the railing on the river side. I hoisted it over and watched it dunk into the water before floating downstream.

Returning again and again, I cleared the deck of over fifteen Glimmer barrels. Goddess, there wouldn't be anything left of the ship if there was that much power behind the blast. Then again, that was probably the point.

I broke into a jog around the outside of the ship and ducked behind a life raft.

I'd found the rest of them.

Yarrow watched on as the remaining barrels were stacked at the bow.

"That's all of it." Bracken came into view, puffing, her face coated with sweat.

"The humans are asleep below?"

She paled and visibly swallowed. "Correct. The cruise staff are bound. We made sure to tell them we represent the Strays from the Triangle. We'll let a couple of them free on the way out to make sure word reaches the human government. As you asked."

My jaw clenched. *Bracken, this is wrong and you know it.*

Yarrow sneered down at her, then lifted his head. "Everyone

off. Let's light it up. We'll be first on the scene after the damage is done. The king and queen will hear of this from us, and we'll be given the resources to deal with the Strays once and for all."

The twisted part was that he *believed* he was doing the right thing, I could hear it in his voice.

The fae dispersed, and I didn't waste any time dodging forward to repeat what I'd done to the barrels in the hull.

"Kallik?"

I whirled to find Bracken translucent and facing me. "Bracken."

She glanced over her shoulder.

"How could you be part of this?"

She dropped her magical cloaking. "Because sometimes it's best to live to fight another day."

I ignored her and grabbed another barrel. Fuck. There were more of them down this end.

Bracken hovered, indecisive, and then started helping me. Another barrel went over, then another.

A shout went up, but I kept at what I was doing, completely focused on my task. I could not let this happen.

Bracken glanced at me. "Kallik, that's the signal. They're going to light it up!"

I didn't speak a word, still grabbing and tossing barrels as fast as I could. There were still too many left.

"I'm sorry," she whispered.

Listening to her leave, I didn't break from my task until a hand grasped my arm in an iron grip.

My curved blade was unsheathed in an instant. Faolan let me place it against his throat.

"What the hell are you still doing onboard?" he growled in my face.

"What does it look like?" I shot back, sheathing the blade and grabbing another barrel.

Faolan trailed me to the railing. I threw the barrel over, and then my legs were swept out from beneath me, and I was free falling, chasing the barrel into the water.

Panic filled me, and I sucked in a fear-filled breath.

That. *Bastard.*

I barely had time to tuck my legs under me before splitting the river's surface. Freezing water closed over my head, stealing the miniscule amount of air from my lungs and obliterating all thought with it. Thrashing blindly, I somehow made it to the surface, choking for air.

The cold water would be enough to kill a human—quickly—but not me. My magic gave me heat.

Faolan held the railing, looking down at me.

My gaze shot to the base of the ship, where a torch roared to life in the shadows.

Despite my panic, my tongue cleaved to the roof of my mouth as the fiery torch looped upward and onto the first deck near where Faolan was standing.

"Jump!" I screamed at him.

He glanced back as a catastrophic *boom* seemed to rip the

very fabric of the world in half. Purple fire exploded into the sky a blink before the ship vibrated and then puffed outward, with a sickening whine, as the ship's outsides were drawn in.

I screamed as the power of the explosion catapulted me underwater again, shoving me all the way to the bottom of the river.

My ears rang, but I kicked off the rocks and pushed upward again, only to be engulfed by a wave rocketing outward from the ruined ship. Flailing desperately, I fought against the river's hold and eventually pulled myself up onto the rocky shore.

Panting and choking, I drew what strength I could from the lichen and riverside plants. It gave me enough to crawl out of the water and cough up the remains of water in my lungs.

I got to my feet and staggered to the bank, where I sank my fingers into the soil and pulled hard. Warmth prickled my toes and fingers. "Thank you," I whispered to the surrounding plants.

My ears stopped ringing.

My breath calmed, evening out.

Faolan.

Bursting upward, I shrugged off my sopping wet cloak and forced my legs into a run back upriver.

He couldn't be dead.

But how could he possibly be alive?

Panic drove my legs faster than I'd ever run. The rocks pulsed icy blue underfoot, helping me along, and I drew from the trees with frantic abandon as I closed on the docks again.

My chest seized. What *remained* of the docks.

Only the far ends had survived, and those pieces were smoking and in danger of going up in purple flames.

The cruise ship was gone. In pieces. And the smaller boats seemed to have been obliterated without a trace.

My heartbeat pounded in my ears, my exhales wheezing. He'd ... he'd been on the river side of the deck. He would have gone out into the water if anything.

I swallowed hard and skimmed over the river. Debris littered the rocky border of the water. Parts of pajama-clad human bodies. A child's toy still clutched in a tiny hand.

Bile surged in my throat, horror and grief threatening to drop me to my knees. He couldn't have survived, I knew it in my heart, but I kept looking.

Blinking into my magical vision, I swept the surrounding area for his unique dark tendrils.

I closed my eyes.

Nothing. Pain speared my chest. I'd come to kill him. I should be happy someone else had done the job.

I should be relieved. Except from the carnage I knew that hundreds of humans had to be dead, *pulled* to pieces by the blast. The horror of that alone was too much to comprehend without Lan becoming just another of their number, unrecognizable from the damage to his body. Gone in a second.

Torn apart.

A ragged breath left me, and I wasn't sure I'd be able to take another.

Relief was the last thing I felt.

A sneering voice carried on the air, and Yarrow and his crew appeared from farther upriver.

Cold fury filled every piece of me. *Blood lust* surged through me with such intensity my hands shook. I tucked behind a tree on instinct, creeping closer to them in a crouch as they celebrated.

"It's done," Yarrow said, grinning broadly.

My eyes skimmed over Bracken's tear-streaked face and the faces of the other assembled fae. Some of them obviously didn't feel so flash about what they'd just done.

But they'd played a part in it anyway. I had not one shred of sympathy for them—not even Bracken.

"I will contact King Aleksandr immediately," Yarrow was saying. "By all appearances, we have just arrived on scene. Help any living humans you can find. Cordon off the area. You know what to do. Make sure they recognize we are not with the Strays."

Part of our training, how to defuse a situation with humans. It sickened me to see him use it this way.

Yarrow split from the others, drawing something out of his pocket. A radio, it looked like. I slunk through the scrubby plants after him.

This time I wouldn't hesitate.

I didn't stop him as he moved farther and farther into the forest. The less chance of additional company, the better for me.

Yarrow had to die.

And I had to survive. Rubezahl had to be made aware of this ploy to turn the world against the Strays.

Yarrow stopped in a small clearing, but instead of using the device he carried to call my father, he pocketed it and drew his sword with an echoing ring.

"Mutt." He turned, a smirk on his face. "Kind of you to join me. I'd begun to despair that you would once more . . . leave me wanting."

I left the cover of the thick fir tree and drew both of my curved short swords, glad I hadn't given in to complete panic and shed them in the water. "Yarrow. You murderous swine."

His smirk widened beneath cruel eyes. "Justice. That's what this is."

"Terrorism is the word you're looking for," I growled, my voice thick with anger and barely restrained tears.

His face hardened. "The king sent us to hunt you. To bring you back for questioning over the disappearance of the fae realm. He also ordered us to investigate the local Strays, and it quickly became clear that they're conspiring against the courts, you along with them. Except we haven't been able to find solid evidence of that yet. So yes, I gave the situation a nudge, but I didn't frame the Strays for anything they wouldn't have done in time. Cowardly beasts. They're behind all of this, and our people deserve to know. If a few humans had to die for justice to get in the door, so be it. Just a few dying for the good of many."

A *nudge?* He was reducing the murder of hundreds of

humans—of Lan—to a fucking 'nudge'?

The truth hovered on the tip of my tongue, but I swallowed it back. Nothing good would come of telling him what had really happened to the fae realm. The king and queen were well aware the Strays had nothing to do with this. They'd just needed a scapegoat to pin Underhill's demise on until they figured out how to get the realm back. With all that in mind, Yarrow's recent actions might actually be welcomed by them, not condemned. I mean, raising public ire against the Strays would keep the courts' shortcomings and failures from becoming general knowledge.

I circled my wrists and walked a ring around Yarrow. Drawing energy from the forest had restored me. Coupled with the thrumming fury in my veins, I'd never been more eager to fight. To deliver real justice.

Faolan was dead. It should have been Yarrow, not him.

"This ends now," I said.

"Tell me, mutt." Yarrow circled with me, countering my effort to get closer. "Did anyone come with you tonight?"

I didn't answer.

"Didn't think so. Uptight bitches don't have many friends."

Thanks to Yarrow, I had one less. But I wouldn't let him get in my head. I needed to get in *his*. "What about bastards?"

His self-satisfied sneer dropped faster than a giant's turd.

"That's what *we* are, after all," I continued. "*Bastards*."

Yarrow's eyes blazed with fury, but unfortunately, he didn't lose control. "I should thank you for coming alone. I guess that makes you the only witness. The king did want to question you, but you're a clever mutt, I'm sure you can gather why that can't happen."

Dark blue magic erupted from my right, joined by a burst of pale green to my left. Two Seelie fae strode into the clearing, uniting with Yarrow to form a ring around me.

"I want to say it's not personal," Yarrow said, edging closer. "But the truth is, I've waited to slit your throat for a good long time. Goodbye, mutt of no house."

CHAPTER 23

I shifted my stance as I took in the two Seelie fae who'd joined us in the clearing. Both men, both big guys. The one wielding the dark-blue magic was wider across the chest and had an angry red scar across his cheek. The smaller of the two held tight to his pale-green magic like he was afraid it would slip away. White-blond hair fell to his shoulders, and he kept nervously tucking it behind his ears.

Dark Blue was the more dangerous of the two for sure.

All of that I took in with a single breath. No time for dawdling when people wanted to kill me.

Testing one foot against the ground, I slid the toe of my boot across the mostly frozen slush. That could work in my favor against heavier opponents.

"You can't say goodbye yet, Yarrow," I cooed. "We haven't had our last dance."

I turned and ran toward him as I pulled up my magical sight, tracking every thread of magic around me. In doing so, I caught a glimmer of a deep gray magic glittering out in the trees.

I ignored it, focusing on the asshole I was about to kill. Yarrow laughed and swung his sword right for my neck.

I didn't even try to block the blade.

Locking eyes with Yarrow, I dropped to my knees and used my momentum and the ice to slide straight toward his widespread legs. His height worked against him, his long legs providing an easy target for me. I went between his legs and leaned backward as I drew my swords up, cutting through both his inner thighs at the same time, slicing through muscle, tendons, and arteries.

I'd thought about how I'd fight him for years, and this move . . . this move was at the top of the fucking list.

He screamed and stumbled to the side as blood gushed into the dirty snow and pine needles.

I spun on my knees and was on my feet facing his back in under a second. I could have run him through right there, but I wasn't a backstabby kind of girl. I'd much rather stab him in the face.

The Seelie with the pale green magic came at me fast, shocking me. I'd expected him to run when things went sideways for Yarrow, not step up.

I kicked Yarrow in the back toward the approaching fae, forcing him to catch his leader. Yarrow bellowed as the soldier dropped him to parry the killing slash I drove toward them both.

I couldn't be slow about this—not with two, or potentially three, against one. Yarrow rolled to his side, bellowing like a wounded beast, and I kicked him in the ribs for good measure, hoping it would shut him up. Or at least hurt like hell.

"You always were spineless," I snarled as the Seelie fighter slid under my guard and snapped a fist into my jaw in a bone-numbing uppercut. Stumbling to the side, I saw stars, but the slashing of his sword prompted me to sweep my right blade up on sheer instinct.

The impact of his sword on mine sent me teetering farther off balance as the tip of his weapon cut through my clothing and flayed the skin over my ribs, but at least my awkward parry had kept his blade from driving straight through my guts. A grunt was all I could manage as the pain cracked through my adrenaline.

Magic slammed into me from my left, and even with my eyes closed I could feel the shadows in it. Seelie magic, but darker and deeper and colder . . . like the river water pouring over me again. Yep, the scarred guy was definitely the more dangerous of the two.

I blinked my eyes open as I was driven to my knees, arms and legs bound with the Unseelie's magic, completely helpless as both fighters stood over me. But out in the trees the source of that glittering gray magic ghosted closer, eyeing us all. Its movements were wraith-like—unnatural—and I kept my attention on the men before me. Odd fae creatures sometimes appeared around the spring equinox, but my gut told me this one in particular probably had a darker reason to exist than most of us. This one was a fae creature the humans liked to look for on a regular basis and were deeply shaken if they ever found it.

"We could kill them both and take the credit for helping the survivors and taking down the Strays." The one with deep-blue eyes to match his magic had a cold smile. "That sounds like a plan, doesn't it?"

Yarrow was howling. "Damn you. Help me up!"

I turned my head, about the only thing I could move as the two fae advanced on him, the way they walked signaling exactly what they intended to do. They both held their swords loosely at their sides, adjusting their grips.

Yarrow was a dead man.

He seemed oblivious as he snarled and extended a hand for their help. "I need to get my legs seen to before I fucking well bleed out, you idiots. I can't slow the blood with my magic."

Dark Blue took Yarrow's hand, pulling him into a semi-upright position. As he did so, Pale Green swung his sword at Yarrow's neck.

Yarrow saw the move in time and jerked Dark Blue forward so the Unseelie took the blow instead, in his side.

The magic holding me was gone in a flash as Dark Blue took the blow. I was up on my feet and running toward the brawling men.

I wasn't going to get another chance. The Seelie and Unseelie had their backs to me, but my qualms about killing them from behind had me squirming, so I did the only thing I could.

"Oy, fuckers!"

They both turned as I raised each of my swords, driving the tips under their ribs and into their hearts at the same time.

Their twin looks of surprise were intense and almost simultaneous, their faces slackening as they slid off my weapons and collapsed on top of Yarrow, pinning him to the ground. I'd never actually killed another fae before. Maybe I would feel sorry later, but right now?

I was in survival mode.

Yarrow screamed, "Kallik, don't do this. Don't kill me. I can make you rich, my family has money. If you want, I'll marry you. You can—"

Oh, brother.

And he'd suddenly remembered my name, had he?

"You can die alone, Yarrow," I said softly, the fight leaching out of me as I thought of Faolan, *killed* because of this man's greed and hunger for power. How many humans had died for him? Hundreds. Children had died. Parents. Siblings. The horror of it tightened my throat and I struggled to breathe around it. He deserved far worse than the death he was about to be given.

"Buried under the bodies of the men you would have turned on eventually . . . if they hadn't first turned on you. As you die, you can think of all the mistakes that brought you here today. Think of all the innocents you've killed."

He blinked at me, confusion written clearly across his face. "You aren't going to kill me?"

I stared at him, noting the pallor of his skin. A smite more blood loss, and he'd lose consciousness forever. But his question remained unanswered as the gray glittering magic drifted closer, until it was only twenty feet away.

What was it?

I lifted my hand in a sign of peace—thumb and first two fingers touching, ring and pinky finger flared, palm toward the one approaching. It was an old signal that Bres had mentioned offhandedly years ago.

The oldest fae will recognize it, and they will know you do not come with thoughts of harm.

The thump of heavy feet could be heard through the trees, and the stench of something long dead wove toward us. Some of the glittering gray magic parted through the trees to reveal a twelve-foot-tall creature covered in chunks of long, thick black hair. Its arms hung to its knees as it skulked forward.

This was what the humans called bigfoot, and he'd been watching the whole fight.

Hoping for a feast.

I took a step back and bowed. "As you will, my friend."

Yarrow tipped his head to see who I was talking to. "No. No, Kallik, don't! Don't leave me!"

"The world needs balance, Yarrow. At least your death will

sustain another." I turned my back on him and listened to his screams until the sound cut off with a violent snarl and the crunch of bone and flesh.

Honestly? Part of me had hoped he'd suffer longer.

Part of me wanted to have been the one to kill him. But . . .

Releasing a breath, I sheathed my weapons and ran back toward the site of the explosion. Faolan, what was left of him, was there, and I had to find him.

My heart lurched in a terrible, twisted way as I imagined finding pieces of him floating downriver. I picked up speed, drawing heavily on the surrounding land, only a small part of me noticing the ash floating down to coat my shoulders and the taste of honey on my tongue.

A sodden figure sat on the bank of the river ahead of me.

A ghost. It had to be a ghost.

He turned, saw me, and stood. Then we were running toward each other, both of us sprinting like we were in a race for our lives.

Our magic touched first. The eruption of that connection stole my breath even before he caught me in his arms. There were no words as he cupped my face, frantic gaze searching mine. In the dark black of his eyes flecks of color swam, like pieces of gemstones that had been chipped away and left there to be found by any who took the effort to seek them.

I wrapped my arms around his neck and hugged him close, gasping back a sob. "I thought you'd died."

His arms snaked around my waist, and he buried his face

against my neck.

"I couldn't find you after. I thought . . . I'd been too slow," I continued babbling.

I couldn't let him go, and my magic seemed to agree with me. Around us ash fell so thickly it might as well have been snowing, and that taste of honey was still thick in my mouth. I pulled back enough to make sure I was truly seeing him. My fingers found their way to his cheek, and I slid the tips along his face and into his hair.

In that moment, I didn't care if it was forbidden for good reason. I didn't care about anything but the look in his eyes, which told me he was feeling this too.

He pressed his forehead against mine, and I could feel him fight the bindings weaving us together. Our combined magic had gone rogue, and for me, at least, it felt right. *Good.*

"I can't," he whispered. "Orphan . . . Kallik. I can't."

"I can," I whispered back and pressed my lips against his, drawing his bottom lip into my mouth and biting it lightly. He groaned, and our tangled magic burst into life around us. I couldn't get enough of him. From the frantic way he slanted his mouth over mine and pushed me up against a tree, he felt the same way.

Every fantasy I'd ever had for him blasted to the forefront of my mind. I ran my hands over his face, chest, and waist, tracing every ridge of muscle and every line of a poorly healed scar, distantly wondering how he'd gained them.

Faolan reciprocated, finding that sensitive spot just along the curve of my waist that made me shiver with anticipation and rubbing his thumbs across it on either side. Our combined magics sang hot through our blood. It was heady. Overwhelming in its intensity. Confusing.

All-consuming.

Which was the only excuse I had for not hearing or seeing the others coming.

Hands suddenly clenched around my arms and ripped me away from Faolan, and I blinked in confusion at the Unseelie who'd gathered around us.

Separating us.

Our commingled magic screeched to an unholy halt, and rage like nothing I'd felt boomed through me like a thunderstorm.

Power consumed me. Of such force and speed that I didn't understand anything other than I had to obey it. I whirled, yanking my short knife from my boot to drive it into the Unseelie holding me. He reeled back, clutching at this stomach.

Lan.

He was beyond a row of others. Others who didn't matter.

Others who had to die.

Spinning, I stole the sword from the injured Unseelie and launched at those keeping me from Faolan. Without remorse or even thought, I brought the hilt of my weapon down upon a head. I delivered a savage punch to the jaw of a male fae. One more.

My metal met the metal of a female, the last who foolishly

stood between us, but she was nothing in comparison to the sheer power filling and driving me. Bringing the blade down with crushing force, I kicked her weapon away when she cried out and fell to her knees.

Kill.

Return to him.

I lifted my sword high to deliver the killing blow.

"Kallik!"

That voice. His voice. I frowned, stumbling slightly at the edge of horror I could hear in his tone.

Lan moved around the terrified woman kneeling at my utter mercy, and in a whoosh the foreign compulsion flew from my body, leaving me empty of the incomprehensible power that just took me over. That made me . . . I stopped short, breathing hard and blinking away the remnants of a stupor. And horror struck me through to the bone in its place.

Groaning Unseelie littered the space. Some were tending to those I'd rendered unconscious. My eyes settled on the man I'd stabbed, widening as his rattled breath came to a terrible, leaden halt.

Silence filled the trees.

Goddess. What did I just do? How . . . ?

I stepped back and stumbled over a limp arm of the fae I'd punched and knocked out. My gaze shot up to see Faolan where I'd left him, his eyes as wide as mine felt.

"What happened?" My teeth chattered. I mean, theoretically I knew what had happened, but . . . how?

Something just *consumed* me.

The kneeling female clambered to her feet and looked from me to Faolan. "Boss, we have to kill her. She's lost herself to the madness once, and it'll happen again. You know it."

No. It wasn't madness that just took me.

It . . . *was* it? I covered my mouth with shaking hands.

But the loss of control disappeared as quickly as it had arrived. No, that sensation was something, but I couldn't believe it was madness.

Faolan nodded as he pulled his sword from its sheath. "I'll do it. The rest of you round up the others. Get to the Seelie and ask them to meet us at the docks. We have damage control to do."

My panicked gaze landed on the now-still fae that I'd stabbed. He was dead. Killing another fae in self-defense was one thing. Letting Yarrow die fell into that category. But this fae, he hadn't deserved his fate. The other Unseelie left, the injured supported as they left me and Lan alone.

Quiet hung as thick as a shroud in the forest, and I went to my knees.

I just killed an innocent. And madness or not, the penalty for that was known to all fae.

Grief rolled through me in a wave so thick I couldn't breathe. With a struggle I spoke slowly.

"Tell Cinth I'm sorry," I whispered. "I didn't . . . I didn't mean to do this." I couldn't even look at him. Couldn't lift my eyes for the shame that was weighing me down.

With my head bowed, I reached up and parted my hair at the nape of my neck so the blow would be clean. "Tell her, please, Lan."

"And what would you have me tell myself in the dead of night when I hear your name whispered on the wind?" His voice caught, and I lifted my gaze to his face.

The darkness in his eyes was filled with gemstone colors again. I could see it more clearly than ever before as it swirled outward, chaotic and agitated.

"You can remind yourself that I'm sorry. I'm sorry that I didn't . . ." I whispered, my voice catching on my tangled emotions.

I shook my head, I couldn't say it, even now.

I was sorry that I hadn't told him that I'd loved him since I was a child. That *he* was the one person who'd gotten me through training—because I'd wanted so badly to prove him wrong. To prove I had more to me than any other woman or orphan he'd met. Maybe I'd wanted a home and freedom and my own money, but I could have had that as a Middling fae. I'd reached for Elite status because I wanted to show him I was good enough. That if he'd ever wanted me, I would be able to stand with my chin high at his side.

He was the rugged, quiet boy who'd held my hand when I'd cried for my mother, and told me that it would get better.

He drove his sword into the ground between us and went to his knees. "I can't do it." Reaching for me, he ran his fingers over my cheek and down my jaw, then pulled back as if I'd burned him.

"You have to run, Kallik. Run to the sanctuary, wherever it is. Pray that it's well protected enough to keep you safe. Rubezahl . . . he can calm you if you need it."

"I won't endanger my friends. I have to find the entrance to Underhill. I have to. If you're truly letting me go, then that's my only hope. I need to finish what I came here to do."

He groaned and closed his eyes, resting back on his heels. "How did she know?"

I frowned, my heart thumping as our two magics tried to tangle again.

I made myself lean back, too, to clear my head. "What?"

"The Unseelie queen said I would need to understand Underhill before the end of my journey. Underhill lives and is sentient, Kallik. The entryway can be anywhere it chooses. It *creates* the weaknesses in the veil that allow us to pass through. You only have to be worthy to open the entrance."

He stared hard at me.

I kept my eyes locked on his. "What does that mean? What else did she tell you? If you know what's going on, then you need to tell me, Lan."

Faolan held out his hand, and without thinking twice, I took it.

He lifted my palm and placed a kiss on my wrist, right over my pulse. "I don't know why any of this is happening. She gave me only one thing to go on. Follow the heart of Underhill, and it will lead you to the door."

CHAPTER 24

"The heart of Underhill," I repeated, then blew out a breath. "I'm glad that's not cryptic or anything, because if it was, it would make my life a lot harder."

Faolan didn't smile.

I squeezed my eyes shut. "Sorry, can we . . . just get away from these bodies. I—"

He pulled me to my feet. "Let's go."

We wound through the trees a ways before some of my shock abated. "Faolan, wait. Where are we going?"

"I have a few things to tie up, and then I'll go with you."

Fear was the first emotion to strike me. I stopped in my tracks. "No."

He glanced back, expressionless. "We need to figure this out together." Moving toward me, he reached for my face.

I shied back, eyes wide. Heart pounding.

His hand remained frozen in the air. "What is it?"

"You know what. Something happened back there after we kissed."

Faolan couldn't come with me because something beyond my comprehension kept pushing me toward him, and madness followed in the wake of the connection forged by our magic.

"So we won't kiss," he growled.

I shook my head. "I want you to come with me, Lan. I do."

"But you'll go alone regardless of what may befall you."

And him. A fae was dead because of me, and yet my guilt and horror paled in comparison to the gut-wrenching grief I'd felt in those moments when I'd believed Lan was gone forever. "Yes. After searching for this 'heart', I'll head to the stray sanctuary to warn Rubezahl about what happened here. You can't go there anyway."

"I'll go wherever the hell I please." For perhaps the first time ever, his voice rose in anger.

I smiled at him, not daring to touch him again despite how much I wanted to. "I'll be okay, Lan. Truly."

The gem-like depths to his eyes faded, and darkness reigned there once more. "If this is what you choose, Orphan."

My smile faded. "This is what I choose."

He bowed slightly. "The Seelie king and Unseelie queen will

already be aware of what has happened here. Though Yarrow is gone, they will use his gambit to their advantage against the Strays. Kallik, it is likely a war will follow."

My gut churned. "I know. But if I can find Underhill, I can stop this."

Faolan's mouth opened again, but after a pause, he closed it and instead curled both of his hands to fists. "Go now. Search for the heart if you must, but it's imperative that you get to the sanctuary soon, Kallik."

A wrinkle formed between my brows. "Why?"

"The queen doesn't often divulge information or interfere in the natural process of things. If she does so, then there is usually much at stake. Just promise me that you won't delay overlong in going there."

Wariness surged through my chest as he averted his gaze. Did he still know more than he let on? Maybe something he couldn't tell me without breaking his liege oath? "I'll do my best." Touching each of my weapons to ensure they were in place, I nodded to him and glanced up to get my bearings from the sun.

There was only one problem. I couldn't fathom what the "heart" of Underhill meant. From what he'd said, the realm was apparently sentient and could appear to someone of worth, but I couldn't sit around waiting to see if it considered me worthy. I needed to go looking for it.

The Triangle had always hosted Underhill. So I'd take Faolan's directions literally and go to the heart of the Triangle, the deepest and most inhospitable area. The outcasts' meeting point was in the same direction, so I wouldn't need to veer far from the path our party had been following for the past several days.

"Kallik?" Faolan said quietly.

Glancing back, I arched a brow.

He took a breath and spoke slowly. "Happy spring equinox."

That was *today*? I was so out of touch recently. I couldn't even force a smile. "Happy spring equinox, Lan."

I set off without another word, settling into a jog that was much slower than the sprinting I'd done over the past two days. Fatigue pulled at me, but soon the heat of exercise cleared my head—for the time being at least.

Eventually, the horrors of this morning would penetrate my mind and haunt me. When that happened, I wanted to be as far as possible from the remaining Seelie and Unseelie at the docks.

The streams and rivers blurred by as I ascended and descended the rolling terrain, at times clawing and scrambling up crumbling cliffs.

According to the Unseelie queen, Underhill had some measure of *intention* within its fabric. Oddly, this made sense to me. Even in the fake version of Underhill that I'd trained in, I'd always sensed another layer to the realm, a consciousness or presence behind it.

Perhaps I'd looked at this wrong.

If Underhill was sentient, then perhaps it had made the choice to withdraw. Maybe we'd had nothing to do with its disappearance.

My steps faltered, and I slowed to a walk, approaching a nearby stream.

After drinking deeply, I crouched by an unmoving part of the water and stared at my reflection. This was my preferred depth of water—the kind where I could see the bottom.

Goddess above and below, I'd seen better days. My hair was caked with blood. A shadow lurked behind my soft lilac eyes. Bruises, scratches, and cuts I hadn't felt or noticed marred my skin.

The sun was high in the sky now, and I sighed, tearing off my tunic. Washing what I could from the woolen, fae-made garment, I set it to dry over a boulder and located some moss by the water, using it to scrub at the dirt and blood covering me.

I then tended to the cut on my side.

Not too bad.

Wiping at my leather pants, I stretched out along the riverside and closed my eyes. Just a small rest before continuing on my way. Had I been in Unimak, I would've slept all day in preparation for the spring equinox celebrations, which lasted until well past dawn. No one had to work on equinox days. Even in training, we'd had the day off and celebrated with a better than usual meal.

But there were no cherry and beetroot tickles or Fae Honey to look forward to tonight. I was alone, half naked, and weighed down by exhaustion. I needed sleep, but my mind wouldn't stop whirling. This all had to be connected somehow.

Me and Faolan.

Underhill.

Seelie, Unseelie, and the Strays—maybe even the humans. But how? That was a question that didn't have any clear answer yet.

Was there something wrong with the heart of Underhill? Had someone . . . injured it? I grumbled, and finally felt my thoughts loosen to the oblivion of a stupor that might be as close as I could get to slumber after the events of the morning.

Voices whispered to me.

"The entrance opens to those who are worthy."

"The spirits are angry, but they will guide you."

MY FINGERS WORKED eagerly to free the lynx from the snare. Most of the pelts we came across when lucky enough to secure a lynx were on the brown side, but this pelt was pure white, the telltale black dots spreading across the creature's back a stark and beautiful contrast. I couldn't wait to get a better look.

"Kallik, dear one."

My mother's bronzed and smiling face filled my view as I looked up from the lynx.

"Tláa?" I responded.

She knelt beside me. "When we take nature's gifts, what must we do?"

My cheeks reddened. "Thank them."

"Yes. This animal has died so that we may live on. Its pelt will

warm us. Its food will sustain us. We must let the spirits know that we will not waste their gift. Not one part of it. Knowing that, they may choose to keep giving us such things."

I mumbled my apology and glanced down at the beautiful, dead lynx.

"You know what to do, dear one," my mother spoke in soft, lilting Tlingit.

Rocks scattered as I sat up with a gasp, not immediately recognizing my surroundings.

The stream trickled to my right, and I dragged a hand over my face, almost groggier for having rested.

I glanced up, groaning when I saw the sun was all but gone behind a mountain range in the distance and the air around me was cooling once more.

Fuck. My nap had gone on far longer than I'd intended.

Forcing my aching body to stand, I staggered to the rock and shrugged into my tunic again. Perhaps it was best to run during the night anyway. I'd left my cloak at the docks and running would keep me warm.

Stretching and moaning a few times, I crouched by a fast-flowing section of the stream to drink again.

Light poured over me, and I spat out a mouthful of bone-chilling water, drawing my blade. I almost laughed when I realized what I was reacting to: the moon was full and shining down through a gap in the trees.

Almost.

My mouth dried as I rose, water trickling between my fingers, forgotten. The moonlight illuminated a path leading west. It held the slightest gray shimmer to it. Someone else might have found it beautiful, but it only reminded me of the monstrous creature that had consumed Yarrow.

I scanned my surroundings for company, and as I did, a memory surfaced in my groggy mind.

The spirits, the voice had said over the radio. *They will come for you on the night of the full moon.*

A violent shiver racked me that had nothing to do with my half-dried tunic. It was a full moon tonight *and* spring equinox. Magic permeated the air, and I knew it wasn't a coincidence that I'd dreamed of my mother.

The mysterious forces that governed magic were trying to tell me something, and I'd be an idiot to ignore their messages.

Swallowing hard, I crossed the stream, only hesitating briefly before I set foot on the shimmering gray path. My shoulders eased when nothing happened. Instead, my mother's reminder rang deep within me.

"Thank you for this gift," I said quietly to the moon.

Then I broke into a run down the path.

CHAPTER 25

The glittering path hummed beneath my feet, bits of snow melting with each stride I took, making my way clearer.

My side where the blade had cut across my ribs ached after the nap that had gone on far too long, but I ignored the wound as I loped my way through the crisp night air. I swept the area, eyes searching for surrounding danger.

The time I'd spent sleeping had cost me.

Faolan had all but said there would be a hunting party sent after me, and that meant I had no choice but to get to the heart of Underhill ahead of them—if that's where this path even led.

Doing my best not to think about what would happen if I didn't reach my goal, I kept putting one foot in front of the other.

Even when I heard the crack of a crossbow bolt loosing behind me.

I ducked and rolled but wasn't quick enough. The bolt slammed into my right shoulder and spun me hard to the ground. Biting back a curse, I blinked through the pain and shoved to my feet, launching into a sprint. A series of howls rolled through the air behind me, and my heart stuttered with fear.

Fae hounds were our version of werewolves. They were fae who'd been transformed into monstrous beasts, bound to the task of hunting down criminals.

And by the sounds of it I had at least four behind me—if I was lucky.

I could have whispered a prayer to Lugh and the goddess of the fae. But I didn't. Whether I really was mad, solstice was being extra funky this year, or something else was going on entirely, I knew who I wanted on my side right now.

"Spirits, guide me," I whispered in Tlingit, and the light of the moon brightened as the path suddenly veered left, into a heavy patch of forest.

I didn't question the change in direction.

There was no *time* to question it.

Another crossbow bolt slammed into a tree trunk right by my head, and I dove to the right, using the trees as hand holds and shields as I kept running. They were out to fucking kill.

The smell of the pine trees was overwhelmed by a rush of wet dog and piss, and I rolled around a tree, grabbing for my sword with my left hand.

More wolf than dog, the fae hound's eyes locked on mine. At his side was a shimmering image of the fae he'd been. Like a double vision, the dog and man attacked as one, jaws clamping down on my already numb right arm.

I screamed as the hound's teeth tore through my flesh and dug down to the bone. A light flashed, and the sensation of electricity seared through the bite—a lightning bolt that made me arch back and clamp my teeth together and I struggled to breathe.

My eyes rolled as the light faded and the flash of power evaporated with a sharp whistle. I hit the ground gasping for air, feeling singed inside and out.

Next to me, the fae hound lay with his tongue lolled out of his mouth, eyes empty of life, body already stiffening. I didn't understand what had happened, and there was no time to figure it out.

Hurry, you must hurry.

I blinked up at the whispering spirit that now stood on my path, the form indistinct except for its beckoning hand. The figure was cloaked in a mist that spilled off in pulsing waves, hiding its shape.

I pushed to my feet, every joint aching as I stumbled forward, following the spirit.

"What happened?" I mumbled. Tasting blood, I realized I'd bitten down on my tongue in the throes of the powerful bolt of . . . magic? Electricity? All I knew was the power hadn't come from me *or* the hound.

The spirit's words floated clearly through the air. *Underhill wishes you to succeed. Her power is legendary.*

Figured that Underhill identified as female, the fickle bitch. Because if what the spirit was saying was true, I was pretty sure Underhill had somehow struck me and the hound with lightning a second ago. If the entity had enough power to do that, then surely she could have aimed a little better and *just* blasted the hound.

All that aside, did this mean I was close to the heart of Underhill? Close enough that she could reach out and affect the world around her? And who was this spirit person leading me?

My jog was nothing more than a stumbling run. I tried to pull on my connection to nature, and although the magic did bolster me, it couldn't heal the heavy toll taken on my body. I wasn't *that* strong—only time could heal some things.

For the first time, doubt flickered through me. I was young and fierce, but was I really the person destined to open Underhill once more? The bastard child of a king. The king's *only* child, whom he still wouldn't recognize as heir.

Orphan.

Outlaw.

I'd fumbled my way here, and look at me. Half-dead and bleeding from multiple wounds. Tears tracked down my face, and I knew in the back of my mind that this doubt wasn't just from my injuries or the hunting party tracking me—it was from the shock of killing those fae, and the knowledge that I likely wouldn't survive the night.

As that thought settled over me, I stood taller.

Bres . . . he'd trained me for this moment. He'd trained me to take each fight as if it were my last. And with crossbow bolts and fae hounds hunting me, it sure as hell seemed like this was my last battle.

I'd make those who came for me work for it.

I let my eyes drift to half-mast as I pulled on my magical sight and let it overlay the glittering path at my feet.

The world lit up. Not with colors. With spirits. All around me, spirits stood vigil, and beyond them I could see the figures of fae moving past my position, almost as if . . .

My mouth bobbed. They couldn't see me.

Hurry.

I picked up my feet and moved on as best I could. My limbs were deadening at a pace that wasn't natural, even for my injuries. Was it Underhill again?

No, Underhill wanted me to find her. She wouldn't purposefully slow me down.

My gaze landed on a fae carrying a crossbow, and I frowned, recollecting the bolt in my shoulder.

A wound that I couldn't feel at all. My shoulder was numb. Shit. I reached for the base of the bolt, and my fingers came away sticky with blood, but I felt nothing.

"Fuck, it's a sedative," I mumbled.

Silence, the surrounding spirits hissed at me.

They weren't covering my noise? Ah, crap.

Fae bodies scrabbled toward me as the spirits fled. Something slammed into my good shoulder, taking me to the ground all too easily, and I went limp under the hand and weight.

My head landed in a rather convenient patch of moss. That was nice at least.

"Watch out for lightning," I slurred, feeling the drag of the sedative. "It'll get ya."

I rolled my head to the side to find the glittering moonlit path still there, so close. The spirit from earlier beckoned me forth with one hand, but I couldn't do a damn thing about it. "Can't do, friend. They gots me," I babbled. "Gots me good."

"Bind her. Captain Faolan—"

That caught my attention.

Maybe Lan would rescue me. Maybe he'd get me out of this . . .

But no, I was dragged to my feet. I didn't spare Lan a glance, my gaze still locked on the spirit beckoning to me. The spirit that had finally seemed to realize this girl wasn't getting anywhere soon. It stepped aside and pointed to a massive tree.

I blinked a few times to focus my vision.

It was a doorway.

A doorway etched with the symbol for Underhill!

"No," I shrieked and thrashed, throwing those who held me away. My arms were bound behind my back, my feet hobbled, but the sight of the doorway to Underhill was enough to spur me forward, to grant me the energy—or at least the will—to fight those who grabbed for me. "It's there. Underhill is there, you fools!"

The words ripped out of me, and the fae turned to where I stared.

Faolan's voice was soft. "There's nothing there, Orphan. Nothing but darkness and forest."

Fury ripped through me. "Take my hand and see for yourself."

The words were garbled. The sudden energy that had fueled my last-ditch effort to succeed drained away with the force of a spring thaw.

The sedative pulled me down. Down. Darkness coated my eyes and stole away my last view of the spirit turning its back on me.

"I'm sorry," I whispered to the spirit, to Underhill herself. "I'm so fucking sorry."

◇◇◇

THE BUMP OF something under me stirred me to wakefulness, or a semblance of it. What a shitty hangover.

Had I gotten into the ogre's brew again?

I tried to roll over, my tongue swollen. All I could taste was blood. Blood? I blinked and stared up at the night sky. I was in a wagon of sorts, if I had to guess.

"She's stirring. Now what, Captain?"

I didn't know that voice. But I damn well knew the one that answered him.

"It is not on us to decide her fate," Faolan replied. "Her life is not ours to take."

"She's a criminal," the other man said, his voice cutting through the last haze of the sedative coursing through my blood. "Any other criminal we'd behead right here and leave the body to feed the forest."

I didn't move, just lay quietly. My bonds were tight, and if the burning against my wrists was any indication, the rope had been woven with iron filaments.

Dammit, how far had we ventured from the glittering path? I had to get back there.

"She . . ."

"Just because you care for her doesn't mean you can keep her alive, my friend. She can't be a pet. You said it yourself, the madness took her. She killed one of our own." The man's tone softened and there was a muted sound, like a hand thumping a shoulder. "You can't fix her, no one can now."

"The queen specifically asked me to watch over her. She said to bring her back to the Unseelie court if there was any doubt of her survival," Faolan said. "Those were my orders."

What. The. Hell. Was. This? Why would the Unseelie queen give two shits about me?

"What would our queen want with a nobody Seelie? You're not thinking clearly."

"Believe me, I am," Lan said.

"I think it's best if I gather the rest of the team to deal with her. You're too . . ."

Faolan snapped, "She's not a nobody, Maxim! She's the bastard daughter of the Seelie king."

Air lodged in my throat.

Right there, *right there* my world crumpled like a ball of paper. He'd known all along the king was my father?

My mind frantically assembled the pieces. He'd been watching over me from the start, not because he cared, but because someone had commanded him to. The mentorship program . . . he'd been assigned to me from the beginning and I'd thought it was just fate. My father had put him there to keep an eye on me.

And now?

The Unseelie queen hadn't wanted the Seelie court's unwanted heir out of her sights.

The other man spluttered in denial for some time before Faolan convinced him of the truth.

"And you think the queen truly wants her?" the Unseelie asked. "Why?"

There was the sound of feet in the crunching snow, and I closed my eyes as someone stood over me. "I don't know what the queen wants with her, but I know her orders. Our job is to obey them."

Did she think to ransom me? That shit would not go in her favor—dear old Daddy didn't give two figs about me. But I said nothing. Maybe I could find a way out of this mess yet. As long as I was still alive and on this side of the dirt, then I had a chance of making things right with Underhill.

The morose attitude that had tried to swallow me earlier had lifted. So Lan had known my secret all along. By now, I was well aware that loyalty was a foreign dialect to most fae.

He was no different.

Fucking *ouch*. I'd rather a dagger to the back than to hear those words from his mouth.

"Our best bet would be to get her back to the water. We'll take a boat, and from there—"

Another set of feet approached and the energy around me changed. I dared to peek out through slitted eyes in time to see Seelie magic flare up above me.

"Captain Faolan," a voice boomed.

Shit.

Bres's voice.

"General Bres," Faolan said as if they had just happened to meet on the street and were exchanging pleasantries. "What can I help you with?"

"You have a prisoner of ours," Bres replied coolly. "Who also happens to be my trainee. She put up a bit of a fight, did she?"

The man from earlier, the one who'd called Lan a friend, jumped in. "She killed one of our men. The madness took her and she—"

Bres snorted. "I doubt that very much. The madness will

never take this one. Were they attacking her?"

There was silence for a leaden moment. "They pulled her away from a . . . heated moment," Lan admitted. His team fell quiet. Yeah, I bet he didn't want to confess he'd been kissing the bastard child of the king.

"I have trained her for the last eight years in Underhill." Bres should have said *Fake* Underhill, but I remained quiet. "There is no way that the madness could have taken her this quickly, but I have no doubt that if she felt threatened she would have done all she could to survive."

Neither man was right, really. A foreign force had consumed me in those dark moments. I hadn't felt threatened by the Unseelie ripping me and Lan apart, but the power that took over had.

That power *wasn't* madness, however, I was almost certain of it. Just what it was, then, was anyone's guess.

Bres continued, "I will relieve you of your duties regarding her. She is Seelie, and I will take custody of her in keeping with the prisoner accords between our two courts."

Hands cinched under my arms and dragged me upright.

I thought Bres would take off the ropes, but he didn't. Of course he didn't. I dangled with my feet just above the ground.

"I know you are awake, Kallik," Bres said.

I opened my eyes to stare into his face.

"Your king wishes to speak with you. You should not have run," he told me.

I glared. "Knee-jerk reaction to people hunting me down,

what can I say. It's nothing personal."

He grunted and motioned for his men—over thirty of the king's *personal* guard, all dressed in deep golds and blues. I was carried by my feet and wrists, dangled like a pig on a spit.

I stared back at the wagon, meeting Faolan's angry gaze for a heartbeat. Whatever. Fucking liar.

"What was the situation they pulled you from that made you fight so hard?" Bres asked.

I didn't answer. "Yarrow is dead," I said instead.

Bres strode beside me and glanced down. "I would expect no less if you two went head to head. How did he die?"

"Why am I still bound if you're going to talk to me like I'm not a captive?"

Bres gave me a tight smile that was just visible in the night. "I've missed you, Kallik." He looked ahead. "I believe you are aware that Queen Consort Adair hates you?"

What? Really? I almost laughed. "I'm aware. Which is why I wish to be as far from the castle as possible."

Why were we speaking of Adair though? Shouldn't this conversation be about what I'd supposedly done to Underhill? Maybe he'd know the answer to something that had preyed on my mind. "Was the Oracle ever found?"

His gaze on me was sharp. "You wish to seek her?"

I locked eyes with him and threw caution to the wind. "I have a few questions for her, seeing as I was right there when Underhill shattered. The fake one, as you know, not the real Underhill."

Bres snapped his fingers, and I was unceremoniously dropped to the ground, my aches and pains reminding me that I was far from healed. His men backed off until it was just me and Bres.

My trainer grabbed me around the throat and hauled me up so we were nose to nose. "Unless you want every man here put to death, I suggest you shut your mouth." He shoved me back with a thrust. I hit the ground with a solid thump and a groan.

Bres snapped his fingers, and the men came back and picked me up once more.

He knew that the Underhill we'd trained in was fake. He knew that I'd shattered nothing more than an illusion.

I peered at him. "Are you going to kill me?"

Bres didn't look at me this time. "King Aleksandr will decide your fate."

"You're taking me back to Unimak, then." A statement, not a question.

My fate was bound once more to the my father's whims, though I doubted this time he'd merely get his guards to cast me into an orphanage.

CHAPTER 26

Maybe one day I'd fly into Unimak and not feel like a fugitive about to face the chopping block.

But today wasn't the day.

Hands and feet still bound, I had to reek. The half-assed wash I'd had at the stream in the Triangle was two days ago—and hadn't really made a dent in the clean-up job I required at this point.

I guess being clean for my execution wasn't a big deal—who cared if I stunk?

Dead people didn't care about personal hygiene, right?

I closed my eyes to block out the view of my home island below, imagining for the hundredth time what might have happened if I'd made it to the doorway etched into the tree.

Nearly saved the world. But didn't. Fell down at the last step.

They could put that on my gravestone.

I opened my eyes as the craft landed with a few bounces on the Seelie airstrip. Once the engines had whined to a halt, a guard crouched by my feet and unlocked my shackles. Behind him, Bres winced, probably predicting what was about to happen.

Yeah, I was pissed and this guy just became a volunteer.

I snapped the base of my heel straight into the guard's face, enjoying the thick crunch of his nose. Blood sprayed through the cabin, and I regarded Bres in the wake.

"Got that out of your system?" he asked.

I smiled. "Not nearly. I'm not dead yet, am I?"

Wisely, he approached me from the side, gripping my upper arm as he escorted me from the craft. I wasn't quite desperate enough to attack Bres. Yet. But I'd take other volunteers if they gave me the opportunity.

"The king awaits," he told me as he ushered me through a side door instead of entering through the front of the small, glitter-infused terminal building.

Goodie. "I would like to wash and dine before seeing him."

Apparently the promise of death brought out the sarcasm in me.

The king's personal guard flanked us on all sides, and Bres didn't speak further as I was marched to a trolley. I had no idea what day it was, but it had to be a weekend judging by how many tourists were on board.

"Clear the trolley," one of the guards boomed. "All unauthorized personnel exit the trolley immediately."

Cameras flashed through the windows, and I glared at the lenses of eager tourists desperate to catch a glimpse of a real-life fae criminal. A woman blanched as I caught her eye. Yeah, I likely looked as rough as the creature that had eaten Yarrow. Couldn't blame her.

The trolley lurched to life, and Bres shoved me into a seat as we ascended the peak of the island.

Was it weird that this felt kind of normal?

I choked on a laugh, half delirious. Bres shot me an incredulous look, and I hooted, stamping a foot on the ground a few times as my entire body shook with the ill-timed mirth.

"I'll say this for you," he murmured when I was done. For now. "You're one of the braver trainees I've ever had. I had high hopes for you."

The comment sobered me.

Because I'd had high hopes for me too.

I'd had dreams. But those old dreams—a home, regular coin, safety—seemed so insignificant when stacked against the real issues of the fae. If the king ordered my death, who would fix Underhill?

She'd come to me—shown *me* the path to the doorway—and Faolan had told me she only came to those deemed worthy.

What happened if I never got there?

Madness. Mass death of humans and fae. War.

"You've arrived at the first tier! Have a fae-tastic day!" the automated trolley recording announced.

Lugh's left nut. That better not be the last thing I ever heard.

I was escorted through the first tier. The streets were packed, and we soon attracted a trailing crowd of fae and tourists, who murmured their disappointment when we passed through the castle gates and they were forced to remain behind.

High status fae dressed in their evening finery turned to gape as I passed, and although I couldn't resist the urge to lift my bound hands to wave, my mind had sharpened enough to grasp I was truly walking to my death.

The courts had too much to hide.

And I knew everything that they'd tried so hard to keep hidden.

I'd been a dead woman walking from the moment Fake Underhill shattered—it had just taken me a while to discover the truth.

"A prisoner for the king," a guard said to two heavily armored soldiers guarding huge double doors I'd never been inside. They definitely weren't taking me to the ballroom where I'd declared my career choice.

The soldiers uncrossed their gleaming spears and stood aside.

The doors creaked, swinging inward, and Bres released my arm, gesturing me ahead of him. Suddenly, I really did wish to be clean and well rested. I always felt unprepared to see my father, and my current state only made it worse.

I walked forward, eyeing the high-ceilinged stone chamber. It was far less ornate than the rest of the castle—less pompous and gold, colder. It looked like the kind of place where real business was done. That didn't seem to bode well.

The guards before me parted to reveal my father sitting on a simple throne, a gold circlet atop his head.

My gaze flickered to Adair as she rounded the throne, trailing her hand along the high back. Her nose scrunched as she took me in, and she covered her mouth.

My lips twitched as I glanced back to the king.

Fury etched the lines of his face. I frowned at the gray in his hair. Was there more than there'd been two weeks ago? Fae didn't age that quickly, certainly not someone of his power.

"Why have you brought her before me in such a state?" King Aleksandr spoke.

Just behind me, Bres stiffened. "We were informed that you wished to see her immediately, your majesty."

"You caught her two days ago."

The trainer's discomfort ramped up a notch. "Yes."

"And in that time, you did not see fit to treat her with dignity?" Silence reigned.

Kind of nice to see Bres squirm for a change. I withheld my smirk though—because imminent execution and all.

"Kallik," the king addressed me.

My insides froze for a full second. He'd *never* addressed me directly. Not to my memory. "Yes, your majesty?"

The king's gaze roamed my face. "You fled for the Triangle. Why?"

Because I shattered the illusion you bastards put in place to trick the world. But part of me still hoped I could get out of this, and speaking the words aloud was a certain way to get dead quick. "I decided that life in the Seelie court was not for me."

I could see by the look in his eyes he didn't believe a single word that had come out of my mouth. Even so, I fathomed that I'd passed some kind of trial by not declaring the truth in defiance.

Defiance was for the rich and powerful. Not for the weak and outcast.

"You expect us to believe that? You think we are that foolish?" Adair's over-sweet voice rang through the chamber. She held her hands clasped in front of her body, perfectly demure. But her eyes were all but glittering with hatred. Yeah, I was not her favorite person.

I answered her carefully. "I'm not in control of what you believe. I simply know what I know."

"And what, exactly, do you know?" The king leaned forward on his throne.

My mouth dried. I knew too much, but no one would thank me for saying so.

I straightened. "I know the fae are in trouble. And that everything possible must be done to prevent what would be a horrific fate for all. I know that there are enemies everywhere."

Adair scoffed, but my father did not.

His eyes flickered with the same horror I felt to my core. Or was that just a child's hope blinding me to his true coldness? This man had sent a force after me, a team that had dogged my footsteps since I left Unimak. If not for my skill and some good fortune, one of those Seelie could have delivered a lethal blow.

This was the man who'd never acknowledged me. Who'd left my mother to fend for herself instead of owning up to his walk on the human side.

Because of him, my childhood had been rife with fear and self-doubt and hurt.

"Yes, Kallik," the king said softly. Adair's scoff cut off and she glanced at him in shock. "I agree entirely."

"Aleksandr," she whispered to him.

He held up a hand and glanced at the two soldiers to the right of his throne. "Take this Elite to a guest chamber. Make sure she is brought food, allowed to bathe, and have a maid sent to dress her—"

"You cannot be serious, darling," Adair cut him off.

The king turned to face her, his face fearsome. She inhaled sharply, her eyes rounding before she lowered her eyes, bowing her head to him.

"It is time." He spoke the words so softly I barely caught them.

My father surveyed the room. "See that it is done and that she is treated with the courtesy and respect due to a fae of the highest status in our court."

From the corner of my eye, I saw Bres jerk.

The two soldiers marched forward, and my lips numbed as they reached me.

What the hell was going on?

I focused over their shoulders, watching as Adair stormed from the chamber through a side door, only pausing to throw me a look of pure loathing.

The king stood also. "Go, Kallik. I will see you shortly. And then we will speak more."

I STARED AT the gown. The gold gown. "You're certain?"

The human maid bobbed a curtsey. "That's what the king sent, my lady."

In the last two hours, I'd eaten and drunk my fill and soaked off the remains of gore from the Triangle.

My mind had been working overtime, trying to figure out what was going on. Because something clearly was.

I was being treated as a hero and not a criminal.

I was being dressed in *gold*.

Maybe that should have come as a relief, but fear had flooded my body and mind so completely, I was surprised it didn't come spilling from my fingertips to cover the marble floors, gold-embroidered curtains, and four-poster bed in this enormous excuse for a bedroom.

With the maid's help, I slipped into the dress, standing still as she tightened the laces at the back. The ruthless corset held the strapless dress in place over my chest, giving said chest an almost Hyacinth level of cleavage. Its flowing chiffon sleeves were just for show. I shoved my feet into the slippers—they'd taken my boots—and stared into the floor-length mirror.

The maid had arranged my brown-black hair atop my head and pinned pearls in place. They gleamed in the light, picking up on the hues of my soft lilac eyes, seeming to make them sparkle brightly.

"Beautiful, my lady," she murmured in awe.

Beautiful.

I looked like them, the fae of the high court—if you discounted the still-healing scratches and dings on my skin, the wounds from the crossbow bolts. Amazing what a change of clothes and a bath could do, and a little fae medicine, but it didn't stop me from wavering on my feet. I needed sleep in the worst kind of way, and the warm bath had stripped me of the last fumes of adrenaline.

A booming knock sounded. "My lady, you're expected in the ballroom."

My heartbeat tripped. The ballroom?

Footsteps never heavier than in these softest of slippers, I crossed to the door on autopilot and found five armored guards on the other side.

The one in front smiled. "This way, my lady."

My lady this. My lady that. One word from the king, and

suddenly I was everyone's best friend.

Of course, I knew better. I'd had twenty-four years to understand what the people around here really thought of mutts like me, and a gold dress and a few polite words wouldn't erase that.

I followed the guards through the wide hall and then down a grand, sweeping staircase that couldn't be more different than the servants' stairwell they'd made me use when I first returned to Unimak.

Frantic murmurs reached my ears, and I stumbled slightly, half from fatigue. A guard steadied me, murmuring some idiotic concern on my behalf.

I stared at the ballroom doors as they opened.

Was this still an execution? Because the only other possibility was . . . *impossible.* Sweat slicked my palms as I walked forward, setting tired eyes on the empty thrones.

High-ranking fae stopped their conversations to stare, and I got the strangest sense that they already knew something I didn't. But of course they did. My father's councilors and advisors sat at the front of the group, their scrutiny more intense than the others'.

My guards stopped me to one side of the stage, and I did my best to appear as though the unyielding attention of what had to be several hundred fae didn't bother me.

The over-excited herald I recalled from last time appeared and brought down the tip of his golden staff on the ground three times. "King Aleksandr and Queen Consort Adair!"

I fought not to lick my lips.

One way or another, I was about to find out my fate.

The king didn't spare a glance for anyone as he entered, and Adair's usual smirks and simpers were nowhere to be seen. Instead, she'd schooled her face into a mask of pity that did not bode well for me. Stopping at one of the front tables, she spoke briefly with a large, kindly looking man—the king's brother, my uncle Josef, though I'd never thought of him in such terms. Her stopping there seemed like a strange thing to do when she'd soundly ignored everyone else. Stranger yet because his eyes, so like my father's, swept over me after. A sad smile tripped over his face, and he looked away.

Yeah, not good.

The royals continued to the stage from the opposite side, and after they'd taken their thrones, everyone else sat.

Everyone but me.

I just lingered awkwardly at the front where every soul could stare at me.

My idea of a fun time.

The king rose again and lifted a hand for silence. The confused murmurs died away, and he regarded his subjects solemnly. "Tonight, I called each of you here to bear witness to a monumental occasion."

Sweat trickled down my back as blood rushed into my ears. This was the exact type of battle I hated—one whose outcome had been predetermined—by someone else.

He gestured to me. "Kallik, please join me on stage."

My knees shook, but I forced them to obey as the guards standing before the three steps parted.

Fuck. Okay. Holding my dress up a little in front, I climbed the stairs and peered numbly ahead to my father's outstretched hand.

This was a trick.

This had to be a trick.

Striding forward, I had no option but to take the king's hand. His breath hitched at the contact, and I frowned as he swallowed slightly before once more facing the audience of high-status fae.

"Just over a fortnight ago," he said in an emotionless voice, "I sent a force of Seelie to the Triangle to investigate the demise of Underhill, as you know. What I did not impart is that we sent an Elite fae ahead of them discover how Underhill might be restored. This fae has a unique set of skills and came highly recommended by her trainer."

This was a full-blown lie.

I knew it. Bres knew it. Adair knew it.

Others must surely guess.

The king glanced my way, and frustration bubbled within me, almost strong enough to overpower the dread seeping through me.

"But there was another reason this Elite fae was selected," the king spoke to them again. "Her station has been a closely guarded secret during her childhood to allow her to grow up in safety, so she might understand all the fae here on Unimak. It is my privilege to now reveal the truth to my court at last." He held my hand aloft. "May I present my sole daughter and heir to the Seelie throne, Kallik of House Royal."

Gasps rang out as the fae burst upward to get a better look at me. But their gasps quickly turned to screams. I gazed back at them, ears buzzing with white noise.

"*Death comes.*" A spirit's sorrowful whisper echoed in my mind as my father's hand went limp in mine.

A strange gurgling noise interrupted my shock, cutting through the static, and I turned toward the king.

Just in time for his fingers to slip out of my own, to watch him topple forward off of the stage, his eyes blank, an arrow embedded all the way through his throat.

CHAPTER 27

I n a single blink, I'd gone from being offered the highest honor and position a fae could have, all the way to the bottom of the literal barrel.

I sat in my golden dress inside a jail cell deep within the castle, the cold air sinking all the way to my bones. The rest of the island was temperature-regulated, but no one cared about prisoners.

Trained. Hunted. Captured. Elevated. Dethroned. Executed. Well, that last hadn't happened yet, but I was pretty sure it was on the way.

I pulled my knees up to my chest and leaned back against the stone wall. My wrists still bore the marks from the iron-infused rope. My ribs ached. My body hurt all over.

KELLY ST CLARE and SHANNON MAYER

And yet the worst pain was from my twisting thoughts.

Looking at all the pieces, at where I'd ended this journey, my gut feeling was that I'd been set up from the very beginning. Someone who'd understood my magic would break the illusion of Underhill had set me on this path.

The only person I could fathom who'd do that was the Oracle who hadn't raised her head since the moment she'd made me swear my oath.

I closed my eyes, seeing the blood spurt out of my father's neck, seeing his eyes dead to the world. There was more shock attached to the image than grief.

He hadn't even hit the ground before Adair pointed at me and screamed for the king's guards to apprehend me. The voluminous skirts weighted me down, but even if they hadn't, I wouldn't have run. I knew a trap and my situation had all the earmarks of a well-made one. Why run from the inevitable?

Footsteps on the stone outside my cell echoed against the stone walls. I opened my eyes and turned my head to watch what happened next.

One of the guards opened the door, and Adair's voice rippled around us. "Shackle her to the wall."

I didn't fight their hands as they lifted me up and pinned me to the wall. Again, the dress was part of the issue. The other part was knowing there was no way out of this, that it had almost certainly been planned and set into motion long ago. Maybe from the moment I'd left the orphanage for training, maybe even before that.

The guards' gloved hands clamped the iron shackles around my already raw wrists. I let out a long, low hiss as the queen consort swept into the room.

"Tut tut, no need to be an animal." She snapped her fingers and the guards left us, shutting the door behind them.

"Afraid of me?" I asked softly, narrowing my eyes. Maybe I couldn't kill her with my bare hands shackled and all, but there was no need to be nice. Death was coming for me, and she was a bitch.

Might as well go out with a bang.

"No." Her lips curled, ruining the perfect façade of beauty she normally held tight to. "How could I be afraid of someone whose death is assured? A mutt who, under the direction of Rubezahl and the Unseelie queen, not only destroyed Underhill, but killed our precious king? Of course, you hired an assassin to do it, but we all know it was you. As soon as he named you his heir, you had him killed to take the throne." She sighed and brushed a hand across her cheek as if she were crying. But there were no tears.

I leaned into the shackles, ignoring the searing pain against my wrists. "Even if I die, Adair, you will still have the madness to deal with. The loss of Underhill will cost our people everything, and I could have stopped it."

Her eyes flashed. "You know nothing. There is no madness. That is a threat we used to keep our people bowing to us."

I shook my head, thinking of the brawling men at Rubezahl's

home, of the young giants who had gone mad and tried to kill us. Of Cinth's parents. Of my own brush with whatever madness had taken me in the forest. "No, I've seen it in action."

Her smile was sharp. "Did you? And who was nearby? The Strays' leader?" She laughed as she stared at me. "The look on your face is priceless. An open book. You know, you did me a favor by running. That fool was going to make *you* the heir. He thought you'd bring the human and fae worlds together. That was why he—" She grimaced and there was a flash of pain in her eyes. My father had knocked my mom up a year into his marriage with Adair. He'd been unfaithful.

I didn't want to feel anything for her—she was a monster. Yet I could see that his betrayal had wounded her deeply.

I frowned. "Why are you here, Adair? You've already sentenced me to death, and you're well on your way to starting the war you apparently want. Are you just here to gloat because you set me up and killed my father?"

She turned her face back to me. There was a glitter of tears there now, and a quick widening of her eyes confirmed what I suspected. She'd killed him, even if she hadn't done it herself. "His death was coming, one way or another, the Oracle foresaw it. I could not stop it, so I took the best path for myself and our people."

The heat in my wrists was near unbearable now, and sweat beaded on my face and along my spine as I struggled to remain calm in the face of the queen. "Again, why are you here?"

She turned her back on me and rapped a knuckle on the door. It opened and the guards stepped in. "Leave her in the shackles. Her wrists can burn down to the bones for all I care," she said. "She deserves no less for the death of my beloved."

The two guards bowed to her as she swept past them, her scarlet and black skirts dusting either side of the doorway.

I slumped against the wall as the door shut once more. Using the edges of my skirt, I awkwardly stuffed the material between my wrists and the shackles. The glittering gold material wasn't thick, but it helped and I breathed a sigh of relief.

"Why did you come to me, Adair?" I whispered. "So I knew that you would use my death against my friends?" Both motivations rang true, yet I sensed there was more to it.

The day slid into night, and I could hear the guards change twice outside the door. I contemplated an escape attempt, but I was dressed in a glittering golden gown, with nothing to change into. Even if I managed to get away, I'd be pinned down in an instant. Above me, the sound of the funeral horns rumbled through the stone as my father was laid to rest with a speed that surprised me. Usually a royal funeral was planned for weeks. Unless of course someone knew he would die soon. Just like Adair had said.

Tears gathered in the corners of my eyes. Not because we'd had any grand relationship that had left loving memories. No, in some ways it was far worse than that.

I had nothing to remember him by but the pain of not belonging, of not being good enough for him. The grief that flowed through me was for the things that *should have been.* The love that I'd missed out on—holding my hand when I was learning to walk, teaching me the best way to connect with my magic, whispering to me that the dark held no monsters that he couldn't slay. Things that fathers were meant to do with their daughters.

A sob caught in my throat, and I curled around myself as my shoulders shook.

Grief for all that hadn't been and now never could be tightened in my throat, and with those emotions swirling through me, I cried myself to sleep.

"You can still save them." My father's voice lifted my head, and I stared at him in shock.

"Still save who?"

"Our people. They are lost in the wilderness, Kallik." He smiled at me. "Your name is Tlingit, chosen by the woman who carried you for nine months, who loved you for five years, and who loves you still."

"You mean my mother," I pointed out dryly. His smile didn't slip but instead grew wider.

"You know the meaning of your name?" he asked.

"Lightning," I said. "It means lightning or lightning strike."

Those words tugged on my memories, but I couldn't pinpoint why.

His body shimmered, and my mother stepped out of the shadows of the cell, dressed in thick furs, her hair braided over one shoulder. "When a forest is dry and dead, it can be burned up by a single bolt of lightning. The lightning starts a fire that cleanses the forest and allows for new growth. Healthy growth."

She held her hand out to me and I took it, no longer feeling the shackles on my wrists. "You are that spark, Kallik. Your father knew it. So did your mother."

I frowned, her words sparking a deep unease inside me. "*You* are my mother."

She sighed and looked to the fae king. "She will understand soon."

I JERKED AWAKE, wrists burning and slick with my blood. The door swung open, and two guards slipped in. The one on the left was Bres. His eyes were . . . sad . . . as he took my shackles from the wall but did not remove them from my wrists.

"It is time."

There was no way for me to get out of this. No way for me to escape death. Was that what the dream had been about? A message that I would be reunited with my parents soon enough? Heart pounding, arms bound behind my back, I let them push me up the tight stairwell.

More than once I stumbled over the voluminous dress, but I barely registered it. I could hear the murmuring of a thousand voices in the distance. A public execution, then, not that I was surprised.

"How?" I asked the one-word question knowing that Bres would understand.

"The queen has asked that you be . . . drowned."

My knees locked, and I ended up on the ground. I could face death, a beheading, even a hanging.

But death by drowning?

Adair knew my fear better than anyone, having created it.

"Get up," Bres snapped.

I fought then, for the first time since I'd been taken. "Bres, don't do this!" I thrashed, head-butting the guard to my right hard enough to send him flying. But the damn skirts made my kicks less than effective, and in a matter of seconds they had me pinned to the ground, a new set of shackles placed on my ankles.

They dragged me to a small room where two women waited. There was no modesty as I was stripped of the golden gown and a knee-length sackcloth dress with no sides was yanked over my head and belted at my waist.

I tried drawing on the energy of the ground, but my indigo magic flared to life, spluttered, and was then drawn into the iron shackles.

By the time we were out into the open courtyard of the castle, I was shaking and sweating from pain and frustration. I kept trying to drag my magic to me, and it kept dissolving into the iron shackles—something that was to be expected with this kind of binding.

A gallows of sorts had been set up on a platform with a large tank of water below it. The wooden stairs we climbed had been freshly stained, and the smell of newly cut wood filled my nose.

Adair stood waiting for us at the top of the platform, my uncle Josef standing next to her with an arm around her waist, comforting her.

There was no point in trying to talk my way out of this. Bres dragged me to the lip of the tank. A diver was in the water, and he took the end of my shackles and dove to the bottom of the tank where a round ring waited. He slid the long end of the chain through the ring and waited.

By all that was holy to me . . . they were going to tie me to the bottom of the tank and let everyone watch me drown.

The shaking started in my knees, and it worked its way up my body until my chains rattled. The pain in my wrists and ankles was distant now, my nerve endings nearly dead from the constant contact of the iron.

"For the crimes of destroying Underhill and plotting the murder of our beloved King Aleksandr, you have been sentenced to death by drowning, Kallik of No House."

I didn't even know who spoke—my attention was on the chain that had been pulled tight, dragging me toward the water. As my feet touched the edge of the foreboding surface, I gasped and looked over my shoulder at Bres.

On his shoulder sat a red crossbill.

I shoved back the hope that it was an avatar from Rubezahl.

Another sharp yank on the chain, and I was plunged into the

water. I sucked in a big breath and let my body be yanked down. Not because I didn't want to fight.

But because the diver had to go by me. If I tried to escape now, he'd stop me.

I opened my eyes, the water blurring things as I watched the diver secure my chain to the bottom of the tank.

Outside the tank there was a jostling of bodies as people gathered closer to watch me die.

These were the people my father had wanted me to save.

Focus, Kallik, focus! I chided myself. The diver—a water fae—swam by me, his blue hair floating as if there were a current here.

"You deserve this death," he said, his voice crisp and clear as though we weren't underwater.

And then I was alone. He was gone, and I was surrounded by the leering eyes of the fae watching me as I dropped to the bottom of the tank and stood there, facing them.

Maybe you should just die with dignity, Kallik. Like your mother.

Maybe I would have if I hadn't seen *her* at the tank.

Cinth.

Her hands were splayed against the glass, and I struggled to get closer. Goddess, I didn't want her to have to watch me die. How was she even here?

She smiled, though it wobbled a little, and mouthed two words. "*Hold on.*"

Lugh's left nut, was this . . . a rescue? When in my life had I ever been saved? I'd always had to be the strong one. The one who held shit together.

There was a sudden deep boom that sent a shockwave through the water, and a stream of bubbles escaped my mouth.

Outside the tank I could just make out bodies fighting. The flash of swords. And then the sharp crack of an axe against the tank.

It didn't break.

My chest thumped hard with the need for air.

Hold on. I just had to hold on.

Another blow from the axe. Cinth's eyes pleading with me. Screaming. An explosion.

I couldn't see.

Couldn't breathe.

They weren't going to be fast enough. I was going to drown.

More bubbles escaped from my mouth. I couldn't help it.

I took in a lungful of water. Burning, I was burning from the inside out.

Flashes of my life cascaded through me. Faolan, Cinth, Ruby, my father and Adair. My mother's smile as she caressed my cheek.

My magic spooled out around and through me, deepening in color until the indigo was nearly black, filling the pool of water.

I needed to get out of there.

Your name means lightning.

Like the lightning that had struck me in the forest, throwing off the beast attacking me. Could it be my lightning?

Clinging to those words, I pulled on the magic in and around me with all my might. A blinding blaze lit up the dark indigo magic, and the tank shattered from the massive bolt of lightning. Glass exploded, water rushed out in every direction, and I dropped to my knees.

Coughing and gagging on the fluid in my lungs, I barely registered the hands that were on me, stripping the shackles off and throwing me over a very large, broad back.

A snort and a bellow ripped through the air, and then someone was holding me upright on the back of one of the land kelpies as they mowed down any fae in their way, racing away from the castle and through the streets.

I clung to my rescuer's hands, clung to the impossibility that I was still alive. "Cinth!"

"She's coming, don't worry about her," Lan said in my ear, his body warming mine. "We've got you, your majesty. I've got you."

And just like that, I was in Faolan's arms, being carried away from certain death.

But call me cautious . . . I suspected I was far from safe.

Because as long as I was alive, every sin of Adair's was waiting to be exposed.

"We aren't done with Adair," I said. "Not by a very long shot."

He smiled at me. "I was counting on it."

ACKNOWLEDGMENTS

SHANNON MAYER

I couldn't have done any of this without Kelly, her wicked imagination, her eye for detail, and of course just being the amazing person she is! What a journey this series has been, I am grateful to share it with not only Kelly but with all of you. May you love this world as much as we loved creating it for you. (PS, now that I have seen her acknowledgments, I see that mine are woefully inadequate #MustTryHarder)

KELLY ST CLARE

Thinking back, it was when I saw Shannon put a beer can up a chicken's butt that I knew we had something special. Lo and behold, here we are eighteen-odd months later releasing our story to the world. I really do need to give a huge shout-out to Shannon for 1) Opting to write with someone suffering from acute pregnancy brain—and then baby brain. Which hasn't yet resolved... When does that resolve? And 2) Doing the lion's share on the behind-the-scenes admin work for this book while I entered motherhood and all its sleep-deprived joys. Thank you, friend. The support was—and is—real.

A shout out to the awesome team who helped us to get this story reader ready. An uproarious bellow to my wonderful readers who are always so encouraging and down-right enthusiastic. And an earth-shattering battle cry to my incredible family, Scott the Husband, and our precious new addition, Bonnie Frances.

And to you, the person about to enter this world…

…Happy reading ;)

Made in the USA
Monee, IL
03 October 2021